Harr

THE I

Namarrkun
Bristol

Namarrkun Publishing,
Rock House,
Bridgewater Road,
Bristol UK.

First edition published 2015 in the United Kingdom. A catalogue
record for this book is available from the British Library.

ISBN 9780993285424
UK edition

Designed and Set by Namarrkun

www.namarrkun.com

Acknowledgements:

Irene Allen:
forever there

Yve Brooks:
for her spiritual guidance & friendship.
www.yvebrooks.org

Aileen Collins:
for her spiritual guidance, help & encouragement.

Steve Griffiths:
for his friendship and advice.
www.artworkingltd.co.uk

Cherry Mosteshar:
for editing services.
www.theoxfordeditors.co.uk

Victor (Emmanuel):
a deceased Buddhist monk that apparently guides me.

All things that happen, happen for a reason. Newton's third law of motion states that for every action there is an equal and opposite reaction. Our environment is changing at a faster rate than we have ever witnessed. If I'm honest, it scares me, although, I don't know what can be done about it, with any certitude. So, I dedicate this book to all those enlightened beings who can't understand why all those who should, don't.

"World peace must develop from inner peace. Peace is not just mere absence of violence. Peace is, I think, the manifestation of human compassion."

Dalai Lama

"And God created great whales.... and God saw that it was good."

Genesis 1:21

"Trees are the earth's endless effort to speak to the listening heaven."

Rabindranath Tagore

Chapter I

Inti, the Laughing Sun laughed and laughed and
laughed. In a petulant gesture he swung his burning
cloak in blazing trails across the horizon. The tall, forest
treetops burst in a swathe of crimson gold.

Far below on the forest floor Wee Tree, diminished by
his giant, parental kapoks, watched as Inti's blinding
light illuminated the canopy above. "Every day," he
thought, "no matter how often I watch Inti sink below
the trees, I never bore. How does he do that? How does
he make the light dance so brightly? Where does he go
when the light goes out?" He always had more questions
than answers. It felt like his small, cellulosic mind
would explode.

He wondered if anybody else noticed but nobody did.
Nobody seemed to notice Laughing Sun; not even Three
Toes. He hung from a tree with one long, dangling,
hairy arm tediously edging its way forwards at about
one metre per fortnight, teasing out the next grip with
such intense concentration that he was completely
oblivious to the sun above. Wee Tree watched the slow
sloth and wondered what it would be like to move, even
at an imperceptible pace. He tried to ruffle his roots but
it was no good; they were intrinsically bound to
Pachamama.

Then there was Tat, the tarantula. She had dug a huge hole under the massive buttress roots supporting a kapok. Hearing something rustle, she was out. Demonic, hell-fire, flying, frighteningly fast, her feet skimming over the earth as if the very soil itself was scorched into ruby-red, scolding cinders. In mid flight she had scanned the world, targeted her prey, oppressed it, parcelled it in precisely cut leaves, rolled it into a ball, then dispatched it down her hole before Three Toes had even thought to blink.

How is that? Could it be that Tat is so fast that she does not have time to think about Inti's dancing lights? Wee Tree's brain began to feel like wood.

He took one last look up towards the ebullient sun as it pierced the edges of a few lingering clouds. Dead, docile, dumb, dark clouds. They appeared to Tree like deposed ancient kings and queens. Laced in their crimson-edged gowns, dejected, drawn on their tattered, battered thrones across a reluctant sky. It seemed that their pulsating, bloodied edges ached with malevolent intent.

Wee Tree watched as the blaze from all that brilliant, blinding light died away to leave no trace but darkness. Staggering – always! Complete blackness. An infinite intensity of absolute nothingness plunged the world into darkness. Big, powerful, all embracing, smiling Inti with his explosive radiance, his effervescent gift of life, had crawled meekly away. Wee Tree wondered how the

2

most powerful Element in the world could be dismissed like a subservient minion. Other Elements began to stir.

For a while nothing reigned. The fool clouds acted like transient, feigned monarchs that puffed and bluffed and pretended to be. Within that blank, black night the moon stalked the shadow of Pachamama.

Under that shadowy cloak the good hide and the bad emerge. Plundering, prevaricating predators have preened their plumes, honed their nails, flossed their fangs, their darkest nightly cloaks covering an eager encounter. Their hopes of skulduggery heightened by the pretentious infallibility of invisibility.

Unknown to the dark night that has no humour, a laceration slowly appears in its tenebrous gown. The nights creep on and the tear gets brighter and rounder until the hole reveals: Monocled Moon. The bustling, furtive nightly secrets are shown; illuminating the illicit to all. The moon, joyous in its concealment, reflects the mirth of the Laughing Sun. There are no secrets amongst the Elements, only pure, shining honesty. The good smile, the bad shrink. Another day begins with a Laughing Sun.

Wee Tree was watching Three Toes. He was not much further along the same branch than he had been a few days before. Tree could see where he was heading: a lush, tender, toothsome cucura. Hanging, gravity-averting, tantalisingly enticing. So slothsome it had "Three Toes" written right across it. The rich, ambrosia aroma drifted alluringly, straight up his nose. It slapped his taste buds. He could hardly contain himself. The sweet fragrance was melting his senses into a boiling soup of insatiable desire. His eyes focused on nothing but the cucura. Every muscle engaged as he urged his frame into top gear. Wee Tree could see his back leg gently releasing the branch. First one toe, then the next and finally the last. The leg dropped half an inch then hung there in perfect, static symmetry before easing forward with unruffled calmness. Not a single hair trembled against his slick, aerodynamic, cucura-grabbing body. Not even an eyelash quivered. Three Toes was in motion.

Towards the end of the day, Three Toes was so close he was almost evanescent with desire. Spiritual heaven was about to be claimed. It was there. Millimetres from his toes. Just one more leg and the cucura would meet sloth; a union in sloth heaven but the Laughing Sun had completed another day for the forest and it descended abruptly into blackness.

Wee Tree sighed. He switched his vascular system into night use and shut down. With Three Toes it was more difficult to determine one state from another. The daily humdrum business of the feisty forest quelled. The squadrons of manic mosquitoes and busy bomber flies turned off their propeller wings. Millions of drumming, cacophonous cicadas upbeat and over ground, hidden in their treetop canopy suddenly stopped. Within an instant the jungle percussion ceased. For a moment the engines of the earth expired, their manic power generators cut dead. A quiescent curtain of serene peacefulness dropped over the warm, darkening forest.

Slowly the night army emerged from their deep, dark, black, buried beds. One by one, stones lifted, foliage fluttered, leaves leapt, caves hummed and the earth parted. Silently, surreptitiously, the suspicious, susceptible, mean and hungry slipped their covers, cast a cautious eye and perspicacious ear into the death-dark night. Pachamama shivered with the unseen while the covert, tenebrous sky bombinated from the beat of hidden wings. Wings with claws, hooks, spurs, beaks and fangs. Predators abounded: small and large.

Within the colossal treetops of Fly Forest – their cathedral columns holding up the sky – hundreds of circling fruit bats danced and played to their echoes. Skittishly flitting, darting, diving, relishing the perfumes of the air. Sedulously searching, air-light, blood-thin membrane wings supported their hungry bodies in the warm, humid night. Blindingly effortless, sweeping and swooping around concealed forest obstacles, they dashed ever closer to the new, nightly market of rich, fresh, succulent fruit. Prized, fought over, competing fruits. Forest figs and large, melting, dangling jungle grape cucuras. A fruit bat's daydream.

By coincidence, also a sloth's night dream. Three Toes might not move that fast but there was nothing wrong with his ears, nor his nose for that matter. He hung, still as a dead stick. Growing life forms, mosses, lichens and algae had stained his rust red, ginger bled hair green and mouldy. Vegetation sprouted from his compost, camouflaged back. Three Toes was a mobile allotment. Looking and smelling more like rotting, decaying forest debris than any other warm-blooded mammal would seriously wish for. Dead sticks and Three Toes were much the same. Which was just the way Three Toes liked it.

Tree was listening to the bats dancing in the dark and wondering how Inti went out. "But how does he do that? How does he sink in a pool of blood at one end of the forest then pop up from the other end under cover of darkness? He is the giver of all light, he is the brightest Element for kilometres around, yet he goes out at night. How does he do that?"

Thoughts like these bothered Tree as did the behaviour of the animals around him. "Pachamama," queried Wee Tree. "Tat moves like Vivacious Wind. Three Toes barely moves but I'm twenty centimetres high and never move. Why can't I move?"

Pachamama, the Mother Earth, was always there for Tree. "I am the bearer of all life, Tree. I created you. If you went running around like Tat then who would hold the sky up?"

Tree had not looked at it that way. Being only twenty centimetres high, it was sometimes difficult enough holding himself up.

"Why does Inti go out then?" Tree rapidly added, changing the subject completely.

Pachamama had lost the thread of the conversation but had learnt from previous experience with Tree that these things became increasingly difficult. "Talk to Ruminant Whale, she knows about these things."

Inti could not see Whale when he slipped under the sea. He gave Rumbustious Sea a touch on the side and said, "Hullo Sea, how are you? Have you seen Ruminant?"

"Ah! Sun, my old son. Yes, she's down below chasing squid. She'll be up shortly. It has been a mixed day really. A bit of a rough start: bad touch of wind earlier. Gruesome Gale whipped me into quite a froth. White stuff throwing up in all directions. Not had a turn like that for a while. Then Tempest Cloud had a look in. He had a load of water on the brain and threw that everywhere. You disappeared over Tempest's hullabaloo and it all went dark, so I was chucking it, Cloud was throwing it and Gale was whipping it. At that point Ruminant Whale drifted in. She seemed insouciant as usual. I waved relentlessly on top of her, Gale lathered her back and Tempest came all over her. She rode the lot. She humped the waves, roller-coastered their backs, stroked down the big dippers, slid under the erupting washers and continued singing to the world throughout. I don't think she noticed anything unusual. Eventually Tempest Cloud ran out of juice. Gale, for all his huffing and puffing collapsed and my waters returned to sublime calmness. Whale flipped her flukes and sank to the depths. Then you reappeared."

"That's Whale; she has seen it all before. She's been around a long time. When you are the curator of the world's ancient history there isn't much you have not seen or don't know about. It will take a bit more than Gruesome Gale and Tempest to vex Whale. Oh well, good night, it is time to wake up the forest."

On the western fringes of the forest, the Fly Mountains rose vertically up from Pachamama. Mysteries from the dark unknown mingled deep within their high, sepulchre walls. Menacingly, oppressively tall, the mystical mountains dramatically contrasted with the lush, evergreen forest. The pulsating shadows of a wakening dawn flashed upon the inimical ores like effigies of the restless dead until the very rocks themselves appeared to silently move. Pushing prodigious columns vertically from the Mother Earth, their baked, grey, granite blocks soared through the forest's living, green capped canopy. Their towering heads burst through the cloaked clouds disappearing into an infinite aura of veiled menace. Fortresses from another world, their overbearing presence conjured to mythical proportions. They made no pretence. There was no subterfuge of dominion, theirs was elementary dominance by overwhelming, silent, brutal magnitude.

Atop the monarchial monoliths the ancient fountains of life erupted from the binding forces holding the stone together. Earth's sacred waters burst from its broiling core when Pachamama created life. Splitting open the ancient rocks, the spirit-ridden waters forced their cures along their paths, opening and gouging with ruthless indifference. The lines of descent as fickle as life itself.

Those pure, cascading waters that ripped open the primeval mountains flowed out towards the mighty oceans. Along their paths they gouged out trenches across the face of Mother Earth, leaving behind mutilated, disfiguring scars. Scars filled with the tears sourced from the intimate depths of her heart and soul. From those mysterious mountains the Rio Fly swelled into a mighty, flooding, life-giving river to feed a grateful world.

The world upon a world bred its own life. With the awakening of another day, before the sun snapped the eastern line, the half-lights twitched. Shadows jumped. What lives looked dead; the dead looked alive. The mountains towered heavier, darker, probing the outer reaches of the atmosphere. Clouds draped around them like old hobos' coats – tattered and torn, hiding malodorous beings of discontent. Each new dawn promulgated new sounds, screaming, piercing sounds, amplified by mountain walls reverberating over the dark forest below as if the demons of the dead were forced to breathe the stale stench from their own decaying bodies.

Each day, before the new light could trickle its way through the thick forest walls, Tree would listen to those sounds. Most he knew, but in the faint, distant background he could hear agonising, deathly tearing sounds as if something was ripping apart its own living flesh. He did not know these noises but the endless, pain-ridden screams made his cells creep.

He was about to ask Pachamama about it when he spotted a dozen leaves give a quick quiver and then a little leap. Tree would have jumped too, except that he was rooted to the spot. Four pairs of black compound eyes protruded from under the leaves. Each pair surveyed the forest, each oblivious to the other, like independent binoculars, searching with a view. Occasionally a pair would blink. It was Tat. She was scanning. A juicy flycatcher would be a yummy treat or perhaps a young, lardy jungle chicken. Now, there was a thought. Tat could hardly contain herself. Her long, crimped, hair-like black legs rustled and juddered with excitement under her temporary umbrella of dead, crinkly, dry leaves. In fact everything was beginning to shudder like a minor earthquake. Tat's eyes began to roll around in directions that Tat had no control of, so she pulled herself together and returned to a dead pile of leaves with eight, small globes searching above them.

High above Tat in the grey, forest-filtered, half-tones of morning light, Three Toes looked up.

"So, it worked again," he thought in a slow, sloth sort of self-congratulatory way. The cucura was hanging inches from him. The bats' aerial senses had been out-batted. Their finely tuned sense of smell had been sloth-dosed, permeated with the overriding odours emitting from Three Toes' bacteria-infested, composted, mulch-stacked back. He had out-smelt them with the stench of overpowering biological decay. It was chemical warfare – sloth style. He was about to introduce himself to a rather large and overripe cucura.

From nowhere, with a dizzying flutter of radiant blues and blacks emerged Princess, a periander butterfly. Her erratic movement, produced by enormous silk-veined, translucent, softly hypnotic wings, danced under Three Toes' eyes to land on his cucura. Built like a finely honed ballerina, her spider web-thin legs held her fragile body delicately to his fruit, freezing him dead to a stick. Her beauty was as radiant as the scattered sun-rays diffracting from her gently vibrating, mesmerising wings. Three Toes had never seen such beauty. For an instant he had forgotten the cucura, his hunger, the many days he had taken to get there. He had stopped breathing for fear the force of his breath would sweep her away, never to be seen again. She seemed so delicate yet so secure, so in command. Princess, oblivious to a mulch-smelling sloth that resembled a compost heap hanging from a stick, swayed deliciously, temptress-sly, with a surreptitious eye to the dozens of male periander admirers. Hanging behind, fervent with expectation were squadrons of admirers; devoted followers, each enthusiastically hopeful to catch the eye of the most beautiful princess in the forest. Three Toes was bewitched. Had he seen the entourage behind him he would, no doubt, have despaired and brought his senses back to the inner core of his rumbling stomach. For now, though, it was as if he had been transported through the rainbow radiance of a butter-flight, agile-light, fly-light world of blue-black periander butterflies. A world where he was king and she was queen and together they would dance the twists and turns of heaven's endless currents. His wings stretched to the outer reaches of the universe, the cosmic winds would pick up his feather-light body and transmit his love towards the vapours of immortal time. She would transcend the universal light and wrap his feather-light frame with her warm, limitless, expanding heart, showering him with unconditional, universally endless love.

It was a loud, ear-splitting crack that reassembled Three Toes back into a sloth. It was also a downward, hurtling sensation that, although he still held the branch, gave him the impression that gravity was the predominant force at that particular moment. Three Toes was not wrong.

Luck was with him today, for although Princess was now a long gone, distant dream in another royal world, a large pile of dead leaves was his fast-coming new one. Three Toes crashed into Mother Earth with the dead weight of an exploding meteorite. The earth rocked. The forest momentarily went silent.

Tat had a mental seizure. She heard this bolt of lightning and rotated her two main eyes in a heavenly direction. They relayed the very bad news that the sky was falling down. If ebullition was the force of outrage then Tat exceeded this with a perfectly synchronised, multi-legged acceleration never before performed in the history of tarantulas. Not in the least in Tat's family heredity, for she was the fastest, the most nimble, eight-legged, sideways thrusting spider to have scavenged the land. She was the most advanced model of Tat-propelled arachnids in any modern, living forest. She had just pulled the last two legs into a hole before the whole of the world went flat above her.

Three Toes was on his back with his eyes tightly closed. He was still holding onto his stick. The only difference, that he could work out, was that he was now forty metres below where he had been half a second before. It had occurred to him that the only other major difference was that he was now holding up the stick and not the other way around. He meditated gently on this rapid turn of events. It is funny how, in just one instant and for no reason of your own making, your world as you knew it no longer exists. What you depended on once now depends on you. Once you were top of the tree, now you are not. It was while he was in this ruminative state, pondering the affairs of life and the indecipherable turns of misfortune, that he suddenly remembered the rum facts of life's basic values. Whether at the top of your tree or below, somewhere amongst all of this used to be a wild, ripe, fleshy jungle cucura. Love and butterflies are all very well, but a well-built sloth has to eat.

Three Toes dared to open an eye. Only one at first. Too many may have dazzled him and would use twice the energy. One would do for now. He opened the left one. It felt nearer. The stick looked pretty much the same as before. He still had four sets of toes dug into it with four legs in more or less the same position. To all intents and purposes, stick and sloth were an entity. This was one of those moments where the courage required to ascertain the truth is possibly too much for most run-of-the-forest sloths, but Three Toes was made of sterner stuff. Prising open his right eye, he slowly bent his head backwards to the spot that had grabbed his attention for the last few days of his life.

A nauseous, perturbing sensation pervaded his inner sanctum. It started from a numb space somewhere behind his eyes and settled sickeningly, dolefully, in the centre of his empty belly. The cucura had gone. Three Toes was sick.

Tat, too, was sick. The smell was awful. It was dark. It was unmentionable, like rotting vegetables spewed from a vile, bile-belched belly by a malodorous breath.

She was going to be really sick if she didn't get out of this rotting, spider coffin. Her hole, while comfortable enough for a serendipitous escape from some stalking, spider-eating snake, was not what Tat would wish for as indeterminate long term accommodation. However, the front door was immovably secured by something heavily, hideously and unimaginably rotten. There was nothing to do but to hold her breath and sit it out.

Tree had been watching passively in a stoical tree way. The wisdom of a Wee Tree may not be that of Ruminant Whale but it did, as it occurred to Tree, appear to be somewhat more abundant than Three Toes'. Stealth and cunning are two virtues but the slothful slowness of Three Toes seemed to take the contemplative approach to the finest limits of masterful redundancy. He could have stretched an arm out a month before and now be on his way towards another larder. It was all so unnatural to a small, static tree, but having watched forest life in its entirety, the sloth way was as paradoxical as it was perplexing. But there was no disguising that Three Toes was no naive animal; he had developed chemical warfare to flawless perfection; he was muscular, powerful; he had formidable armoury. Such an impressive animal didn't achieve those attributes on a diet of one cucura per fortnight. So why was he lying on his back crying? Tree had no answer. Pachamama was being elusive and Whale was not to be heard, so he decided to wait and see.

Gradually, the numbness of brain began to clear. Three Toes, being a sloth of exemplary analytical prowess, surmised that if the branch with sloth had descended to Pachamama then so had the branch with cucura. A slight but imperceptible grin spread across his round face. The uninformed perhaps would not have noticed, but to a sloth it was a whopping great smile. Gently but punctiliously he held the branch with his back feet while releasing his front arms to create a huge, hairy, curved net above his head. Slowly he bent his head back then brought his arms together, pushing up the dry, dead foliage and debris so it spilled over his arms like a giant sieve. The unknown, heavier forest elements moved towards the earth while the lighter waste dispersed like water over a hairy dam wall. His arms closed together drawing in bits of earth, stones, wood, some dead beetle shells and one big, juicy cucura. There, right towards his

16

toes, was the sole focus of this mighty, tactical, fruit-enslaving combat machine. Letting the debris fall through his arms he rolled the fruit onto his right toe, then bringing it to a wide-opening, smiling, curling mouth, he dropped it in. His lips closed around it. He caressed it around his molars momentarily before crushing the succulent, sweet flesh and slopping those fantastic flavours over his drooling, obstreperous tongue. Thirty thousand taste buds ignited the gustatory nerve of a fastidious sloth's well-being.

It was a relieved Tat when a chink of light filtered into her coffin. The odorous pong of death also began to diminish. Cautiously edging her way through the crushed wreckage of unwanted forest, Tat thrust some eyes above her tomb. There, not more than one metre from her was the rear end of a three toed sloth. It walked, with what Tat thought was a swing and a swagger and if she was not too sure about that then she also was not too sure she could detect a soft but self-satisfying, sloth-styled hum emanating about.

Tree had found his answer: sloth was the pinnacle of masterful tacticians.

Chapter II

A penetrating easterly had been blowing the high ridges
of the forest's peaks for several weeks. Its cool, cutting
edge trimmed and sharpened from the oceanic
frontiers. It wasn't going to give up. Its day had come
and the day was going to dance in the beauty of its
tooled precision. The land cooled after the fervid
summer months. The mountains sent a shiver along the
highlands of the forest's spine. Vivacious Wind,
penetrating and sharp, knew his time was almost there.
By battering the Mother Earth with indefatigable
tenacity, it knew the Elements would talk. It was their
time. It was Tempest Cloud that picked up the calling.
He had gently and inconspicuously collected over the
freshly cooled mountains and grown. The temperature
dropped. The clouds deepened. Their numbers swelled,
bellying obtusely until one could not be distinguished
from another. Their amalgamate, shapeless forms
pushed higher. They grew into mighty, colossal war
columns, towering into the diminishing skies,
expanding, rampant, festering, all-encompassing
tumours smothering the world with their sullen
resentment. They blackened out the Laughing Sun and
grew darker in colour and mood, their power and anger
agitating the cowering life below.

Tempest Cloud rocked the tops of the mountains, clinging to the slopes like lost survivors holding out for the slenderest of hopes, descending, determined, demonized under their accumulating weight. They massed ever higher, ever blacker, ever angrier. Inflated with power and energy their columns marched, uncompromising, down the hills onto a flinching forest. Their moment arrived. Monocled Moon opened a spectacled eye above the western horizon, then closed it quickly. Tempest Cloud was not to be denied. Their bellies exploding with wrath and power, their drums beating their intentions to all that lived and everything that died. Life lived in fear and fear fled.

The corrosive collisions ripped through those bellicose, berating bellies, stripping away nuclear binding atoms as easily as petals from a flower. For as they collided, those broken particles intensified their combative manoeuvres. Million-volt white light, fire and thunder bellowed eardrum-splitting, stomach-churning war cries, leaving none in doubt as to their intentions. Fly Forest went black, dead black. Even the sun's spy, Monocled Moon, was extinguished with no polite prose. No negotiation. Indubitable subservience demanded by unchallenged dominance. Vivacious Wind roared and Tempest charged. It shook the sap out from the deepest, throbbing roots of the strongest kapoks.

Finally the rains came. The forces, no longer capable of holding back the masses, their sides split open. The attack began, exploding into Mother Earth like driven bolts torpedoed from a mega-watt power machine with a vile temper. It lashed the land and the seas, lighting the skies with electric fire-storms. Its anger cracked open the air, atom by atom. A nuclear parasite, it split the cosmic forces with tenacity and fear. Fly Forest was blasted from the mountains to the ocean's shore and back.

The days turned into weeks. The weeks into months. The torrential bombardment ceaseless; the atomic assault uncompromising. Tempest Cloud was a mighty Element. Even Inti wondered where he found the energy. Every other Element had been subdued and disciplined into second place. There was no reckoning with Tempest Cloud and Vivacious Wind. Finally, Cloud's temper subdued, his payload diminished and with it, his power and testiness. Monocled Moon passed a respectful wink to the cloud. Inti, from the other quarter of the sky, returned it with a reverent smile. The Elements were impressed and passed out the message. A caring, southerly wind was the first to pick it up. He held the tired cloud, pulling the fragmented spent forms together then drifted him off over the seas. To rebuild, replenish. The Elements paused briefly then nodded a silent acknowledgement of respect. Pachamama had seen it all before. Balance was restored, the land nurtured. Ruminant Whale archived a memorable note. Somewhere a cock crowed. Tat dripped from her hole and hung herself out to dry.

The Laughing Sun's warm grin greeted Whale. She was waiting, looking dead east towards the exact spot that Inti would appear. The first thing Inti saw in this bright, new, fresh day of a world was Whale looking straight through him. It happened every day. He didn't know how she did it. Whale used his fresh, early morning, vibrant, infrared wavelengths to carry her songs across the world. To every plant, to every breathing creature, she sang a little love, a little history, a little reminder that we all need each other. She sang into his heart with the very essence of her lifeblood so the whole world could understand how we are connected and how we all need each other to flourish. Laughing Sun, of course, had no idea Whale was using him for this purpose. All he knew was that she sang to him every morning. For every morning, for the last one hundred million years that he could think of, Whale had done this. He'd consider it the end of it all if it failed to happen; and to be honest, the day would not seem like it had started if Whale wasn't there to greet him. After one hundred million years or whatever, one gets set into one's routine. So, there was Whale looking at him with her two too-big intelligent eyes every day and she would sing to him. Just him, the two of them; his own beautiful lullaby as he hung, gently rising out of Rumbustious Sea. He felt a slight swagger, a solar shift, a shaking of his pulsating neutrons as the world's only appointed curator of its ancient history sang to him. It was part of the solar system; life would not exist without it. It started the day on the right note. So Sun smiled, Whale sang and she smiled back.

An old albatross was in the skies behind Whale. He could see her clearly heading dead east towards Inti, her calf close by, pounding into the waves just away from her port flipper. He sat in the air currents listening to the harmonies of Whale's song. Connecting with her love and relating to her messages as he had every day in his long life. He felt privileged this day to be so close to the world's curator. Not that the song was any less transfixing, but such close proximity to her massive frame and small, vulnerable calf placed his physicality into perspective. Inti's light, throwing amber, ember-speckled lanterns off the tips of Sea's splintering waves, shredding over Ruminant Whale's grey streamlined body, resembled thousands of dancing stars. Each excited by the meaning of life, of a truly precious and unique world sung only as Whale could. The Laughing Sun laughed and laughed and laughed.

For some reason today, the old albatross reflected compunctiously on life's flight path. Perhaps it was Whale's song. Perhaps it was seeing her with her newborn: the old, the new. Perhaps it was Inti's magical light show, harmonising with her indisputable wisdom. The old albatross knew not, but he could not stop his mind tracking back to those tragedies that affect the course of life. Maybe it was something in Whale's song. He had flown this passage a thousand times. His mind allowed the nostalgia within the comfort of familiarity. He was coasting effortlessly, his twelve foot wingspan planing just feet above the rolling waves of the southern ocean. Occasionally, he would allow his wing-tipped, primary flight feathers to nip the top off a wave – more from boredom than a lack of concentration. The wind-lashed spray whipped white froth from the waves against his weather-beaten face. A face that had prevailed against every element that Mother Earth could throw at him. A face that took the world head on. Nothing fazed him; he was an old school Southern Royal Albatross. Today though, he allowed his mind to drift, to drift back to that dark, sad summer; that tragedy. A vicissitude of chance, a fickleness that has no effect on a planet, but a devastating, life-disturbing severance to any one albatross.

"Why was it me?" he thought, then dismissed it quickly. He had analysed it often enough.

It was a summer of unusually heavy storms, many summers ago. He had returned to his rock as he did each year. All the Southern Royals returned to the same island. It was rich in sea life – sprats and squid were abundant. Rumbustious Sea kept a munificent larder. A staple diet for a large variety of seafarers. A favourite place of the young: easy to catch and palatable. Even Whale was not averse to a large lunch.

"I wonder what else disappears down her massive throat?" he idly pondered.

He always arrived slightly earlier than his mainstay contemporaries. It guaranteed him the highest, westerly facing rock. Now though, it was known as his. Nobody would challenge him for it. A respected patriarch of the Southern Royals, he had gained respect in the time-honoured way: perpetual presence and dignity.

Each year he stood on that rock. Ready to meet his partner. He would stand indefatigably anchored no matter what weather Vivacious Wind hurled at him. Day after day he would stand on that rock. His big-billed beak pushed unfalteringly into the screaming, pressure-packed winds. With resolute fortitude he scanned the horizon seeking the one love of his life. The one bird he had promised to stay with for all his life. The only one he wanted to stay with. He could recognise her the moment she popped her beak above the horizon several kilometres away and she would see him – statuesque, the proud figurehead of a gargantuan flotilla. He would be there standing head and shoulders above the world, looking directly at her. No matter from which direction she came or on what day, he found her; he never dropped his gaze until she stood next to him.

For days, for weeks, he stood on that rock seeking, scanning, searching. Standing on one big webbed foot, then the other, then he would shuffle back to the first without a break, twenty-four hours a day. His beak pushed hard into the relentless wind, his necked outstretched. The mighty, intimidating wind blowing back the tears stained with the white whipped sea salt, wrenched from the atom-stripped oceans. His heart barely able to beat, the shadows of torment cloaking his soul, fuelling his anxiety, smothering all rational thought. He knew not whether it was night or day. He didn't care. She failed to show. For several years thereafter he would stand on that rock, facing those south westerlies, those gut-wrenching, pertinacious winds, watching that mighty ocean, watching for that one speck on the horizon. That one speck that would light up his heart, his whole life and turn it around again; turn night into day, day nightmares into daydreams. It never arrived. He never saw her again. He never fully recovered from it.

Even now, after all those years, a wretchedness can tear at his heart. Inexplicably, nonchalantly, dropping into his thoughts like an oil drop onto still water, it dilates and smothers. In a slice of a second it can turn him from carefree to inconsolable. No warning, no presentiment, it's a neurotic bomb: it goes off; he crumbles instantly. No fight, no resistance, instantaneous surrender. Now though, he is used to it. It is as much a part of him as she was all those years ago. He has learnt not to dwell upon it; he allows it to shatter him, then he dismisses it. Life's experiences dissemble the pain.

An enigmatic half smile crossed his face as he was adventitiously lifted by an eddying spurt of air tumbling up from Rumbustious Sea's cross-currents. It reminded him of another occasion when he had been caught in a mighty electric storm. He could see that there was no way he could gain sufficient height to gently bob over the top. These were colossal, compacted thunderheads, stockpiled towers, stacked cumulus upon cumulus. Even with his accumulated flight miles he had not witnessed anything like those bomb beating monsters in front of him. So, he dipped a wing and cut a gracious curve towards the south to nip around the least voracious wing of the beast. Unperturbed, he gained a little altitude, cruising effortlessly with an equanimity of a seasoned flyer but subconsciously, cautiously, he monitored Tempest Cloud.

The strong, westerly winds suddenly turned towards the south. Tenaciously stinging, Tempest Cloud whipped him into a frenzied, unbalanced psychotic. Cloud raced across the heaving, panting air like a deranged demon screaming from having his sides torn open then smashed together by unstoppable hammers. Albatross, completely out of control from the relentless, senseless pressure waves was pushed southwards. He was consumed and then the lights went out.

Day and night fused into a rancid, black, boiling cauldron of splintering atoms, haphazard pressure strikes, pummelling and buffeting from all angles. The tumultuous erratic pressures under his enormous, air-gliding wings caught him unawares, turning and flipping him like some worthless flotsam on the tumble-turning waves. Wings designed to catch every breath of air to transport his large, sea-soaring, world-wandering body thousands of miles with little effort. Now, those huge wings fought against him as each maelstrom gyred him into a new dimension, a new plane. Each time he closed in his wings, regaining some control, regaining his plane to rescue his line, he would be smashed into another pressure pot. No longer interested in where he was going, he concentrated on staying above the demented Rumbustious Sea. To gain height he knew he had to open his wings but each time he did so he was shredded and thrown into another voracious vortex. Mega-volts of lightning exploded over his battered body sending him blind, for how long he never knew. Still he held his line and prayed to the Elements that he could hold it straight and not go down into a snarling slab of a bad-tempered wave spitting an all-consuming appetite. The winds pushed him further south, getting colder, getting exhausted. The storm lasted days and daylight died. His muscles, toxic from fatigue, failed. His body no longer responded, his mind numb; blind, he tumbled from the sham sky.

He briefly remembered a searing pain in his left wing, then oblivion. When he regained consciousness the storm had passed, the seas rocked soothingly, the sky above was veined with whispering, white clouds lit by the Laughing Sun. The pain in his wing was still there but he could not move it. Slowly, he worked out from the shapes around that he was on a ship, one of those small flerd-made machines that he would curiously notice way below him. The little, tin, bobbing boats made him smile; the irony was not lost on him. It was weeks before his strength returned and his wing recovered. It never was quite the same again: a bit bent with a dihedral at an odd angle but he could still whip the top off a careless wave.

Every year, he returned to the rock to look for a mate. There were some around. Most turned him down: some didn't like his bent wing, some didn't like his cavalier attitude. One or two, he thought, were perhaps okay. He wasn't sure though: these new birds, somehow, looked a bit flighty.

Today he was due to return. His mind raced back to his last encounter. She was a bird after his own heart: aloof, discerning, bright but not supercilious; style with humility and a big heart. He remembered how his heart trembled, his feathers ruffled. It had been a long time since he had felt like that; he did not know that he could still feel that way. He remembered thinking, "Be brave, boy," and so he had moved close to her. She didn't back away. It had encouraged him to be bold, so he slowly stretched out his neck, both feet firmly anchored to the rocks, had closed his eyes, prayed, then gently, ever so gently, tapped his beak against hers.

Would she be back this year?

Far below the soaring albatross, Whale was ruminating on the high seas. She had all the time in the world. All the time for her newly born son. She also knew that there was no time at all. The balance of the earth was shifting. It had done so several times in the past. Now it was on the cusp of doing so again. The old stories she had been told had similarities with today's events. Life was going to be tough from here on, although she was not sure how; only her stories survived from the ancient past.

Over the last ten thousand years or more the earth was stable, everything lived in harmony. There was a mutual balance. The whales had developed their intellect, their spiritual essence. They required nothing from the world other than sea, air and food. They had transcended the physical and had touched the heights of ethereal enlightenment. She had descended from the highest lines and become revered over the globe. One day, too, her calf would touch the ethereal pinnacle and transcend the physical by right of worth and birth to become the Curator.

Whale reflected on this and the more she did so the more a sense of sadness deposited itself upon her. She mused back to the days of her fathers. How once there were thousands of pods, each with hundreds of whales. They spanned the globe. Each pod specialised in

Pachamama's history, each sang to the world. Their own song, their own music, their own wisdom. The whole world filled with music, knowledge, tolerance and compassion. She never knew such days but the stories from her foremothers filled her with wonder. Now, it was gone leaving just a hint of sadness.

She would have loved to have lived in the days where all were connected. Each species with its own strengths working towards a totally enlightened planet. But her kind were hunted and killed in the recent past. Why? She did not know, nor did anybody else. Her ancestors sang each day, but it made no difference.

"Why do they not hear our songs? Why can they not listen to our wisdom? Must they kill all of us? Surely to live with acceptance and to enjoy each other's quirks and ambiguities is far more fun and entertaining than living all alone. All other animals and plants connect and listen, why cannot they; do they have to take all and give nothing back? Everything on this planet lives in harmony, in synchronised balance, each dependent on the other but for some reason the flerds cannot connect to others, they prefer to destroy. Even the simplest of living cells hear our songs. Not the flerds ..."

Whale's thoughts trailed off. She pondered with melancholy on the tragedy they were promoting, but more so for what she knew would happen in the future:

the Elements wouldn't tolerate an unbalanced world indefinitely. They never had done.

Her calf that had been dive-bombing with Rumbustious Sea had become a little bored with the gently rolling Element that covered most of Pachamama's skin. He was now pushing his tonne of puppy fat into Whale's abdomen. Dwarfing the calf, she brought down her large, left flipper onto his back, plummeting him fathoms beneath in a broiling cuss of foam and bubbles. The small calf, rolled and winded, came scooting back to the surface, drawing a huge lungful of air before engaging all engines to power into his mother's side. He turned fast but knew what was coming. He was far too slow for his powerful mother. She smacked again with her flipper, this time rolling over onto him using the advantage of her seventy tonne mass. She caught him square, catching him on the top of his head. He spun into a swirling, uncontrollable nosedive. Half concussed, half winded, he spiralled back down to the calm, cooling layers below Sea's rough, jagged edge. The coldness of the ocean brought his senses back; he levelled himself and gained control. He loved this game with his mother. She always won. He swam back up and rammed his nose with all his might into his mother's nose. They bonked noses several more times then sang to each other with their secret, signature song. The bond between them strengthened, their love unmitigated, it could never be broken.

The Elements were relaxed. Monocled Moon hung in the still, blue-black sky by an invisible force that none could see. His eyelid half closed, drooping like a lonely, fresh-filled tear off an unemotional face. He watched the world, no words, no opinion, no judgement. Yet Monocled Moon was in partnership with the Laughing Sun and was part of the pair of the most formidable forces Mother Earth and all who dwelled upon her could know. A dominant, domicile Element that affected every living cell by nothing more than his sheer presence.

Inti was high in the sky and in full view, laughing to everybody and nobody. Vivacious Wind was away, presumably whipping wild elsewhere and Rumbustious Sea behaved like a scolded schoolboy who had been caught out and was now trying to regain respect. The Elements have the power of life. They all work together, for one affects another. Their dependencies and interrelationships are complex and total. They may be unpredictable but they are not ambiguous. Rumbustious Sea can wash your leaves or wash you away. Vivacious Wind can move a leaf or a tree. Inti can warm you or chill you. And Pachamama? Nobody could predict her. She would be as serene as an angel one moment then she could split her sides through some tumultuous, provocative, bellyache. Fire and venomous explosions would rip from her, destroying everything around and occasionally, everything that's not around. She was the most unpredictable element. She could kiss you or kill you. She created, she destroyed. She was indifferent to it all, or so it seemed. Everything that lived and breathed were her children. She did what was needed for the benefit of all. Sometimes though, the all could not see that.

Today, she was talking to Tree. Tree had been listening to Whale; he couldn't understand why flerds would wish to kill all the whales. It troubled him. Whale had been singing to him during the night but not in her usual high, sing-song fluent-flipper, flippant manner. Her harmonious melodies would normally melt a smouldering heart into the warmth of a caressing Mother Earth. Like she and her foremothers had done since creation. Today though, there was a tiredness to her tones, her mind distant from her normal, synchronised harmonies. Tree felt her. All felt her needs.

"Why don't flerds like whales?" he asked, puzzled.

Pachamama knew of the flerds' bellicose tendencies but she tried to be neutral when explaining the actions of her children. It wasn't for her to say who was good or otherwise. She maintained a balance. The flerds were pushing the boundaries, it was true. The Elements had already issued warnings.

"It's not that they dislike them. They don't understand what the whales really are. They either kill to eat or kill because they are afraid."

Tree persisted: "But why would they wish to kill all of Whale's family? She is so warm and wise."

"It is complicated Tree. Not every creature is enlightened. Some, like the flerds, have little or no concept of the benefits of coexistence. They have something called ego that interferes with their ability to promote their inner selves above a simplistic, basic level. I'm not sure that I can explain that to a tree. No offence!"

"What's ego? Inti is enlightenment, does he have ego?" Pachamama was beginning to feel the earth opening up and the chasms getting deeper, but as she was the only perpetrator of ground-opening-up and she was the earth, it was all becoming a little self-consuming.

"Think of it like Tempest Cloud blocking out the Laughing Sun, then nobody can see the light. Some creatures fumble around in the dark before they get drenched?"

"But that's a good thing!"

"Yes, but not if you're drowning." With that Pachamama wished Tree an enlightened day and fled.

Chapter III

Tempest Cloud was playful – nonchalantly tossing blazing, electric daggers between himself and Pachamama. Flashing, sparkle-sharp blades bounced off their booming boundaries, cutting irregular, zigzag, razor-edged serrations, with stinging strikes. Occasionally, the haphazard daggers slipped between the clouds towards the highest point on Mother Earth in violent, dancing arcs. Momentarily Cloud grinned. A rapid, unhesitating smirk spread across their black faces as they witnessed the devastation on the unsuspecting, trembling beings below. No time though for any self-gratifying, stentorian belly laughs as daggers ceaselessly catapulted from all and to any. Tempest Cloud tossed them with insatiable, malevolent recklessness.

Amidst the lightning strikes, a tree is hit and falls in the night. Tempest smiles. Inti laughs. Tree is agog, sunlight blazing onto his leaves. No fickle half-lights. Fully fledged Inti rays shone straight onto Wee Tree's leaves. But one of his near family are down, roots violently ripped from the earth, upended and rigged amongst other trees. Its mighty trunk prostrate. In its earthbound travel it has collided into two large figs. The colossal impact has smashed through branches which crumbled like dried sticks under rampaging elephants.

The momentous top-heavy forces, too much for their shallow buttress roots to resist, snap-levered away tearing trenches from the tenuous soil. Proud pillars to the sky no more. They lay helpless, dying, ready to be consumed and rotted. Their mammoth carcasses down, symbols to their immensity, protruding amongst the wreckage of busted branches, shattered shrubs and a scattered carnage of rooftop leaves. Wee Tree sensed the emptiness.

The fallen trees were immensely important as sources of food and shelter for many forest flora and fauna. For the several thousand displaced cicadas that view was not necessarily shared. The crashing cacophony of the trees' descent had drowned the drums of rapid-beating membranes forced by their impromptu but imperative evacuation. Their neighbours were also not so enchanted with the uninvited intrusion which instigated an immediate problem by suddenly doubling the housing occupancy. Even though they were over-packed and crowded it was still no deterrent to their basic instincts. When the Laughing Sun turned his incessant drive to scorch the world, it was the sign for the millions of invisible cicadas to drum their beat together, new neighbours and old and once again the forest became alive to the sound of their machinery.

Those enormous, rotting lumps of degenerating timber attracted all forms of life seeking to benefit from the unexpected bonanza. Animals, insects and birds congregated from miles around to feed and breed. Sparkling sunlight had revivified all the latent, buried, dormant seeds dispersed over countless years. They absorbed this new energy and transformed the forest floor into a seething, fertile, multifarious tangle of flora, algae and moss.

It was the moment all young rainforest trees wait for. Some never find the energy-giving light, but from adversity new life flourishes and the forest regenerates. This was Tree's moment but he had to move fast: competition was immense. It was a once in a lifetime opportunity. Although the fallen trees had decimated others' lives, for Tree, this was life. It was his turn. He could feel the power of Laughing Sun on his tender, receptive leaves. Already, energy began to flow through the fluids in his vascular system. It felt as if his cambium sides would blow a rupture. The power was his. He could feel it. He would become a Titan of the earth: a mighty kapok. Like his ancestors, he would hold up the sky and feed the world.

Tat meanwhile, was dead to the world. That was until she felt the world move. She wasn't too sure at first whether it was the enormous crack reverberating down the tree's trunk from the first lightning impact, or the tremor from ripping roots that initially caught her attention. Either way, she knew it was serious enough not to hang around and dwell on such things. Fortunately, the momentum of several hundred tonnes of tree hurtling through the air was a jog compared to a nimble, lightweight Tat who was about to have her home annihilated. Not to mention her fresh, yummy, lush larder of dumb, flightless jungle chicks. That thought, though, did not linger. She scorched from under the homely roots as a hot rock from an enraged, exploding volcano. While fast and capable in her own, nimble, leggy evacuation, she realised that any wrong turn would produce a meeting with the unforgiving tonnage of accelerating, earthbound hardwood and would be little contest for a small tarantula.

With each passing moon, the fallen trees slowly decomposed and Mother Earth reclaimed her offspring by gently reabsorbing them. Most creatures moved on to more upright trees close by. Some plants died on the fallen timber but others were encouraged and embedded their roots into the decaying wood to assist with the trees' demise. New creatures emerged, for what was once somebody's home becomes another's. The rotting timber provided nourishment to many beetles, larvae, ants and fungi; all ably assisting with its return to the earth.

Trails of sagacious ants were at work chopping and logging the decaying wood into valuable food. Organised highways developed from the monster food store to their subterranean garden cities. Slowly and sedulously the biggest plants on earth were removed by some of the earth's tiniest creatures.

Amongst this decaying activity a banded anteater lay on his back. When the burnt, buff brown, dusty, dry leaves began to crawl, crackle and rustle, gently whispering their surreptitious existence way down under the cicadas' screeching treetop cacophony, then it was time to look closer. Banded Anteater with his head stretched out and his long, protuberant proboscis stuffed unceremoniously under the root of a gnarled garlic tree, certainly thought so. It was a tough decision though: was it worth the effort to roll over and seek out a noisy leaf, or better to continue the current mopping up project towards the demise of those rather juicy, little, red ants. It was always going to be a tough decision but they were beginning to bite the insides of his ears.

"Just one more slurp," he thought.

Well that was never going to happen. You cannot just have one more slurp when it comes to succulently, provocatively delicious red-bellied ants. But then again those dead, dry leaves don't rattle on their own and the nips in his ears were becoming bothersome. A decision had to be made, after another slurp, on one of life's quandaries: to seek adventure and possible bigger red ants, then again possibly none, or to stay stuck and suck the current larder dry.

"Oh suck it," he thought. The curiosity would gnaw away at his little brain, as these little ants were doing in his ear. It could wreck his day. He could not stand it any longer, nor in his disposed orientation could his ears. He sprung onto all fours with excited enthusiasm. In his rising spirit his long, sticky tongue swung uncontrollably from his mouth with all composure lost. Such was the exuberance of the demented organ that it became in imminent danger of being trampled by two rampant forefeet.

Banded anteaters might be short on brain but there's nothing wrong with their hearing, even with antagonistic ants gnawing away at their drums. There, on the other side of a decaying branch, was the music from a pile of leaves. Anteater stretched, magnificently and commandingly he thought, over the branch and peered like a monarch at his people, ready to deliver a sermon before a feast. Well, forget the sermon: Anteater was never big on words; he was an action anteater. Watching deliriously, his head swinging from one side to the other, he maniacally stared around. The earth moved with rippling eddies of marching leaves and twigs. He looked wildly to the right, then to the left. All around was a black, moving carpet rustling to a melodious, earthy beat. Thousands upon thousands of tiny, black ants were scouring the landscape. It was a wild, wobbling world of a throbbing, bobbing, seething, black mass of convulsive ant waves. The floor beneath their endlessly tireless legs vibrated and quivered, producing an amplified, mellifluous, jungle humming ant beat. It was warm, fruity and sweet-sounding to Anteater. Within the fever of the moment he was suddenly brought back to earth by his long, lathered tongue slapping into his ears. He slurped it quickly back so fast that its end whip-lashed the tip of his nose sprinkling his eyes with sticky, silvery saliva. No sooner had he pulled it back when it ungraciously slopped to the other side. It dangled tantalisingly above the long, frenzied, determined lines of marching ants. He pulled it back in. He pulled himself together. He did the best thing he could in the circumstances. He leapt over the fallen log scything his nose widely from left to right. Lashing lovingly in every direction, the momentum catapulted his tongue to the extremities of its fixings. Massive carnage was inflicted on the unsuspecting ants. Swathes of black lines disappeared down a long, black snout stoked by a tenacious tongue before being expertly swallowed and gobbled. The freshly stripped tongue exploded out again faster than an ant could twirl a tango. Lashing vehemently at every black hum-beating ant in sight he demolished the colony. It was mightily, militarily impressive. It was fashionably antisocial. It was intoxicatingly euphoric to a small banded anteater.

"What good fortune," he thought, "to seek adventure and follow one's ears, followed by one's nose for the antidote towards lethargy. And what good fortune to have a long nose with an even longer tongue. How could you not wish to be one of the most advanced species with the longest proboscis in the world at a time like this? Unlike those flat-faced, inadequate creatures with diminutive, minuscule stumps. What use is that? No use at all. No, it's simple enough, the longer the nose the more advanced you are; a worthy species for Pachamama."

With a belly full of ants and the fortuitous percipience of an advanced species, together with the added good fortune to be a banded anteater, he trotted delicately away into the forest. Happy in the knowledge that he was at the pinnacle of the animal kingdom he paused and looking back thought, "And to think, not only am I the best-looking banded anteater in the world, I'm also the brainiest."

Tree had been watching Anteater trying to control his out-of-control tongue when he noticed a boulder move. Not a gentle, discreet, inconspicuous move. The sort of move that if a boulder were to move then that would be how Tree would expect a boulder to move. This move was an impervious, moody move that defied all and everyone to interfere. It was not performed with any finesse either. This was a move with attitude. Mother Earth rebounded from each impact. Tree felt it through his roots. It was also not skulking under the cover of fallen tree debris. This was a bold, brash boulder sat conspicuously in a bare, brown patch of unloved dirt.

It was curious to Tree. He had good spatial awareness in his small part of the forest, or so he thought, but as far as he could recall the thing had not been there in the morning. Nor had it ever been there. Now, in the dying light of the day, there it was: a rock. A bust your bones, bumper great, grey rock – that moved! Tree watched it with rock-solid attention.

Then it happened. There! He saw it. The boulder leapt ten centimetres high and two metres along. A cavernous, gaping mouth instantaneously opened up and a whiplash trunk of a tongue shot forward. Two spotlight eyes emerged briefly in flight, then the whole thing collided with the planet and returned into a rock. Tree rocked. The dirt patch scattered debris into the sky as if a meteorite had exploded into it. When the planet stabilised, its axis realigned, dust settled from the air and a surprised flying beetle had unexpectedly disappeared. Overcome by a powerfully slimy, sticky tongue, it was now in the gruesome, dark depths of a rather large Savage Foam Frog pretending to be a rock.

Tree looked at the giant. Savage Foam Frog looked at a cricket. The cricket looked blank.

"This is not a fair contest," thought Tree, "a galloping tapir would think twice about taking that thing on." But then what was going to stop him? He was a formidable creature that cared not a flying beetle about anything else. He bounced his mass exactly where he wanted and nothing out there was going to stop him. "And that," presumed Tree, "includes me." The next moment the cricket had disappeared. Savage looked like the epitome of innocence. Tree hadn't even seen it happen.

Tree had been so intent on watching Savage that when he looked up, Three Toes was gone. He had only taken his eye off him for perhaps half a day, now there was no sign at all. "He couldn't have shifted any more than his body length in that time," thought a bemused Tree. Not only was he not there but was nowhere, anywhere. It wasn't slothfully possible.

Three Toes was oblivious to Tree's attention to his whereabouts. He was high in a fig tree wedged into a fork between two branches. His rust-brown, mouldy hair camouflaged him perfectly against the dappled green, brown and silver hues of the big fig. He was as inconspicuous as the bark he hung off. Pontificating upside down, lodged between the branches in idyllic equilibrium, he mused to himself, "There is just as much food here as there is down there." Those indigestible fig leaves would satisfy his acidic, grinding stomach just as easily as that new, fresh succulent fodder now ramping up through the floor. "And," he continued, "I don't waste a week racing down, a week getting dirt under my nails, then another week racing back up again. For all I know, while gorging on this new-found fad stuff, somebody else might inhabit my trees and gorge themselves in my larder while I'm getting dyspepsia on that foreign junk. On top of that," he paused mid thought, reflecting gravely on the insidiousness of the prospect, "my carefully guarded tree of fructuous cucuras is reaching that critical point requiring onerous surveillance to protect it for my cucura-starved belly." Just the mere thought of such a calamity brought a lump into Three Toes' throat. His eyes welled up sending his lofty view of a cucura-filled treetop world into a watery, hazy mist. He clung rigidly to his fig forks, staring manically towards his protected larder.

Three Toes looked like a stick, or more precisely a jumble of sticks woven together with matted, dead leaves. His spine nestled neatly into the cleft of the two branches. Three big, brown, brawny, bushy legs protruded stick-straight up away from his outstretched body. His powerful, curved hind claws slipped perfectly around two branches, securing an immovable vice-like lock. His right arm did the same in the opposite direction encircling a higher branch. The left dangled flaccidly towards the ground. Nothing moved, not a quiver, a wobble or a tremor. Three Toes was a tree. To all on the ground, it appeared as a very credible extension to the fig's natural, knurled branches.

It had taken the rest of the day for Wee Tree to find him. Yet there he was, a mere eight metres higher up the same fig. Keeping his eye on him, Tree spoke to Pachamama.

"How does he do that? How can you lose a creature that hardly moves the moment you take your eyes off him? Everything else in this jungle runs, scuttles, scurries, hurries, scampers, scrambles, flies, dives, or slithers. All possessed with a demonic mission, but not Three Toes. He just hangs there. Even when having sex he is in no rush: six days it takes him. Five and three quarters just to get to where he wants to be. With Tat it's five seconds at the outside and the suitor doesn't hang around. Look at Jaguar. He can catch anything and kill anything but he doesn't kill Three Toes because he can't find him. Nobody can find him. How is that, Pachamama?"

"Three Toes has adapted, Tree, look at his coat. It is the same colour as the trees. Look at the thickness of his limbs. They are also the same size as the branches he hangs off. You see the mould growing from the tops of his arms. It matches the mosses on the bark and blends with the leaves of the fig trees. So you see, Tree, when Three Toes doesn't move, Three Toes doesn't exist. He is a tree. Even if he moves, it is so slow that predators don't see it. Jaguar can't even smell him. Amongst all the other animal odours Three Toes drops off the list as a pile of rotting grass. He is a master, Tree, don't ever take your eye off him: you'll lose him."

Tree drifted off into a soporific state of adoration. Not just for Three Toes but for the whole forest. The fastest creature cannot be caught and neither can the slowest. It was a paradox of the forest but a beautiful, simplistic one. The way everything was so different, yet everything so connected, seamlessly, effortlessly, yet bark-bogglingly complex. Each life interconnects. There are billions of plants and animals and they are all connected. It was too big for Wee Tree. Yet, there it was, in all its complexity. You could sit and watch it work and it would do so with its everyday simplicity without a bead of sap.

Wee Tree was struck into a ruminative state of reverence but this time he kept his eye on the slippery, stationary sloth.

Through the bush emerged an elusive visitor: a small group of Indian flerds. Tree watched them with concern. He knew what they were from listening to all of Whale's stories – flerds were not good news. He watched ruefully, willing them to go away. The group decided to settle on the far side where the fallen trees had created a small clearing. They did not behave like the other animals of the forest. They had wrapped dead animal skins and dried leaves around their smooth bodies. Most of their bodies were hairless with the exception of their heads. Sprouting from the tops were peculiar tufts of shiny, sleek, silky, black hair. Some had long tufts flowing over their shoulders while others only had a small dome of cropped hair on the tops of their heads. Most had dry bones of differing lengths protruding from their faces, ears or noses. All of them had multi-coloured feathers sticking out of them and coloured beads strapped around their bodies. Unlike other creatures they didn't start rooting through the ground or foraging for food. Instead, they cleared the forest floor and then cut down branches and leaves. The butchered plants and trees were then piled together in a number of nests forming a small circle. Tree gave a shudder and was grateful that he was further away. Even though he had grown several more metres he still felt very vulnerable.

What was odd about these creatures was when all this destruction had been completed they then sat under it and set it alight. Tree watched on with interest: flerds fascinated him in a scary way. Whale had sung all about them; he knew this was a dangerous animal. When dusk began to fall white smoke filtered through the roofs of their nests. It was all very odd; he had never seen such peculiar activity.

Tree watched into the night. Partly because they interested him and partly because he didn't want to be taken unawares by a brutal attack for no reason other than for just being there. Whale had said that they performed unpredictable, vicious and violent things to the detriment of everybody. If that was the case then he wanted to see it coming.

When all activity ceased, peace descended for a short period. Tree thought they had all gone to sleep like the day animals. Just when Tree was becoming a little less uneasy, odd wailing noises emitted from under the pile of sticks. It was a little like the howler monkeys but without the charm. For quite some time the whole group seemed to join in with this activity, then for no apparent reason they all stopped together. Tree presumed from exhaustion.

After two days the flerds had secured their camp, lit fires, caught food and prepared offerings to show their appreciation to the Spirits and Elements. The shaman, who had remained apart from all the daily business, had spent his time mixing potent powders ready for the night's ritual thanksgiving.

After the daily bustle had long ceased and Inti had disappeared, the indians sat around a smouldering fire. Yoppa powder was placed in a small bowl and warmed on the edge of the fire. At the given hour the shaman passed the bowl around. Within the bowl lay a small, hollow bone. Each flerd inserted one end into the powder and the other up one nostril then snorted up the concoction. They repeated with the other nostril then passed it on to the next flerd. When all had inhaled the potion they sat around the fire chanting to the spirits. The hallucinogenic drug slowly began to loosen the mind from its conscious strings; it allowed them access to another world inhabited by their ancestors. They chanted throughout the night, inducing themselves into a stuporous state where their bodies became moribund, their souls became spirit. Surrounded in the still, spiritual night air, their ancestors unostentatiously arrived. Wailing and howling they danced with their own reflections until, wide-eyed, they saw the mirror of their souls.

The Fly Flerds believed that life and death begin and end within the sacred depths of those ancient, sepulchral Fly Mountains. The source of the eternal waters is also the origin of their own beings. When their spirit is taken from their bodies it passes through Tempest Cloud and travels to Inti, the father of all life. The sun bears no life but feeds and nourishes and the soul that is life itself is offered back to the sun. The body of each is consumed and returned to where it was borne by Pachamama. In this way the essence of the spirit mountain is returned to the bosom of Mother Earth whose very breath gives life. After life there is death, the sun and moon, black and white, male and female. After death then life and so it begins again. There is no beginning and no end; it just is. Thus is the Indian principle of duality.

One by one the flerds collapsed, stone-still, prostrate with the silent, dancing dead; only the shaman remained to dance with the spirits alone.

In the morning Tree explained all this to Whale. He was quite relieved, if he was truthful, because he had feared they would sneak up on him in the middle of the night and cut him down. So when Inti broke through the canopy he was thankful to find himself in one piece and not cut-up and discarded in a pile with the others.

Whale explained in her usual sing-song way: "These are indigenous Fly Indians, Tree, members of the flerd group of animals. They have developed in isolation from the others and consequently their powers of communication, awareness and intellect are more advanced than the common flerds. Although they are different from the other species in the forest they are also part of it. It is their world too, they look after it, and the world looks after them. They are more like us, Tree: connected, as a whole, for the benefit of all and the respect for Pachamama."

He felt a little foolish having worried throughout the night. He did not want to be a pile of sticks. His relief quickly transmuted back into confusion.

"So, if they're brighter than the average flerd why then have they butchered those other trees and turned them into a pile of sticks?"

"They only take a few, with the old and the dying giving way for Inti to shine his light onto the forest floor. This new energy is received by the young, they force upwards and the forest is replenished and never dies. In this way all life continues."

Amazed by how simple this all was, he began to wonder why flerds had such a bad reputation. It was then that he remembered what Whale had previously sung to him and became confused again.

"So," he started with a little trepidation, "when the flerds killed all your forefathers is that what they were doing: weeding out the weak and dying?" Tree wasn't sure if this would upset Whale, so was a little nervous as to what Whale's reaction would be. But she was as gracious as a gentle giant could be in her honourable position. Just as a small tree had hoped for.

"Ah Tree, if only," Whale paused and allowed a little reminiscent sorrow at the full horrors of the slaughter, then continued with no hint of her thoughts, "no, they killed indiscriminately, old and young alike. The Indian Fly Flerds are a different species. They consume what they need from an area then move on. That area then regenerates to provide food and shelter for the future. So the cycle continues as it has done for thousands of years." She wanted to warn Tree what would happen if the other flerds continued with their thoughtless wrecking as had others in the past, but decided it was not her position. She was the oracle of all knowledge not a prophesier of doom.

Tree was comforted from talking to Whale. Her soft voice sang sweetly no matter what was happening. She was so imperturbable that Tree wished he had fins so he could swim and soak in her knowledge.

Chapter IV

The summer progressed and Inti rose towards his
highest position over Fly Forest. Full-faced and laughing
at the cloudless, blue skies, he achieved his polished
performance with such nonchalance that Tree
considered it bordering on the casual. Inti, though, was
magnificent and beamed beautifully above the green,
vibrant forest.

The Indian flerds had stayed around Tree for many
months. They became part of everyday life in Fly Forest.
Each day they swarmed in and out of their wooden
nests with the same tireless energy as the busy,
bumbling bees. At night the activity slowed with the
creatures showing a contemplative quiescence while
sitting around the fire. Smoke drifted upwards towards
the roof of the world and some diffused gently, silently,
from their nostrils and mouths. It was a peculiar sight
for Tree. Initially it alarmed him but always intrigued.
Slowly he lost his fear of these paradoxical animals. He
was not chopped down. They followed their own routine
each day, so Tree kept his eye on them as he did with all
the others.

The day arrived when Inti reached his highest point of
the year. The flerds were busy preparing for the sacred
celebration. A large collection of wood was already piled

in the clearing. Pairs of flerds were painting each other with coloured stripes and patterns with dyes obtained from plants and the earth. Black, red and white berries interlaced with animal teeth and claws had been made into necklaces and bracelets. They had plaited their hair, then woven in multi-coloured seed pods and vivaciously bright feathers. Food had been collected ready to offer to the spirits at the precise second of Inti reaching the highest point of his solar cycle.

The shaman sat alone mixing his summer salutation yoppa potions to release the spirits and please the sun. He was already painted in vivid yellows and reds contrasting evocatively against a myriad mixed base of white, black and ochre paints. Plumes of long, exotic feathers radiated from his head in a vibrant array of extravagant colours. Claws from the giant anteater and large cayman teeth adorned with red and black seed pods hung around his body, portraying his spiritual strength as a powerful guide for the tribe.

While the flerds were busy with their preparations, a young female started crying. She became the centre of much attention. An older matron took control by organising the others. The males raced around collecting wood to stoke the cooking fire. The females stayed to comfort the wailing flerd, holding her hands and rubbing ointments onto her sweating body.

While Tree watched this busy commotion the old shaman sat alone. Unperturbed by the activities he continued mixing his herbs, smoking and singing to the spirits.

After the initial burst of activity an edgy routine seemed to settle over the group. The distraught female continued to screech at intermittent periods with only the matron to comfort her. The females painted each other's bodies; the males cleared an area around the large pile of sticks in the middle of the nests. The shaman, crouching by his own fire, continued to chant and smoke. Tree, still intrigued with smoke emanating from a being, sensed a new force around him. There was a touch of electricity in the air. He looked at Inti for inspiration but saw only a big, laughing, round-faced Inti looking straight down at him. Yet, there was energy about that he had not felt before. His hot sap was running up his trunk in tingling fluid tunnels to reach the tips of every leaf before emanating towards the universe.

Tree spoke to Ruminant Whale, "Hello Whale, Inti has a twinkle in his face, the native flerds are acting strangely and I've this twinkling feeling running through my cells. I can sense an energy around, like an awakening, but I can't put my leaf on it. Have you any thoughts about it?"

Whale sang back, "It's the summer solstice, it's the point where the tilt of Pachamama begins to reverse. The energy changes. That is what you are feeling, Tree. It is going to happen very soon. Some flerds are connected with this and celebrate the change by passing thanks to the Elements. Watch the flerds, Tree, they are very connected. The shaman is a wise, old flerd, anything can happen."

Wee Tree was transfixed. "How can that be?" he thought, "some flerds are connected, some are not. What's the difference? How can you tell one from the other? Another paradox from this forest but there's no denying, there is an energy." If Tree could have lifted his roots and run with his burning, sap-pumping power to the tips of his reach then he would have exploded from the ground and raced throughout the forest in a foray of upturned roots and fluttering leaves. Inti's strange energy, the excitement of the unknown, that hint of curiosity, that small sliver of intrigue about the unpredictable flerds, that is what made it all so interesting. There was always something new in this paradoxical forest and he wanted to know about it.

The flerds were seated around the burning fire. A pipe and bowl of powder was passed along, each flerd snorting it up one nostril then the other. A lone flerd beating a low base to his drum, banged out a throbbing rhythm. The shaman sang and danced. In one hand he held a razor-sharp knife which he swept swiftly, agilely close to his twisting, bare torso. "For an old flerd he is remarkably supple," thought Tree. A sacrificial howler monkey, tied up by his side, looked ominously on. The shaman's great headdress of feathers swayed and swilled above his small, willowy frame writhing to the vibrations and evocative energy. Gradually the group was swallowed as a whole into a hypnotic trance. They danced around the fire in magical, unconscious waves. Wind-blown feathers and beads involuntarily swept by the moving air chased the dancing beings beneath. Hypnotised by the chanting and the flickering flames they danced themselves into the sleep of the spirits.

Inti rose high. The shaman stopped abruptly, dropping to his knees. Drawing his knife high in one hand and collecting the monkey with the other he raised them both towards the sun. The others dropped too. The beating drum ceased. Silence spilled over the forest as if commanded from on high. All the flerds looked up at the great, white, burning Inti, now directly overhead. Tree, too, gazed at Inti, perplexed at what he was about to do that somehow he had never done before. The fire glittered, sending light in crackling, spitting cuts into the dark, silent seams of a seemingly suspended forest. Still holding the monkey and knife, the shaman slowly brought his hands together in front of his face as Inti touched the highest point. He was about to draw his knife to slice the howler's throat and throw the sacrifice into the fire when an ear splitting shriek cut the forest apart. Whatever their stupefied condition was, all heads turned towards the source of the cry. They looked in awe at the wailing, supine female flerd in the hut. A gasp rose from the group as there, on the fresh reed mat, lay two bloodied babies. They had arrived so fast into the embracing arms of Pachamama that nobody knew which had arrived first. The helpless twins quickly found each other and wrapped their arms and legs together, tangling up with their umbilical cords to produce a living knot of contented flesh. On seeing this, the shaman wailed in unison with the mother. Drawing the knife across the monkey's throat, he tossed the gurgling sacrifice into the flames of life. The Laughing Sun laughed and began his journey back again.

By the end of the flerds' ritual thanksgiving, all the dancers had collapsed from fervent emotions and too much yoppa powder. The shaman, kneeling next to the mother, collected the young in his arms. She was still lying on the earth, exhausted, but meeting her eyes with his he beamed broadly at her. His three remaining yellow, teeth flashed a warm, gummy grin. He said, "You have produced two daughters at the height of the Sun God, Ah Kinchil. This is no coincidence. It is a great prophecy, Ocillo. You must be very careful with these two, they are here for a reason. You will name them Chil and Chel." With his message passed on he handed back the children and returned to his fire to continue yoppa-snorting, meditating and mixing more ceremonial body paints.

Ocillo looked at her two pale babies. A warm, sensual glow spread throughout her body. She felt their beating hearts against her bare skin. The words of the shaman resonated through her thoughts: "Why has he picked Chil and Chel? Are they not unlike the Sun God's name, Ah Kinchil and the Rainbow Queen's, Ix Chel? And they are so identical, as pale as a full ghost moon and with such radiant, deep, sky-blue eyes. Never have I seen such children amongst our people. Our olive-skinned bodies are topped with straight, shining, black hair. My beautiful, unblemished daughters have not one hair between them. Our eyes have the colour of rich, dark brown, not unlike the moist, freshly picked juvia nut. You are so alike my babes, but you are not like us. How will I know which of you is Chil and which is Chel?"

The old shaman returned to Ocillo and picked up the first born. "This is Chil," he said to her softly.

"How do you know?" whispered Ocillo.

"Feel her heart, she is guided," he simply replied. With that he took the child towards the fire and began chanting and dancing around the hot embers. He held her straight out from his body, pointing her towards the four cardinal points of Mother Earth. Finally he lifted her towards Inti, chanting wildly before collapsing to his knees with the child still held high. After a long silence he picked up a brush of henna and painted a small circle in the middle of her forehead. He repeated the ceremony with Chel, but this time he painted three small, diagonal lines, one each of indigo, white and henna.

Ocillo thanked the shaman then asked, "They are so identical but I cannot keep them marked for life, it does not seem right. How will I know one from the other?"

The shaman smiled and replied, "They are the same but also complementary, Ocillo. Feel their energy. It is vibrant. See their auras. They are massive, they are different colours. Feel the difference, Ocillo, feel it with your heart."

Tree had seen many births and deaths but never such a performance as he had just witnessed. He spoke to Pachamama, "I know Inti whizzes around you and the flerds all worship him because he is the most powerful Element, but why all the fuss about two flerds being born?"

"Hmm, well, it's not quite like that, you see. In actual fact I whizz around Inti. It is just that it appears to be the other way around. Being a static tree, you may find that a difficult concept because everything else runs around you. Therefore, in your case, they are all moving, which is true. It is all about references."

Pachamama was not making a good job of this and could see it getting excruciatingly complex so decided to move it on rapidly. "It may be best to ask Whale about it, but the reason they are celebrating the birth is that it is rare for flerds to give birth to two. It is rarer still to give birth with no time between the two and to do it at the exact position of Inti's mid-summer solstice. It is also unknown for them to be so white and have blue eyes. The shaman knows all of this, hence the special ceremony."

"But other animals don't do this. They get on with things as quickly as possible."

"Yes, but," here Pachamama paused as she wasn't sure what the easiest answer was, "they don't usually celebrate the solstice as far as I know, so each day is just another day, they get on with things. The flerds like to give thanks to things that they cannot explain in case it comes back to hurt them."

"Why don't all animals celebrate the solstice? Doesn't it hurt them too?"

Pachamama did not know the answer to this and to make things worse, she did not know why anybody would offer thanks to an Element; there was no need as it was all given freely to everybody.

"I think maybe, you should talk to Whale."

The young flerds flourished within the fecund forest. Secured in their nest and protected by Scorching Fire, they grew strong and healthy. Ocillo's bond with them also grew and her feelings deepened. She could distinguish each of them with her eyes closed. By listening to their heart and breathing or simply by the slightest touch of a finger she could tell which was which. The shaman had been right; she could feel their souls, their energy, their very being. She was their mother, their blood was hers. She felt that they deliberately and consciously connected with her. She knew when they were hungry or needed cleaning, or simply holding, before they let her know. The connections grew stronger and she gave the children everything they needed.

Although these were her first born, Ocillo was intuitively wise for her young age and allowed herself to be guided by the skilful shaman. She, too, grew strong, maintaining a daily, constant awareness of consciousness. She recognised when her ego demanded attention by using the children to satisfy her emotional needs. She subdued those feelings and submitted to her own humility with complete joy. The young flerds helped her become more enlightened.

Much of her days were spent with Wee Tree. Ocillo felt comfortable there. It was peaceful lazing away from the bustle of the others. The twins, too, seemed to enjoy Tree's company. They spent the days laughing and smiling which was much the same as Inti. The shaman had named them well.

Chapter V

Wee Tree loved it when the two small, pale flerds came to visit. He had so much more energy and always grew another few centimetres. It made him want to run along the tracks, to chase Jaguar and scare him. Although he could not envisage being able to move around, he could see that it might be fun. Nevertheless, it was a constant mystery to him.

"How odd," he thought, "it would be to lift your roots from the ground and gallop through the forest." He looked across at an ancient strangler fig. It did not exactly pull its roots from the ground but once it had killed its host tree it would slowly move away down the slope to find another.

He was wary of strangler figs; stranglers and flerds. Both could kill him.

Moving, though, bothered him. If he was honest, he could not see how it worked. "How would you know where you were if you were always moving away from where you had just been?" He thought he would talk to Whale. She knew everything.

Before he could sing to her a bright crimson and yellow flash darted through the trees. It took him by surprise and he wondered what was in such a colossal hurry. He forgot all about calling Whale.

A fully fledged, Chestnut Mandibled Toucan pierced the green canopy and settled onto the lower branches of a guapinol negro tree near Wee Tree. Along the length of his beak flashed a startling array of vivid reds, yellow and green, contrasting brightly against his shimmering, night-black, glossy body plumage. His massive, yellow-tipped beak was a third of the length of his body and possibly wider from top to bottom. The dazzling beak lifted the toucan to one of the forest's most breathtaking performers. A big, bright, black-buttoned, probing eye offset from the pale green and yellow feathers around his face resembled a huge bolt that fixed his beak into his cranium. Tree thought perhaps that is what stopped it falling from his head.

"By rights Toucan shouldn't have the strength to drag that beak across the ground let alone whizz it through the air like he does. It gives him an indifferent, multi-coloured ambience. It is far too big for his body and looks like it belongs to somebody else. Perhaps he has flown so fast into it that now his head is permanently jammed there. It doesn't seem to have slowed him down though."

Toucan was power; a lithe, agile, polished performer. His massive beak could crack a nut or delicately hold an overripe berry at its very tip without crushing it. A big pair of muscular aviator wings propelled the agile bird with such awesome power that it sliced his shimmering, jet-black body arrow-fast through the humid air. His wings beat the liquid forest air as a frigate's sail fills with power from its propelling winds. Toucan landed on a small branch as gently as a feather falling into a trickling stream. His sharp, black, bolt-tight eyeball adroitly scanned the forest. His multi-coloured beak shaved the air around; eyeing his surroundings he sang a short, two-toned song. Motionless, he listened through the noisy, ceaseless cicada machine. From behind he heard a whoosh.

"Too big for a toucan," he thought.

The whooshing became louder until it was so close he could feel the air beating the tips of the feathers running down his back. Something large and heavy flopped itself, unceremoniously and with little punctiliousness, right beside him on the same branch. They bobbed up and down for a short period while the branch adjusted itself to the extra weight. Toucan slowly swung his big, bright beak around and looked straight into the knees of a rather large and scraggly Black Vulture. Tilting his head upwards, he looked at his new, uninvited neighbour. There, looking straight down towards him was a pitted, ragged-edged, hooked, chipped beak with a bright pair of orange eyes right above it.

Toucan cocked his head to the right and gave him the big, bolt eye. The broadside display of his bill showed his intent. The bright yellow flashed a brazen message. Toucan reflected on the effects of his display: "That should show him I'm no dead meat. He may be fifty times my size, but if we're talking beaks then he's just been beaked out!"

Vulture half closed his eyes and squinted at the little chap with the big nose. He was tired. All this flapping around in the heat of the day was not his style. It had sapped his energy and he just wanted a quiet spot in the cool under the guapinol negro tree. Where, with any luck, something would have just died by running head down into the tree's dense trunk. It hadn't; there was just Toucan. A showdown with some flashy, egotistical, long-nosed, short-legged, over-opinionated bird bragger was the last thing he wanted. "These youngsters, give them a big, flashy beak and they think they can intimidate." With that thought he dropped his shoulders, hung his head towards his belly forming a big U in his neck and sat looking for anything excitably expired or about to be.

Toucan was feeling triumphant. "Nothing out-dazzles a toucan in this forest. Especially not a Chestnut Mandibled one." He swung his head back in front, letting out another loud, shrill, two-tone song. When nothing happened – nobody arrived, nobody died and more to the point, nobody replied – he slowly realised nothing ever would. "Here I am sat next to this big, black, ugly, melancholic, old, grumpy, death-stalking, wrinkle-featured vulture when all the girls will be letting off energy flying around the bromeliads with other chestnuts chasing their tails all day. But if I leave now, Vulture will think he has the better of me. However, if I stay then all the girls will be twinning the tango and I'll be left with nothing but this old baggage." It was a quandary.

Vulture was thinking, "Vanity fuelled by ego. I may be old but I know my style. Now, is that something dead or did that rock just jump?"

Savage had disturbed a jungle chicken. She was rummaging under a heap of dried debris. Her three chicks following faithfully, imitating, in their own aimless style, her clucking ways, her deft footwork, her meticulous manner as she bent and picked up fallen seeds. Circling behind their gracious mother the chicks crunched and stumbled. They bounced into each other, squabbled, squawked, tripped and fell into ruts. Numerous scuffles started from their awkwardness. Their mother ignored them. She continued lightly, guiding them gently across the adventurous, nutritious earth towards a safe roosting spot. The mother pecked, then stepped; the chicks rustled, then tussled. Unknowingly, they were slowly circling four covert pairs of keenly attentive eyes. A bubbling feeling of uncontrollable excitement was generating beneath the silently scanning eyes. They blinked in unison, reflecting Monocled Moon's shining exuberance. Had the chickens taken a glance over their neatly tucked wings they might have seen eight, faint, glowing alien worlds, shimmering mystically above the decaying dregs of a discarded forest.

Tat was a quiver of suppressed suspense. Her long, black, recoiled legs were straining at the bolts to spring from the earth, but she held tight, her subtle motion-detecting eyes feeding back information about the ghostly, ethereal chicken world. Chicken behaviour was augmented and segmented into the relevant slices of her Tat-sized databases. This is what made Tat the greatest, speediest, nimblest spider of a generation: she thought, she processed, she pounced. She was the best. Then to her dismay the chicken larder moved away. All four sidestepped several chicken-lengths towards an orange-and-cream-coloured, fan-shaped, oyster mushroom hiding under the root of a large cow tree. The mother started pecking and scratching the dry earth under the mushroom for the nutritious spawn that had fallen down. Her three chicks performed a rough interpretation of that. Tat, thinking murderously black chicken thoughts, relaxed from anxious alert state to stand down, then to disappointed state, then she saw it. From the corner of her eye, it was the merest of flicks. A minuscule lightning flash of silver so swift that it defied the eye. But Tat saw it. Her precision tuned, micro-motion detecting eyes had picked it out. Unfortunately, the hapless chickens had not. Their heads buried, savouring the delights from a generous mushroom; their beak-watering preoccupation had momentarily caused their guard to drop. The flick was the taster. The strike followed. Faster than even Tat's eyes could follow. Pandemonium erupted, entropy enveloped chaos: chickens squawked, feathers flew, twigs, leaves, branches, mushrooms scattered. Debris and earth hit the soft-lit skies as a monster anaconda launched herself into the middle of the chickens. She crashed down, demolishing the mushroom as chickens scarpered towards the darkest recesses of the forest. She collided with Mother Earth with a heavy thud, her mouth closed tightly with a few, dark tail feathers protruding from one side. One small gulp ended the performance. Tat couldn't tell whether there was a smirk across her face or not; nor could she tell who had been taken, but there was one thing for sure, there would be no chicken banquet tonight. Not for some.

Over the days Monocled Moon rose higher in the blind, blacked-out sky, his exuberance expanding with magnificent radiance. He grew fuller, fitter, flamboyant; his majestic brilliance unique to a noble Element hung over Fly Forest. The dark night sky silhouetted his distinct cutting-edged gown. His moonlit rays spied a restive, active forest. The gossamer light danced, prancing as nimble as a sylph transfusing through the torn, torpid, tangled trees.

Fly Forest's night life grew increasingly weary of the moon's persistent clarity to illuminate their clandestine ground work. Moon was always affably more ebullient the rounder he became. Wee Tree was still confused how Inti could disappear on one side of the forest then reappear the next day on the opposite without ever being seen racing between the two. It was not, as such, that the mightiest Element was shy in his exploding effervescence, but with all that constant, brilliant light, how did he get to the other side without being seen? It was a great mystery to Tree. So when Moon came along it was always with a bit of relief, for he always felt that he might catch Inti surreptitiously sneaking back the other way, given that there was a bit more light on the subject. Somehow though, Inti was never seen during his crossing. Tree was as much in the dark as the dark was without the sun, regardless of Moon's magnificent, glowing attempts to shed a little more on the matter. Still, somehow, it was reassuring to have Moon there. He spoke to Pachamama.

"Pachamama, how can Sun illuminate the whole forest starting the day from one end, finishing at the other, then returning to that same start the next day without being seen?"

"He does it under the cover of darkness," replied the wise, old Mother Earth.

This seemed so blindingly obvious to Tree that he wondered why he asked the fool question in the first place. If he was truly honest, he felt a bit of a wooden top for not having worked it out. "But then," thought Tree, "sometimes the obvious is so manifest that you can be blinded by it." With that, Tree looked through the open canopy, mesmerised by the magnificent Monocled Moon, and marvelled at how clever they all were.

Chapter VI

Albatross scanned the horizon. He was getting tired. An old feeling began to creep through him; an awful sinking, stomach-frothing feeling. He didn't want to think about it but it wouldn't leave his mind. He stretched his head further into the wind. Further towards the horizon. Why? He didn't know; it didn't improve his vision, but somehow looking into the distance made him feel better, if only because he was putting more effort into it. The relentless wind was buffeting his body, counterbalancing his weight from toppling over the cliff. It did occur to him that tumbling over onto the wave-lashed, ragged rocks below would be a way out, but somehow he could not quite do it. He could not do it last time and he could not do it now. Curiosity kept him alive. Six days he had been there. Six days she hadn't turned up. Just one more day. What would tomorrow bring? He had to know and would she turn up? Would she still remember him? Would she come to him? He had to know and stretching his beak out a little further was all he could do to find out.

Ruminant Whale was cruising headlong through Rumbustious Sea's three-metre swells. She was not so much punching holes through the enormous, unstoppable banks of water as carving valleys through it. Her enormous hulk split the waves open with such insouciant simplicity that she took no notice. Conversely, Calf was swept hither and thither until eventually he found a sweet spot just behind his mother's tail. He tailgated her, feeling slightly smug that he was sponging from his monstrous mother's wake. But then he thought, "If I had a seven-metre-wide tail then I, too, would sweep Rumbustious Sea aside with an idle swipe and an imperturbable indifference." The power and size of his awesome mother continually impressed him. She must be the biggest, strongest, most powerful mother Pachamama had ever borne. He felt the luckiest and safest calf in the seas.

Whale was singing to the world as she was idly demolishing the sea:

"Close your eyes to see the light
Be inspired by Inti's song
Your spirits grow by others' delight
To seek your wisdom far beyond.

Swim through the tides of doubt
The shivering fear of lifeless fright
Find your power to roar and shout
Open your eyes to see the light.

Connect your body, mind and soul
With healing energy in flowing flight
Forgive yourself in all and whole
Close your eyes to see the light.

You are the mirror of your life
Spiritual union reflects your sight
Your soul grows far from strife
Open your eyes to see the light."

In the forest Wee Tree had been listening to Ruminant Whale. She was the Curator and always had something to sing about. Life in the forest was full of confusion and paradoxes, then Whale would sing and remind us that we can live above the forest's constant bustle. It seemed to make so much sense. She was singing about having the wisdom and courage to love ourselves so we can forgive others. In this way, spiritual union would reflect the mirror images of our own lives, then others, too, would follow. By working together, combining energies to create harmony and coexistence. Being a tree it all seemed very complicated. Perhaps it was all this moving around that was confusing. You lived where you were put and provided food and support for everybody around. They in turn did the same for you. It was not as if there was a choice. Failure of one lets everybody down. Why the need to tell everybody?

Tree thought he would talk to Pachamama. She was always up for a meaningful chat and understood so much.

"Pachamama, why is Whale telling us to work with each other when that's what we all do anyway?"

"Whale likes to make sure we don't drift off and forget our basic principles, so she reminds every plant and animal on the earth of what is really important."

"Well, how can I drift off anywhere when I'm firmly secured to this spot?"

Pachamama had the beginnings of another foreboding moment that regularly occurred when trying to explain things to Tree. "You're not a good example because you are unique. Most other species move around. Look at Three Toes for example. He's all over the place, so Whale likes to help him live a connected life wherever he is."

"Three Toes takes a week just to make his mind up. If you set him alight he wouldn't move."

"Well okay, maybe Three Toes was not a good example, but you see my point."

"No! Three Toes is an enigma; he is the most connected creature on earth. He was rooted to a branch for a fortnight looking at a cucura. You cannot get more connected than that."

Pachamama sank a little into her crust. These conversations with Tree always seemed to go the same way: deeper into the abyss. She thought she would try Tat. Tree liked Tat.

"Look at Tat," Pachamama started optimistically, even though she felt a state of precariousness lurking around the corner, "she's forever on the run. Never stops. A gentle reminder every now and then keeps her feet on the ground and makes her a more grounded spider."

"Tat is so cool. Her feet are always on the ground. She's the fastest spider ever. There's not a jungle chicken in sight that is a match for Tat. You can't get more grounded than her, so why tell her?"

The precariousness had rushed from around the corner and quickly overtaken her. "Talk to Whale, Tree. She is the Curator after all." Pachamama made another hasty exit and disappeared to fine-tune a volcano for its next earthly connection.

Whale was oblivious to the Mother Earth's uncomfortable exit and kept her course heading north. The dark blue sea, enriched with energy-boosting ozone, sizzled with power and life. Slowly other whales appeared. Calf could not always see them in the heavy, bubbling, white, froth-foamed swells. While slip-streaming his mother he listened to their calls as their songs mixed with Rumbustious Sea's blithesome, wave-crashing melodies.

Their group grew steadily as more mothers with young calves joined them.

The juvenile whales played tails and fliers with their powerful mothers. They would follow until they reached her wake and then get pulled along for free. At a critical point where the tail moved downwards they would accelerate with all their power to swim over the tail. Those that failed, which was often, sustained several tons of broiling, white water thrust into their underside, tossing them like damp, limp squids out of the ocean before they smacked unceremoniously back into a welcoming sea. The others watched knowingly. They smirked as the bent and battered player returned to the water, where, doubled up and winded, they desperately swam to the surface to recover their breath. Eventually they would be so exhausted they would have to hitch a lift, with the nearest adult that was not already being tailgated, to keep up with the pod. To fall behind at this stage would slow the group and result in some heavy flippers as admonition.

Whale's calf was too young for this game. He swam around all the others watching humorously, getting in the way wherever possible to assist in miss-timing their advances. Without fail it resulted in another victim becoming 'fluked'. Fortunately for calf, the shattering re-entry into Rumbustious Sea winded and dazed them so much that they had not the energy to pick on him. An inward smile usually expanded into an outward smirk as he escaped their comminations and rebukes.

He remembered once being chased back under his mother's flipper by a larger juvenile. Calf had tapped his fluke as he prepared to launch. The young male lost his timing and rolled off the lifting fluke only to be battered by it on the way down. Even he had to back off, as nobody was willing to admonish the Curator's only son and be caught doing so. Calf took his chances; he played to his strengths, or at least, his mother's.

On the other side of the ocean the mature male adults were also heading north. A huge, subaquatic plume of cold, dense, black water was known to push up from the hidden, volcanic floor of the ocean. Rising from the anonymous world below, it powered up the continental shelf, carving a cold wound through the warm, effusive waters several hundred kilometres wide. Rich in minerals and deep marine animals it attracted all forms of life. Tuna, wahoo, dorado and other vicious hunters swept in to seek their pleasures on the unsuspecting life forms. Many larger apex predators arrived: sharks, sailfish, marlin, orcas, squid and rays. Vast shoals of feeding tuna, sprats and bonitos erupted on the boiling surface. The frantic activity attracted the big killers. They homed in towards their unsuspecting prey. The big predators struck with devastating affray. Disorientated and broken apart, the shoals scattered frantically to escape the rapid, giant killers that swung and swirled in menacing circles below. Assiduously, they displayed a casual, open calmness that masked their optimistic verve of the true, accomplished killers they really were. Effortlessly they glided, as silently as light itself under the blue bright, sunlit surface in a luminous, bounteous sea.

The mature male whales swam this way each year eagerly anticipating the prolific plume to converge with their travels. The fruitful bonanza would provide vital nourishment for the months ahead. There were copious amounts of food in the plume to satisfy all the big predators – the huge shoals of fish and themselves. It would provide enough fuel to drive them north and challenge for the right to mate.

The Elements were quiet. Rumbustious Sea was flat with nothing more than a gentle, rolling swell. The whales pushed easily along through the placid waters leaving nothing but a ripple and an oily slick in their wake. Even the clamorous sea birds that were usually fighting and squabbling were cruising in equable circles above the pod. The occasional frigate bird would take a dive if it saw a flicker of a fin catch Inti's golden light. Travel was easy for the mighty whales.

The adults kept the pods moving north. Unlike the Elements and the playful calves, the mothers were not so relaxed. There was a sense of tension amongst them. None had communicated their thoughts but they all knew: the sounds from the ocean were not as they should be. Ruminant set the pace a little higher. The young adults were unsure what to make of the unfamiliar background noises and normally would have ignored it, but they sensed the urgency in the pod and moved closer towards the matriarchs. Now moving faster, the calves could no longer play. The big adults had also gathered tighter together, leaving little vacant sea for anything but the hopeful, opportunist birds circling above. With everybody swimming tightly, there was less chance of whales dropping behind unnoticed.

Ruminant Whale kept the pace of the group. She knew they could not maintain it indefinitely for the calves would tire. She also knew what the new ocean sounds meant. The group was vulnerable despite its size. No males were around for protection. She kept the pod moving in the hope that things would change. Soon it would be dark. Monocled Moon was not about, so the blackest night skies would prevail, offering a chance to pull everybody through.

Darkness descended quickly after Inti sank from sight. Only then did Whale slow up. The pod spread out a little but kept singing to keep together. The younger mothers were still a little spooked because they didn't understand, although all were relieved to ease up. The calves took the opportunity to slide back under the wake and free-ride behind their mothers. Whale continued to swim north.

By morning the group was revitalised. Inti greeted them with his huge, crimson, laughing face. Whale sang briefly straight into him and the world heard her song. Inti laughed. But she was more concerned with the night's activities. The background noises had now materialised into her worst fears. The group was packed tightly together again and moving at maximum speed. How long they could keep this up was uncertain, but Whale knew it would not be long enough. All the horror stories of their elders were flooding back into her memories, few of them showing signs of encouragement. She went through each one in minute detail recalling each action, each thought, each consequence to help protect the group. In her mind she knew there was only one action that could be done, but it broke her heart to even contemplate it. She would have to sacrifice herself and possibly Calf.

She also knew they only had a few hours. If only the males were here then the pod would have more options and would stand a better chance. If only the Oarsmen were here then there would be a different ending. That was it: the Oarsmen. Why had she not thought of them? How do you call an Oarsman? It had never been done in her lifetime. Nobody had even seen one, let alone contacted one. From the stories she had been told, though, she knew they existed. All their stories were based on real accounts. There were no tales by whales, only facts and history. She crashed through the tepid sea invigorated with hope while she trawled through her memory banks for anything on Oarsmen.

She found what she was looking for. Only the elders could call the Oarsmen. Although she was an elder and she could communicate in their language, her position as Curator was privileged but had no part in council. She called the council.

In reality Whale knew she was on her own and it was her responsibility to ensure the group's safety. She now knew that the abnormal, background, ocean noises that had been getting louder were from a hunting flerd death ship. The group was being tracked. Only Whale knew the extent of the flerds' slaughter from the numerous historical accounts. She also knew the tactics – the flerds would kill the calves first, then drag their carcasses behind their killing machines to attract the mothers. That way they would be able to devour every member. For a low form of life they were ingeniously evil. She also knew there would be no salvation, for, unlike whales, they were not capable of compassion.

The elders were spread over the globe as the conference began. So far they had not returned any messages to her. She was not waiting. Whale pushed through the bubbling, black waters while continuing to trawl through her memories. If she could find some surviving accounts then she could understand the flerd strategy in attack.

Unfortunately, the killing ships were very good at what they did. Not many whales escaped, but some did and she analysed those accounts in meticulous detail: angle of approach, speed, sound of their heartbeat, their distance, how they struck and how each survivor had escaped. Each account she logged, correlated, checked and double checked.

The long-awaited message from the elders arrived. They had all spoken and unanimously agreed – it was a serious situation. The Oarsmen had been engaged. Whale could have cried. Her emotions rocketed from fear to jubilation. She could not think or sing and then she saw Calf on her port side and cried like never before. Calf saw the tears in his mother's eyes and tried to nudge her head as they swam, but she was going too fast. It was all he could do to keep up. Although he didn't understand what was happening, he wanted to show that it would be okay, so he sang to her. She cried even more.

Never had the elders engaged the Oarsmen to save a whale; never for any whales alive today, but they all agreed one thing: she was the Curator and every effort must be made to save her and the group. In doing so they had released the most formidable force on earth. Now that it was mobilised there was nothing to stop it. Oarsmen only took orders to complete tasks, from then on all other decisions were theirs. Their vocabulary only had positive words and halting a mission was not positive. Once activated, there was nothing on this earth that could stop an Oarsman.

Whale was getting short on time and options. According to the elders the Oarsmen could take several days to get to her. She did not have that long. Having analysed the steadily increasing volume of the death ship's heartbeat against known records, she knew it would be on them within a day. On top of that, the group was tiring. While the adults could continue at this pace, the young could not. She needed another option.

The whales' wake left an oily trail that stilled and dampened Rumbustious Sea. Bubbles and froth spun from under their wake as their flukes pounded the flat surface. White and Blue Footed Boobies bombed and dived continually. Small fish attracted by the oily, whale smell were battered and stunned by the big flukes, then speared and gobbled by the manic, diving birds. A constant aerial umbrella followed the whales. The deathly-arrowed, trapezoid frigate birds splintered, cutting black silhouettes of darting daggers slashing the taught, silk-soft, blue skies. High above the mad, manic bustling, booby-bombing waters the frigates glided silently, dark archangels whose mission was never declared, never mixed, never hurried but forever composed. Above the hubbub of feverish boobies the sky raiders watched and in an instant the merest glitter from a gill or a fin would trigger a laser-eyed frigate to fold her wings, slice open the medley of flying, clattering boobies to scythe, dagger-bill-first into the frothing chaos. One after the other they torpedoed from on high, leaving their adversaries jabbering, yabbering in clumsy disarray far behind. It was not to the pod's advantage having this towering frenzy advertising their position, but Whale somehow doubted it would make any difference. Most of the whales were oblivious to the birds' consequential pleasures and continued parting the waves with urgent resolve.

Whale took them to the end of daylight before dropping their speed down to a leisurely ten kilometres per hour. All the smaller calves were exhausted. She thought the dark, starlit night would offer them some protection from attack although it would allow the flerds to reach them earlier than she would have liked. However, everybody seemed to relax a little more. The darkness offered them security and most were grateful for it, but only Whale knew that it was the quiet before the storm. Tomorrow the flerds would be with them but the Oarsmen could still be several days away. She did not know how long they would take. It was a dim prospect. She had decided on her final strategy. All the timings from the records were memorised. Any ambiguities and missing information from the accounts she took educated guesses on. By correlating them against other recorded events she could estimate likely manoeuvres. The timings were critical as was her ability to analyse the flerds' positions and actions from their sounds. Half a second too early or too late would be too serious to contemplate. It was a high-risk plan to minimise death and maximise the chances of the pods' survival. The outlook for her and her calf was not an optimistic one.

It was a long night and not much rest was taken. Daylight arrived. The dark night quickly dispersed into clear, bright, blue skies dazzling amber and gold onto the tumbling backs of ocean birds. It was a beautiful morning but Whale was too occupied. Today she had to perform.

Inti popped over the eastern horizon. A slither of a cherry-red crescent bubbling through Rumbustious Sea's distant edges sent illuminated lances of golden rays skimming across Sea's still, reflective surface. "Inti looks magnificent today," thought Whale. She found herself momentarily reflective and wondrous at this beautiful but now paradoxical planet. Thoughts flooded into her from deep within her past; happy, lucky, loving thoughts from all she knew and had met. Instantly, she snapped out of it. Becoming emotional was not going to finish the job in hand. There was no benefit in reminiscing. The past does not exist. It is only now. Turning abruptly, she swung herself to starboard, forgetting Calf was on that side, consequently sinking him in a mass of foaming bubbles. Now facing east she sang. She sang of joy, enlightenment and the happiness of living with peace and love, not only for those close to us but also for others that share the benefits of the Elements' work. There were no signs in her song of the fear, apprehension or the bilious sickness that was convulsing her stomach. No hint that she was being systematically stalked by the ocean's deadliest predator and this could possibly be her last ever song to Inti and the world.

Although they had lost much time, the group had had some rest and were feeling stronger.

"They will need all their strength today," she thought. Throughout the night the adults had sung to each other. Whale outlined her plan. Although there were many tears, eventually they agreed and each went through their part in meticulous detail. Right through the night they practised the manoeuvres at low speed. The last rehearsal was fulfilled in real time at maximum speeds. Even the calves had been told about the plan, although not why. They considered it a game but understood the importance from the attitudes and sharpness of the adults. Despite their young age they were still capable of detecting the adults' doubts and fears. By daybreak everybody was so conversant with their parts that it was etched into their souls.

The pod split into groups. Each group was led by a senior matriarch. The juveniles patrolled the calves, ensuring none wandered off and that they kept up with the adults. Now the groups were travelling fast and had increased their distance from each other, though still close enough to appear as one pod.

Calf was excited. This was a new game to him although keeping up with his mother was tough. He kept calling for her to slow down but she just kept on going. He tucked his nose under her port flank and cruised in her ebb as best he could.

Whale would have preferred to have Calf in another group but she knew that would distress him and he'd come back looking for her, so she developed an emergency strategy that involved Calf should events dictate.

Whale continued monitoring the death ship's distance. They had increased their speed so she knew they could smell blood and would be with them a few hours before nightfall. It was critical timing. She wanted the hit to occur as late as possible, but not so late that the flerds postponed the attack until the next day. They had to be committed today. She adjusted her speed accordingly.

She felt sure from ancient tales that if the Oarsmen were here things would be very different. She did not know how they could help, only by their reputation. It was no good wishing. What would be, would be.

With just a few hours to go before impact, she instructed the first two groups to peel off east and west. Their instructions were to keep swimming as fast as they could, stay together until nightfall, then for each to split into subgroups. Thereafter, every four hours to keep splitting until they were in pairs. The main group, led by Whale, continued north. Anxiously she monitored the death ship. The soundings confirmed that they were still following her. So far, the plan was working. She had to keep it that way. Over the next few hours this happened four more times: the groups split, fled and continued splitting. They maintained the pace. Although all the mothers and calves had split away Whale was still left with a number of juveniles in her group. She had to convince the flerds that her group was the biggest to feed their odious appetite, thus sustaining their effort to pursue them and not any of the others.

The tactics were working, at least for the moment; the ship continued to hunt them down. When the next time marker arrived she signalled the juveniles to split and dive. Like a cascading star-burst following the points of the compass, they swung away and powered their bodies to full speed until their hearts felt like exploding. Over the last dying hours of daylight, their task was to get as much distance away as they could sustain, leaving Whale as the last target and so it was: just her and Calf. By now the noise of the ship's heartbeat was like nothing borne from this earth. Deafening and disorientating it pursued, quickly gaining. She gently sang to calf informing him to stay enlightened, connected and to live with compassion and finally adding to be alert and ready for the time was close. There had been no errors; now, if she could, it was time to save Calf. She knew he was too small for a decent meal and so long as she was an easy target then they would hunt her. Most likely by now they would be maddened to have witnessed a bounty disappear to just one. She, though, was the biggest and she hoped their rapacious hunger would mix with their anger to make irrational, injudicious decisions.

With the death ship now engaged it gained quickly. Whale was counting the sound ticks. Rumbustious Sea was still as flat as her tail. Vivacious Wind had not appeared for days. Now the Elements were not in her favour. Conditions could not have been more impeccable to slaughter a Curator than if the flerd ship had designed it. They were almost on top of her. She was fast, but was nothing like this monster – then its heartbeat hit her trigger mark. She smacked her flukes against the flat sea, turning it into a wild storm of froth and scum. Powering her blunt nose through the tame water she reached full speed. Plumes of displaced, upset sea cascaded into the air angrily returning with wavering ambivalence to their once torpid beginnings. Her huge, pounding flukes deranged momentous tonnages of idle sea. Quickly she accelerated approaching sixty kilometres an hour and briefly outpaced the flerds. It wasn't something she could sustain, but then she did not need to. Calf was left behind but he did what his mother had instructed and veered off to port in a huge sweep, then dived putting as much distance between him and the ship as he could. The rapid acceleration established another two hundred metres between them and the distance continued to increase. This, she hoped, would buy Calf and herself more time. Especially for Calf; she did not want him to witness what she knew could be the only result.

Whale was on another level. Her senses and body had electrified; she became light itself. Listening intently, her mind clear and calculating, she counted the heartbeats. Something would happen. What, she wasn't sure. By the few accounts she had, it could be distinguished and was unique. She was still counting to reach the point to expect it when something resonated above her. It was earlier than expected but loud and unequivocal. Amongst the crashing seas and her beating heart she heard a muffled explosion in the air. Not a sonic sound as she expected, but there was no ambiguity that this was it. The accounts were right. She started the final countdown. After this there was no plan. On reaching zero she swung hard to starboard and smashed into a crash dive.

Chapter VII

The calm conditions and the rose-tinted lights of the evening sun allowed the death ship to fix an accurate sighting to fire its harpoon directly at Whale's head, ensuring an easy, merciful kill. The attached, exploding warhead was designed to detonate after entering the whale's skull before triggering four, large, steel barbs to blow out. Sufficient internal damage would cause near instantaneous death or enough disability to secure the whale, enabling it to be retrieved by means of an attached line. It was well tested and infallible.

Whale's accounts had witnessed this and by rolling away at the exact time when the harpoon was in flight she hoped to miss the deadly encounter. The harpoon was faster than she ever imagined. By adroitly turning she had prevented the harpoon from entering through her blowpipe. Instead it glanced down the side of her head. The warhead triggered. The resulting explosion ripped her flesh away from the bone and one of the detonated steel barbs blasted through her eye with the barbs lodging behind the bone of her eye socket.

Whale screamed involuntarily. It was a short, piercing scream that reverberated around the world. In the next splintering second a blinding, incandescent light split her head in two radiating an agonising, shearing, splitting pain. It ricocheted through every cell, paralysing her body and mind.

In the brief, insensate numbness that followed, she must have passed out. How long, she did not know. It could have been seconds. It could have been months, but then the intense, tenacious pain bellowed uncontrollably bringing her back to the horror of reality. The lapping waves rubbed salt onto her exposed skull. Raw, ripped, racked flesh hung in tattered shreds gushing scorched oxygen-rich, blue-black blood, turning the sea into a magenta mango-coloured soup. Momentarily, hanging limp and docile from her splintered eye socket, the cold, inert harpoon rocked against the whale's rolling, wave-lashed body.

Inti, low on the western horizon, heard the scream, as did all the Elements. Pachamama momentarily stopped spinning. Every living creature held their breath. Tree froze. Never had anybody heard anything like it. The world became silent. All the whales of the oceans shuddered to a shivering freeze. Terror and tears tore through each of their trembling torsos. Calf stopped instantly in his wake. Fear fled through his frame. Turning on the spot he raced back to his mother despite all her precise, unambiguous instructions to the contrary. Calf could see the huge flerd ship standing monstrously high above the flat sea. How he wished to be an Oarsman.

Whale sensed the moment. The tethered cord to the harpoon would soon become taunt and drag her into the ship's stomach. Gathering the remains of her strength, she dived and powered down with every joule of energy she had left to expel. The few survivors and witnesses that there were in the archives advised against this. It was documented that death would be certain on resurfacing due to the huge loss of oxygen-carrying blood and the massive water pressure would render her weak and incapacitated. Whale could think of no other options. Through the debilitating pain she engaged the last of her energy to kick the sea walls deeper and deeper.

The whale line to the ship tightened. The harpoon against her skull locked fast. The pain intensified. Enormous pressure mounted around her eye socket. She thought her skull would be wrenched apart as she fought against the line's tensioning clutch, stripping fathoms away from the surface. The flerds were unprepared for what should have been a simple kill as hundreds of metres instantly whipped off the ship's bow.

Massive blood loss flowed involuntarily at depth. Her oxygen, too, would be used up quickly. According to the accounts she knew that she would last no more than an hour. There were plenty of stories going back a hundred or more years with whales having been harpooned, but she knew of none with an exploded harpoon in the eye.

On resurfacing she would be so depleted of oxygen and blood and with her energy spent, she would be mercilessly slaughtered by the insatiable flerds.

Calf lost his mother. There was no way he could descend to that depth. But he cried with joy as his mother was alive. She had defeated the flerds; her plan had worked. He was so excited and wanted to tell the world how his clever mother had defeated them. Only then did he notice that she wasn't diving in her usual, sleek style. She had turned to one side and was descending at an odd angle. When he looked closer he saw the harpoon wrenching her face towards the surface with a long length of cord curving upwards towards the ship. The taste of blood and burned flesh whisked through his jaws. He then realised it was his mother's death dive. The flerds' ship was playing with her before hauling her into its stomach. There was nothing he could do but backtrack. Tears flooded his eyes. Anger and sorrow combined into an excruciating, sick, numbing pain. Pumping his flukes violently he surged down to be with his mother despite the intolerable pressure crushing his body. Ignoring everything she had told him, he was determined not to let her die alone.

The Elements had spoken. Normally, they did not get involved with particular life on earth, they did whatever was required within their own boundaries. Seldom did they all work together, but this was different. All agreed: nobody kills a Curator. They acted instantly. Inti intensified, burning hotspots into Rumbustious Sea. Vivacious Wind picked up Inti's energy, sweeping into the thermal hotspots, gaining power until he was a roaring hurricane. He swept across the sea, howling and screaming towards the flerd ship. Rumbustious Sea collected wind's anger, producing forty-metre waves, whipped, white water avalanching from their tops, blinding and scything all afloat. Monocled Moon, usually docile and amicable, heaved his mighty, gravitational waves towards the earth. The multifaceted Sea again responded with increased energy by producing massive tides and formidable currents. Catching the mighty winds, Tempest Cloud towered into frighteningly high, heinously raging columns of black, hateful, water-filled cumulus clouds. They sat on top of Vivacious Wind and raced across the oceans. Finally Pachamama, roaring with anger, split open vast underwater trenches letting forth the wrath of Scorching Fire that fuelled deep within her soul. Her tectonic plates stretched and quivered with vehement and unequivocal fury. In doing so she let loose an unrelenting, barbarous tsunami. Now initiated, it raged unstoppably and invisibly across the planet.

The Elements raced indefatigably, doggedly towards the killer ship. The waves from Rumbustious Sea quickly climbed from millpond calm to monstrous, menacing mountains that loomed high and swallowed whole. Huge swelling, pumping, raging waves many times higher than the ship smashed over the top, engulfing it in tonnes of steaming, hissing, bad-tempered surf. Tied by a line that was secured at the bow to an immense, underwater whale, the ship could not move. Worse than only having to survive an unpredicted sadistic-sized storm, they were also tethered by an irate whale that showed no signs of stopping. The ship began to slide under the massive rollers. Over three hundred kilometre-per-hour hurricane winds drove into the ship while Tempest Cloud delivered a blackout of spitting, high-tensile swords of rain and lightning combined. A flerd quickly recovered an axe and with one mighty swing severed the line. The air locked ship popped to the surface only to be swept by a surging wave to its wind-hacked crest. With its engines whining at full revolution as its propellers pitched into the air, it rolled onto its side before it was sucked, pitilessly, savagely down the wave's back side. Forty metres below it briefly levelled into the engulfing belly of the next waiting wave.

The dark, smothering cloak of the murderously engulfing Elements seized the seas in the pitch-black night. Inti pulsated immortal streams of high energy particles into Pachamama from far across the other side of the world. In the night skies the hidden Moon showed a pale, indifferent face, a face that was just a façade which hid his roaring emotions. He continued to pump gravitational waves into the earth. Now working in concert with the sun they both induced a power into the other Elements of nuclear proportions. Wind, cloud and sea were continuously, relentlessly energised. The supply was endless; their reserves unlimited. It was perhaps Pachamama and Rumbustious Sea's tsunami that was to prove the most debilitating. It was due to send a hard message; it would not be received for another half day or so. They were in no rush. She ensured that all other death ships would never leave their ports along any coast of the ocean's rim. It was Whale's insurance policy and the death sentence for all flerd death ships.

The pressure pulling against Whale's head stopped. She felt the harpoon drop from above, hanging heavily across her jaw. The dark, quiet stillness that pervaded those depths was in extreme contrast to the bellicose war above as was the agonising, nerve stripping pains from her wounds. Getting steadily weaker she decided to surface, hoping that the severed line was a good omen of the flerd ship disengaging. It did cross her mind that it was a trap and that they would launch another harpoon when she surfaced, but she no longer had the strength to fight. In a way the relief to escape the pain would be welcome. She did not rush to the top.

With just a few fathoms below, she could see with her one good eye that Rumbustious Sea was undertaking an uncompromising, violent assault of proportions she had never witnessed before. The noise transcending down towards her beat together like a hundred competing hurricanes.

When Whale reached the surface it was difficult to ascertain where the sea started and the sky stopped. There was as much water above as below. The world had turned upside down and was in a very bad mood indeed. Thoughts of the flerd ship being a threat faded. Thoughts of a flerd ship even being afloat seemed highly improbable. Drained and exhausted, Whale reached the surface and, sucking in huge quantities of clean air, she idly floated. The waves caressed her battered body and rocked her up and down. The limp harpoon that had created so much excruciating and catastrophically painful damage lay like a docile dog by her side. Several kilometres of flaccid line aimlessly hung in the lathered sea, sinking and floating with no mind of its own. She lay on her starboard side leaving her wounds open to the Elements. There was nothing more to do but wait for the inevitable. She slipped into unconsciousness.

Chapter VIII

Sea found Whale and wrapped an encompassing eddy around her. Sheltering her from the ongoing fury, she gently cosseted her within the troughs of her mighty waves. Whale slumbered in and out of consciousness oblivious to all.

With continuous heavy blows the Elements pushed the torn, dilapidated ship farther away. Tempest Cloud persistently flicked bombastic charges of lightning into the ship with unaffectionate ease.

Throughout the night the winds and rains blew. The savage bombardment continued unrelentingly. Pachamama's and Sea's tsunami reached the first coastlines. On encountering the shallow water it transformed itself from a mere pressure wave to a twenty-metre rampaging wall of angry, liquid granite. Travelling at over one hundred kilometres an hour it delivered a calamitous impact across thousands of miles of low coastland. It flattened everything it touched.

Calf found Whale sheltering in the bottom of a well of rising water. Rushing straight to her he carefully bonked her discreetly on the nose. There was no response. She was floating on her side but her good eye was closed. Calf couldn't see the other eye with the harpoon. He cried and cried and cried. In his grief he involuntarily sang out his lament. The message travelled the globe.

Every whale in every corner of the earth stopped. Another shudder went through them with the realisation of the implications of murdering a Curator. The elders instantly responded, their songs harmoniously floating across the world's seas. The whales listened in awe. Never had they heard anything like this. Some were so distraught that they could not comprehend and had to be comforted by their families. The instructions simply stated all whales to join together to take the Curator's body back to sanctuary where it could be returned to the Mother Earth. A ceremony would take place to deliver her soul to Inti and to appoint a new Curator. One or two of the older whales had heard of such events but none had ever witnessed one. Usually the offspring of the Curator is appointed after they have spent years in training. She was the first Curator to be murdered. Without exception every whale changed course to begin the journey towards Whale and then on to the sanctuary within the cold, southern, polar oceans.

Steadily, with each passing hour, the whales began arriving. Calf was inconsolable. He refused to leave her side. Some of the larger juvenile males tried to push him further from his mother. Each time they nudged him away he would roll around swimming straight back to bonk her nose. Edging next to her he stuck to her side like a limpet. A senior matriarch eventually swam next to Calf. Staying by his side, she sang low and gently, eventually persuading him to let his mother rest while they took them both south. She took him away but not so far that he could not see his mother's body and kept him by her side next to her flipper. The young males strained to take control of Whale's enormous body. When enough had arrived they slowly, respectfully, turned her south to start the long track back.

It was a gruelling task. The hideous weather made it almost impossible to move as a group with any organisation. The carrier males soon became exhausted pushing a seventy-tonne whale into forty-metre swells against a roaring hurricane. They changed shifts often, making very little progress. With the light fading towards the end of a hard emotional and physical day, Rumbustious Sea had sapped the strength of all but the strongest. Pods of female whales arrived with increasing frequency. Unfortunately, all the mature, strong, male-filled pods were still days away.

The Elements had battered the flerd ship into a floating garbage can. Its decks had been swept clear, the cabin and steering mechanism stripped off. Water had flooded into its engines and fuel tanks. The batteries, drowned in salty water, had shorted together, buckling their plates and were lifeless. Half the crew were lost overboard, the other half wished they had been too. In one momentous day they had been blown hundreds of kilometres from Whale.

At last the Elements relented. All, that is, except Tempest Cloud. He had not finished with the flerd death ship and continued hurling bolts of lightning into the vessel. The other Elements, however, turned their attention to Whale. Vivacious Wind changed direction and pushed them south. He did not know where they were going but whatever they wanted he would help, so he blew Whale incessantly. Rumbustious Sea picked up on Wind and rolled her waves southerly. In an instant the carrier males suddenly found themselves lurching forward, propelled by some of the mightiest Elements.

Throughout the night the shifts changed, more whales arrived. The sea became a thick, corrugated carpet of waggling, wave-bumping whales. They came from all directions, their numbers incessantly increasing. By daylight the sea had turned into a monstrous mass of moving whales. Spreading over several kilometres, the bobbing, black platform hissed and steamed, turning sea into land. Boobies and frigates arrived in their thousands, diving dangerously between their vast, closely packed bodies, scavenging anything that had been shattered by this moving platform.

Inti rose steadily into the sky and laughed.

The mood was sombre as they slowly continued south. By midday Inti, still laughing, noticed a disturbance with some whales towards the eastern edge of the group. The feeling had jumped from a lugubrious melancholy to an edgy nervousness. The whales towards the east became nervous, bouncing into each other, darting and pushing. The perturbation persisted, gradually migrating its way throughout the whole group. Everyone became alert and uneasy. Their speed involuntarily increased. The older ones began to suspect another attack. It would be an ideal opportunity to wipe them out entirely. A flerd ship now amongst the group could slaughter hundreds of them. The animals would have nowhere to go but down; they would be picked off at will.

Unbeknown to the whales, Pachamama and Rumbustious Sea had already eliminated any further flerd attacks. The tsunami had reached every shoreline around the ocean. There was not a port intact nor a ship afloat that could touch a whale. There was sufficient carnage for it to stay that way for a long time.

Towards the eastern flanks of the whales, a number suddenly parted. Ducking, diving, pushing, they forced each other apart. A frenzied clamour set in as dignity and respect evaporated from the white-washed waters. A huge, clear sea channel opened up. Four monstrous creatures cruised in. The anxiety transformed to fright but there was also a touch of awe. Although they could not get out of the way quickly enough there was also a flicker of dangerous curiosity. The fear ricocheted through the group like a rampant virus. Everybody was asking, "What on earth are these things?"

Four Oarsmen had arrived. Slamming into the sea at eighty kilometres an hour with water cascading thirty metres into the air, their blunt heads pulverised the ionised sea into vapour. Huge fountains spiralled over their backs, producing a constant plume of agitated, cascading torrents as it crashed back into the sea. Their speed, power and physicality dominated all. They pushed into the very heart of the group where Whale was located.

Calf, terrified, hid under his new matriarch's flipper, touching her sides as close as he could get. He would have climbed on top to get out of the way if he could. The group stopped. Everybody's attention was firmly on the newcomers. For an instant nobody breathed. Not a fountain in the skies could be seen or heard.

Each Oarsman looked identical: each the perfect physical cetacean of colossal proportions. Weighing over one hundred and fifty tonnes a piece and over fifty metres long they dwarfed even the biggest males. Satanically strident, inviolably indifferent, the sea dripped from their smooth, night-black backs, cloaking their coolness with a billion cascading, glistening diamonds. Their enormous square, box-shaped heads, a third of the length of their bodies, were longer than most whales. A small pinhole, black, unblinking eye, low down towards the back of their heads, showed no sign of life or emotion. Despite its inconspicuous size it could detect a sprat sixty metres in any direction. Their vicious lower jaws, the length of their heads and filled with strong, ivory teeth, could crush and break the spine of any whale alive or dead. They dominated by magnitude and temperament.

In less than two days they had covered over three thousand kilometres. It was inconceivable to any mortal whale. But these were not mortal whales. These were Oarsmen, the pinnacle of evolutionary power to have ever swum in Pachamama's high seas.

The male carrier whales moved quickly away at the sight of the approaching Oarsmen. Whale was left bobbing gently in Rumbustious Sea's southerly pulsating waves. The Oarsmen took command and moved into their positions: one either side of Whale, one in front and one behind. The two carriers swam under Whale and pushed her up to support her total length.

Calf watched with fear, terror, dread, intrigue, amazement, admiration and veneration. He thought of his mother as the biggest, strongest whale of all but now, cradled between these megalithic leviathans she looked tiny, frail and fragile. He wanted to cry and laugh but could do neither.

The harpoon hanging from Whale's eye was obstructing the lift. Swirling behind the fins and tails the harpoon's twisting, tethered cord wreathed a dance along an obstreperous path between birds, beasts and waves. The two carriers split, lowering Whale back to the surface. One bent his head down and with a mighty blow from his indomitable fluke plummeted to the depths with a turn of speed that left all the onlookers awe struck with disbelief. Some moments passed before the Oarsman resurfaced. He crashed through the surface with such speed that half his body launched from the water right next to Whale's head. His huge, black, monolithic body soared into the skies with a cascade of flaying water, scattering boobies in every direction. He arched his body towards Whale. Twisting on his ascent, he snatched the harpoon in his jaw then landed on top of her head pushing her several fathoms under.

Spitting out the harpoon, he dived below Ruminant, pushing her back to the surface as he returned. Her skull had splintered around the socket where the barb was pulled out but the Oarsman's twisting action had minimised the damage. The long, attached cord now whistled quickly past everybody as the hefty harpoon plummeted towards the distant, dead bottom.

Whale awoke. The tremendous bone-fracturing blow to her head induced another excruciating, lightning pain ricocheting across her skull. She jolted with shock and terror from her innermost sanctuary where her subconscious survival instincts had induced a total shutdown. The roaring pain returned again, sending her consciousness into a panic and oblivious to any other feelings she lay shaking and trembling. Amongst the pain and fear she became aware of two warm beings by her side. Powerfully but gently, she felt her body levitating from the sea. The sun's rays warmed her ice-cold back. There was nothing on this earth that could lift her as easily as that. Then she remembered the Oarsmen; they had come. Involuntarily she gasped, a huge plume of clotted blood and stale, acrid air shot into the sky.

The whole group stopped. A single song from Calf's matriarch echoed around the world, "The Curator is alive."

Calf hadn't time to cry. He sprang from the matriarch's flipper and raced towards his mother without even thinking and swam straight into an Oarsman. He raced to the front and turning he faced two Oarsmen. Undeterred, he dived and came up to where he thought his mother ought to be, only to find the underbellies of the same two insurmountable Oarsmen. "The plan clearly isn't going to work," he thought to himself, so he sang.

Whale heard her son and cried softly to herself. She had no idea what was going on. She sang back in their own special song. Calf cried too.

The Oarsmen were unmoved. With the two carriers back in place, one of the Oarsmen took the lead at the head of the carriers and the other positioned himself to the rear. With everything in place the leading Oarsman set the pace, breaking the waters to enable the carriers to tailgate with minimum effort. At regular intervals they all changed positions. By rotating and sharing the load they could continue at pace for weeks if required.

The elders gathered. It was obvious to all that she was in a bad way. Torn flesh was hanging from half of her face, one eye was missing with the splintered, fractured bone exposed to the sea. What internal damage was done, no whale knew. On top of that she had lost a lot of blood. It was imperative to get her to sanctuary where the cool waters were thick with krill and squid before she grew too weak.

With this new information the elders agreed to disperse the group and send them back on their original journeys. The edict sang out. Slowly, starting from the outer edges many kilometres away, the whales turned and headed back north. The Oarsmen, oblivious to their surroundings, pushed on without delay.

Four massive flukes swept the ocean waves into a fermented froth of boiling white foam. The frigates and boobies bombed it incessantly and in an instant the elders were left far behind. Within minutes, the only sign of their existence was the occasional plume of vapour and stale breath rapidly diminishing into the horizon. Even the elders were astonished at the gruesome raw power these animals had. Then they were gone. The elders eventually gave up the chase and dropped back to what all considered a fast cruising speed of twenty kilometres an hour.

Calf was euphoric. She had beaten the flerds and lived. His new surrogate mother had left her pod with another matriarch to accompany Calf to the sanctuary. They followed the elders at an even more respectable cruising speed so that Calf would not get exhausted. Even so, he was bouncing all around her, urging her on to go faster. She kept it steady for there was a long way to go.

Chapter IX

High above Fly Mountain a broad-winged condor soared high on the cool, nightly currents; perfecting a flawless night vigil. Its single, pure white collar contrasted against its moonless, black, night cloak producing a cut-throat shimmer of a distant star.

Far below in the dungeons of the mountain a creature cries. The roaring begins veiled in darkness, screaming from the very depths of extinction. Each night, every night, the earth rumbles low and groans in accompaniment to the creature's demonized cries. Bellowing with pain. Acute, organ-rupturing pain. It roars. It hollers. Its lungs, ripping stale, acrid air over its abused, raw, swollen larynx. Teragorm was bent over a cold rock, iron-gripping claws lashed against it, holding to subdue those crippling, slashing stomach cramps seizing, squeezing the very life from her belly. Bending her head sharply back, breaking her neck towards the stars, she screamed. Her ugly, broken, beaked jaws stretched achingly, vacantly wide. Unmoved and indifferent to the creature's catastrophic consumption, circling, silently, slyly, Condor, confident with his prowess, consummated Teragorm's defences. The acidic, half-digested debris decomposing foully within the creature's belly lays her involuntarily immobile across the rock. She screams with agony. The mountains amplify her torment like relentless, abominable war machines. But oh, how she loves to eat that meat. That oh so sweet, succulent flesh. That insatiable appetite for even a banal flerd. To feast all night. How the dregs of their demise sit bad within her aching, bloated belly. How she roars each day her discontent. Her morning day. Every day. But how she hates those morning days. Within those failing half-lights her red, swollen eyes try to focus through her tears – streaming, biting tears. Green tears, through the putridity of her rotting stomach. Seeking desperately. Seeking out. Out of light. Out of sight.

The mountain goat sentries, scattered strategically, indefatigably, stolidly detached, stand as solid as the timeless rocks that support them. Still as the dead. Indifferent. Unperturbed by the creature's bellyaching cravings. They stand their post. The dark ebbs. The half-lights flicker. The new day.

Teragorm's dying wails echoed throughout Fly Forest. The daily clutter increased as one by one the diurnal animals ignited to the light, each battering the clattering orchestra.

Tree could not sleep. Something demented had been screaming. The events with Whale weighed heavily on his cellulose mind. Day and night he had been repeating her last song. She said she was about to lure a death ship away from the mothers. This was likely to be her last message. It was! He had heard nothing. Other than terrifying screaming, nobody had said anything since. Whale often used to sing in the background. It was what she did, she enjoyed it. He deeply missed her soothing songs each morning but now she was not there he could only hear this distant screaming. It was a very long away off but he could tell it was powerful and painful.

It was not for the better either. These guttural, tortured cries had no message. They had no end; they seemed to go on for ever. "What are they saying?" Tree pondered, trying to get any meaning from them. "Not only that," he thought, "but what is making them?" He decided to talk to Pachamama, "What makes those awful, painful, pre-dawn screams before fading away as the sun gets higher? I have heard many sounds from the forest but nothing sounds like that and nobody ever sees it. What is it?"

Pachamama had heard it. She knew what it was. "For once," she thought, with some relief, "I can answer this without the need for Whale as a backup, so this should be simple." Pachamama started confidently, "It is coming from the distant Fly Mountains, Tree. They are sacred to the indigenous Indian flerds. The vertical walls of hard, barren rock form precipitous fortifications protruding high above the treetops into Tempest Cloud, each a monument to its own righteous destiny. They form a mystical physicality to the origins of the earth. That is why the Fly Flerds revere them as sacred temples, but do not associate these flerds with the savages that have hunted down Whale. These flerds have developed separately; their spirit has intricately woven into the fabric of the environment and connected to the Elements. So life on the top of the mountain is separate to life below. Because the sides are so impenetrable, the worlds digress but the ancestors are as one. There is one creature though, that can traverse this huge, natural barrier and the noises you hear are from this ancient animal. She is called a Teragorm, Tree. A primitive, angry, aggressive, brainless creature that only eats flerds. She stalks them at night, picking off the stragglers in the forest, then drags them back up the mountain via a hidden path known only to her. On top she is in her own domain. There she rips them apart with her serrated, saw-edged beak. Unfortunately, they disagree with her digestive system to such a large extent that it renders her immobile, crippled in pain. She is also allergic to sunlight which makes her eyes sting and her pallid, bony skin burn and itch. The debilitating effect of eating flerds means she cannot move until after they are digested which usually takes her well into daylight. She has a peculiar pact with Condor and Goat. It's a relationship of symbiosis: Condor picks off the leftovers from the flerd and then Goat cleans up. In exchange they guard and protect Teragorm while she is incapacitated. But that takes hours and by then Inti is up and beaming. She's too stupid to change her diet. They tend to live alone but there are many hidden high in the mountains spread across the land. They are an ancient lot up those mountains where the earthly norms have been dismissed, but the spirits remain with them."

Tree was agog. He had not heard of anything that hunted flerds. Nor indeed anything that eats things that disagree with it so badly, that incapacitates it so much that it howled in agony. To eat to that excess, it must be a really stupid creature. He was pontificating on such matters of eating, something to which he had no affinity. Especially as his case was of continual absorption dictated by need. How could you overload?

"So why does she eat what she knows is bad for her?"

"She likes the taste. It's her favourite meal."

"But it makes her ill."

"Yes, we know, but she likes the taste." Pachamama was beginning to get that déjà vu feeling.

"But it cripples her, then she collapses, only to be burnt up by the sun which makes everything worse."

Pachamama's confidence sank a little further. There was no convenient escape route to Whale and she could think of nothing to say other than, "Apparently not."

Tree was about to jump in about flerd flesh and its putrefactive effects on poor Teragorm when a bolt of inspiration hit Pachamama. She quickly continued, "Did you feel that, Tree? The earth moved."

Tree didn't think it had but paused anyway just to make sure then said, "No." Then he added, "Yes," but before he could clarify the ambiguity Pachamama butted in.

"I believe it did. I don't recall authorising an earthquake. I must investigate. Have a great growing day."

Tree was about to tell her that it was a falling branch cracking off a tree and thumping into the earth that she had felt. A large ficus branch lay discarded across the ground. The hefty, severed end, which was once not so long ago attached to the trunk, opened out exposing its split, ragged, vascular tissue. Bark was torn back in long, ragged ribbons as it had tenaciously tried to cling onto its parent trunk before weight and gravity overcame its resistance.

For a while Tree could not make out the cause in the late afternoon's vacillating light. Branches are not known to drop of their own accord unless old or damaged and this was neither. Under the debris of busted twigs and shredded leaves he eventually recognised four feet sticking upwards towards the canopy. It was Green Iguana. The feet seemed in no hurry to move and Tree presumed that Iguana was either happy in his upside down world, or dead. It seemed unlikely that a mere ten-metre fall would kill him, as past experience had shown the animal to be impervious to any physical maltreatment. However, on this occasion there did not appear to be much life under the demolition zone.

Iguana was a noble creature, fully mature and in his prime. He bothered nobody and nobody bothered him. A full one and half metres from the tip of his very long, whiplash tail to the end of his blunt snout, he was packed with powerful muscles encased in an impregnable armoured, spiky casing. Running along the length of his back was a fearsome array of bony spines protecting him from any attack from above. At the end of each of his indomitably strong, stubby legs were five immensely powerful claws. It was these that Tree could see, as could anything else that happened to be looking at the vegetative carnage. Even if they were, it would take some sharp eyes to distinguish a brown, green iguana from a brown, green tree. Iguana did not care that his belly was exposed towards the mighty Elements. Iguana did not care much about anything because anything fancying taking their chances for a quick bite would soon find themselves ripped to shreds before it could lick its lips.

Still, falling out of the tree like that had taken him a little by surprise. He thought he would have needed to amble another metre or so before the branch gave way. He lay there for a short period with half the branch across his belly while he regained his faculties and pretended that he'd done it on purpose.

Iguana lay where he fell. Completely immobile, he relaxed while soaking up the last of the sun's energy. Dappled in tan, fawn and brown-camouflaged skin, he melted into the earth. Even when in the trees he matched the colours and hues of their bark so impeccably that he remained invisible. A large, gnarled flap of skin under his chin showed his dominance, his maturity and also helped him raise his blood temperature to climb and fall out of trees. When he thought that nobody was watching, he rolled over onto all fours and shook off the broken branches. Exposing the full extent of his muscular physique, he trudged off to his hole under a clump of wild banana trees. Wee Tree was impressed; considering Iguana was only twenty centimetres high he must weigh ten kilograms, but his seismic crash into the earth was dismissed with such lethargic nonchalance that you would think he had not noticed.

Tree watched with wooden interest as the daily light began to ebb away. He spoke to Pachamama. "Pachamama, are you still there?"

"Nearly," replied a hesitant Mother Earth.

Not listening, Tree continued, "Green Iguana, that you thought was an earthquake, is camouflaged in dull brown and tan. He's as much green as he is orange or blue; where did he get that name from?"

Pachamama had not the faintest idea, "He is green in a brown and tan sort of way, Tree. Because he hides amongst green leaves he appears green as opposed to, say a black iguana, who is always black."

Fortunately for Pachamama, Princess arrived, taking Tree's thoughts away. It was impossible to tell where she had come from or, for that matter, where she would go. In an instant she flew in one direction then changed it to another. It was as if the slightest of breezes lifted her off course and blew her unpredictably to another. Then again, it could just have been the way her mind worked. Up and down, left and right she swayed an unknown dance to the invisible air currents with effortless style and polished poise, her shadow littered with optimistic, blue admirers all hoping to catch her eye. Each trying to out-dazzle one another by reflecting a shimmer of fading sunlight through their azure wings. Each forever expectant to attract the attention of one of the forest's most alluring and beautiful princesses.

Princess took no notice of the cavorting efforts from the following troupe and landed on the multi-coloured bark of a guarumo tree. There her micro-thin, sensitive tongue gently unrolled to sample the tree's nutritious sap as it leaked from an abrasion in the bark. Folding her wings, she all but became invisible. The delicate hues of cream and golden brown concentric circles etched into the underside of her wings mimicked the multi-shaded silver, beige and bronze bark. She masked with the bark. Intoxicated by the tree's gift of life she became oblivious to the frantic manoeuvrings of her male admirers.

Close by, the Black Vulture was perched on a branch of one of the fallen trees. Not that he was doing much, nor was he waiting for anything to die. Neither was he hungry or feeling particularly sociable. The irascible jostling, flapping and quarrelsome mien of his fellow cackling cronies' manic squabbles had left him somewhat wilting and jaded. He had stealthily slipped away and found this peaceful spot with a little sunshine left to warm his old and ragged wings. Stretching them out to their full one-metre limit, he idolised Inti before settling himself down for the oncoming night.

Lapping up the sultry, soporific effects from the dappled sunlight, he reminisced about those intoxicating, high spirited days when he had to wait to be called before being allowed to eat. Those adolescent, juvenile times when he was at the bottom of the hierarchy. Unfortunately for him, nearly everybody else was also at the bottom. Most of the time there was no issue but as soon as it came to food and sex, he was at the back of the queue. The statesman took first choice in everything: the fittest, strongest hen and the prime chunks of dead flesh, which usually started with the eyeballs then finished with the gonads, if there were any. It had been ten years before he tasted an eyeball. To be honest he did not see what the fuss was about, but he ate them so that all the rabble below knew that he was the statesman and that they were not. An eyeball is an eyeball and a gonad is not theirs and only when he was finished could the elders then move in. Recalling the tantrums and antics they used to get up to while waiting for the scrap ends made him smirk. The strategic manoeuvrings, pushing and blocking that was performed to get to the front at precisely the time the elders stepped aside was in itself an art form.

He was happy just to sit there contemplating life and the forest. Although, should something come along and happen to conveniently die in front of him he might have to hop off and clean up a bit before the ranting riff-raff destroyed the harmony. "But that then," he pondered, "was the true spirit of being a Black Vulture: beautiful, placid, clean-living birds of the forest, that never did any harm nor threatened any living animal. We are one hundred percent docile and considerate. Everybody should be a vulture; the world would be a better place." Although, it was not unknown to give something a sharp tap on the head to help them along the way towards enlightenment, if the occasion required.

While pontificating on the events of his Samaritan activities, he noticed a huge, blue butterfly zigzag her way in a haphazard, random fashion towards him.

He looked down at his drab, black coat then up towards Princess's sky-blue, luminous cloak, dazzling with each beat of her wings. She danced above the fresh, growing grass. Her beauty touched his old heart. She radiated love. A warm, comforting glow spread throughout his body. He wanted to be young again. He could fly with her and follow her to the ends of the earth.

Dreamingly flying, flitting, infatuated with his new love, he danced a rhythmic waltz around an aromatic hibiscus bush, its flamingo orange petals darkening into a burnt, flaming crimson towards the inner depths of its ovarian soul. Princess' fleeting, explosive brilliance powered from her magnificent, velvet wings complemented the vivid greens and burning orange flowers. Vulture swung and turned and danced with her every twist while their love laughed and the Laughing Sun laughed too.

A turbulent rush and swoop in the still, tepid air brought Vulture disdainfully back to his earthly branch. For a brief moment he was trapped between the love lust delights for an ethereal butterfly and the humdrum existence of a startled, old vulture. His mind involuntary returned to reality to see what the blazes had interrupted his fanciful daydreams. The vainglorious, narcissistic Chestnut-Mandibled Toucan had landed right beside him on his carefully selected branch. He sighed dismissively, pulled his wings close to his sides and looked longingly, lifelessly into the hibiscus bush. Somehow, tucking his wings in made him feel more secure. With a brazen, big-nosed toucan next to you, events could only continue one way.

Standing side by side the two birds took no notice of each other but fixedly stared over the grass at the forest's most beautiful butterfly. They were both in love. Toucan did not turn to look at Vulture in case his large beak swung into his belly, knocking him off his perch. He did not want to be seen to start an ugly argument.

Uncharitably, he thought, "It is not as if the bird isn't ugly enough. Besides, which would a beautiful, blue butterfly prefer? An ugly old, washed out, bedraggled vulture, or a vivid, lustrous, multi-coloured, bright toucan with energy, pizazz and the biggest, brightest conk in the forest? No contest!"

Vulture was a little indignant at having his peacefulness destroyed so late in the day, not to mention his imaginative trip to the ends of the earth. Still, he resisted the temptation of tapping the annoying little chap on top of his head in case it started an embarrassing disagreement in such a splendid, tranquil place in front of Princess.

Toucan sang out a snappy, sharp, two-tone whistle, "Hey gorgeous, why don't you swing your beautiful body over here to touch down on my enormous bright schnozzle?"

Vulture could not believe what he was hearing. How could anything be so obnoxiously arrogant and vulgar? But then this was Toucan we were talking about. The black vulture, though, had already seen the dozen or so suitors swinging around the wild hibiscus bush. They were waiting for their chances to attract Princess's attention with their own dazzling displays of radiant blues and purples.

"Still," he thought, "how could one stand in the way of a big-nosed bird's ambitions? It would be entertaining enough to watch Toucan become demoralised by the number and quality of his opposition. A little encouragement in that direction wouldn't hurt too much; would it?" Without further hesitation Vulture emitted a rasping, ear-jarring, toneless scoffing squawk then, without turning to watch the irritating loudmouth to his right, relaxed back with a surreptitious grin and a dark, beady eye.

Toucan nearly fell off his perch. He laughed and laughed. Never in his life had he heard such a cacophonous din. That would scare the dead and all in earshot would wish they were. "Clearly, this ancient duffer is not just battered and ugly but a senile, old fool as well. He also has a voice like Savage Foam Frog with nasal blockage." He stood up tall to flash his vivid, banana-yellow breast fringed with scarlet red lacing. His beautiful black-feathered tail fanned out wide to show the full effect of his fiery red under-plumage.

Pushing his magnificent jet black and scorching yellow beak to the skies, to emphasise his striking body, he sang out crisp and shrill so that there was no ambiguity as to his intent. He settled back with a smug and contented smirk across his face, "There, old boy, that's the way to do it. That's how you attract a lady! Top that if you are bird enough."

Vulture sat expressionless. Princess removed her long tongue from the delights of savouring the sweet hibiscus flower and fluttered up to find another. The entourage from the other side of the bush arrived. They swung around the glossy, green leaves in a disjointed, erratic line of bobbing blues. On catching up with Princess they kept a respectable distance, waving their big, seductive wings. The golden, speckled sunlight filtered through the forest leaves dappling their shining wings into a magnificent, exploding array of moving, jolting rainbows spreading across a fiery spectrum. It moved and jostled, constantly changing shape and size. The brilliance of the display stopped the forest for a brief moment.

Vulture, inscrutable and motionless, strained with mirth to hide a whopping great grin the size of an upturned banana. Toucan, mesmerised by the prismatic display, sat paralysed, numbed and astounded by this unexpected extravaganza. The greens and dappled browns of the forest were suddenly punctuated by this explosive, late evening show. Toucan suddenly felt very uncomfortable and belittled for thinking that he could attract such a beautiful princess, while a sensational troupe of radiant suitors were a whispering wing-tip away. He immediately took off, reaching maximum toucan speed within seconds. Looking only at the tip of his beak he disappeared into the dark forest like a black and yellow dart with its tail on fire.

Unmoved, Vulture spread his wings to catch the sun and laughed and laughed and laughed.

Chapter X

Tempest seethed and simmered far away across the forest's horizon. Mean and ugly, he boiled and brewed, building his towering armoury to batter a scorched forest in his annual siege of winter rains. Massing upon the far side of the vast Fly mountain range his invading forces accumulated, waiting for the final push. The marching orders delayed by Vivacious Wind's late appearance, he hovered, multiplying menacingly up the dark side of the mountains with patient perverseness. He was in no hurry.

Along the banks of the Rio Fly the dormant mosquito larvae, long buried under the dry earth, hissed with itching, expectant excitement. Each larva swelling, stretching inside its tiny cocoon could smell the change. Multiplied a billion times the banks appeared to vibrate to a throbbing, latent, buried breath. A massive, mutilated prostrate animal ready to rise from the dead, never going anywhere, but alive with trembling anticipation eager within for freedom and blood.

The nights drew cooler as the sun sank prematurely behind the growing, impermeable clouds. The twilight zone eroded to a brief message of closure before rapidly collapsing into oblivion, closing the world down.

It was not long before the nocturnal prowlers with their overhead, winged slaughterers and stalkers felt secure enough to venture into the lightless forest. They did so with a fervent zest for life and a hunger within their bellies. Around the trees, mingling through the leaves, filtering from the dusty floor, came eager sounds. They distilled, exuded and evaporated, cyclically orchestrating as a growing sense of confidence emanated amongst the new, unseen inhabitants.

Suddenly a terrifying screech pierced the tentatively growing confidence, slashing the delicate, calm fabric into serrated, nervous ribbons. The mood turned sombre and creatures instantly stopped or fled back to their holes. Hysterical, manic screams emanated from one of the shelters. Flerds erupted from the other six nests. The cries carried far into the still, dark depths of a nervous forest. Momentarily the forest quietened, creatures cowed and listened. The agonising wails wrapped around every feather, leaf and ear. A tense, brittle caution infiltrated everything awake. Even the dead were listening. Distrust and anxiety permeated through the docile darkness. The shaman, holding some lighted embers on two sticks, hurried across the rough ground as quickly as his old legs would allow. He disappeared into the clamorous nest; a warm, red glow emanated outwards with a mirage of dancing shadows flickering across the forest floor. The screaming had subdued on the shaman's arrival, turning into disconsolate moaning and sobbing.

He left the nest with some other males. Shortly, they returned loaded with bowls, cloths, sticks, assorted leaves and water; then they emerged again, empty handed. The wailing and sobbing continued.

A small fire was built up. The shaman and his male accomplices sat around smoking, snorting yoppa and drinking crushed coca leaves. When the desired level of delirium had set in they danced around the fire singing to the spirits. Tree swayed to the rhythms wondering whether the females were wailing in harmony with the increasingly volatile males, or whether they were still only wailing. In his Wee Tree way, he joined in. One by one the flerds collapsed, leaving only the shaman who appeared to be impervious to everything he consumed. He walked, or he could have floated, to the wailing nest leaving his intoxicated colleagues to slumber where they dropped. Eventually it went quiet. The dancers around the fire fell asleep apart from the old shaman; he spent the night chanting, smoking and spraying special powders over everything and everybody to ward off evil spirits.

During the night the shaman left the physical world. He walked through the metaphysical light paths looking for the ancestors, guides and spirits to help him fight the demons possessing the sick and dying.

The new day began before the Laughing Sun could break above Tempest Cloud. A dull half-light broke through the dark edges of the monster trees. The smirking shadows flickered. It challenged the senses. It spooked the timid. It signalled a revolution.

Screaming and sobbing once again shrilled through the trees' enveloping branches. It was a task too much for the shaman. Both of the young flerds died in their mother's arms. Dejected by his failure to exorcise the babies of their demons, he returned to his fire. There was much to prepare. Kicking awake some hunters he instructed them to fetch two animals – one howler, one ocelot – and return with them both alive. The hunters looked at him in disbelief but said nothing. It would take days to find and kill one; to catch two alive in one day was near impossible. They were turning to go when the shaman said, "Be positive and have faith, the spirits will deliver."

The young mother continued to wail inconsolably. Weak and numb she staggered from her shelter into the bright daylight holding the two limp bodies. Her face, drained of colour from the pain of her agony, was soaked in the monsoon of her tears. She stumbled around the clearing, listlessly, wandering vacantly, aimlessly. Deadened to the core, her senses were extinguished and replaced with a padded void of emptiness. Exhausted and unable to comprehend how her two beautiful daughters, gifts to the world, had been taken away from her. "Why?" she thought, the word echoing around her hollow frame incessantly. It was never answered. A matron took hold of her arm and guided her to sit by the smouldering fire. When on the ground, in touch with the only solid thing, she dissolved into a wretched mess of inconsolability. With pity in their hearts and the knowledge that there were no words that could be said, the others turned away to prepare for the twins' passage to the other world. The matron's heart was ripped in two. Silently, she lay down on the raw, warm earth and wrapped her arms around the sobbing, shivering mother who was now her last remaining daughter.

The hunters returned. Out of respect for Ocillo they did not look outwardly jubilant, but inside they were pleased. The spirits had delivered. Within their shrouded bearers were two live, bound howlers slung over two branches. A dead coati hung over the shoulders of another hunter. A hooded, makeshift cage housed their prized catch: a live condor. Although far away from Fly Mountain, they had seen the birds in the distance and set a trap. A coati was quickly killed then set out on a rocky escarpment with the camouflaged hunters hiding close by. It did not take the holy, sharp-nosed, revered birds long to detect the smell of death. Once on the ground the giant carcass-cleaners were easy to catch. The hunters could have caught more but were unsure of the shaman's reaction to capturing a creature so close to the soul of the spirits. In earthly form, they were the bodies of the gods themselves. The condor, wisely, stayed quiet and low. How would the shaman react?

Silent as a butterfly's breath the unperceived hunters materialised before the shaman's fire like the spirits in his doped mind. They floated and glimmered amongst the shimmering haze of the flickering flames. The shaman looked at the thickening, bodily forms then again towards the floating, swirling spirits spinning through the flames. They teased the hot fire embers and twisted through the tangled trees before descending upon the new arrivals. He let them dance around the earthly bodies looking for guidance and wisdom to fight off the demons seeking entry at the weakest points. They hissed at the monkeys, twirling rapidly amongst the bearers and the frightened animals. Gradually the colours changed. The auras smothering the monkeys effervesced from radiant reds and ambers to vibrant greens and blues. The shaman was pleased and flew amongst them as if one himself. Then with no warning, they scorched towards the skies as if Pachamama had blown the earth apart with a roaring volcano. In an instant they turned and with lightning speed, plummeted into the condor and disappeared. Momentarily the shaman was left floating alone amongst the trees before he, too, was sucked into the condor. The world went black, deathly black – no lights, no life, no world, no time; nothing!

He was sucked into another universe. The spirits were waiting for him and guided him along the multi-coloured light ways. Twisting and twirling they shimmered and spun, the colours changing with each

transition across the galactic bands of a rainbow. The
spirits pulled him along, transmuting into his dead
ancestors and long-extinct animals, leaping and
bounding in colourful, galloping herds. The years went
by and he grew younger, stronger and wiser. They took
him to the birthplace of the demons. There he fought.
The fights were tenacious and long but his spear and
shield held strong against their prolonged attacks. In
frustration, the demons twisted into his brain,
metamorphosing into the first flerd he had loved and
lost. She looked deep into his tear-filled eyes. His heart
ripped apart with agonising, melancholic despondency
as she begged him to put down his weapons and lie with
her in the warmth of her caressing arms. He slumped to
his knees, his energy evaporating as love filled his war-
torn, embattled body. His arms slumped to his sides
holding lightly on to his valiant but limp weapons. She
came close, touching his naked body. Her arms wrapped
around his shoulders as she pulled his head gently
towards hers. He felt the warmth of her breath against
his lips. Her smooth, silky legs folded warmly around
his body, his eyes closed as love pumped his scorching
blood through his veins. He felt her lips gently touch his
own, melting into sweet, warm honey. The bright, light
colours changed slowly into a calm, moonless night as
he looked once again into her long-lost, hazel eyes.

The lights suddenly went out, then two intense, bright
spots emerged, growing rapidly towards him. Her
beautiful, brown eyes had been replaced by two sharp,

glistening daggers poised, ready to strike into his own. Instead of his long-lost wife, a gargoyled creature dug its claws into his back, locking his body into its cold, scaly belly. It screamed with a gargling, frothing frenzy, spitting bile from its contorted, agonised mouth. Its intense, dazzling dagger eyes closed and transmuted into dark, lifeless caverns. Its furrowed face contorted as its claws slit into the shaman's severed flesh to rip out his lungs. Abruptly, the gargoyle froze. Momentarily its screams stopped. Pain exploded throughout its icy frame as its ruptured heart shattered. Blood and vomit spewed from its twisted mouth. The shaman's spear had split its loveless heart and embedded itself in the creature's spine, severing its spinal chord. Twisting the spear he felt its razor-sharp edges shred the creature's hardened heart and lacerate the remainder of its organs before it crumpled into the blackness of its own cold, emotionless void.

The flashing, universal aura returned to the spirit world. He felt the power flood back through his legs, torso and arms. Each slaughtered demon fed his strength. They fled to worlds beyond the world of dancing light. His ancestors marched by his side. The condor lit up with golden rays and ultraviolet lights. The demons were chased from the worlds of enlightenment back to the bitter underworld of the black sun and lifeless darkness.

Ocillo, on her knees, was rocking back and forth. Subconsciously she rocked in harmony to the slow beat of a lone drummer. Numb to the world, oblivious to its harsh, incomprehensible realities, she cradled the twins' bodies close to her heart. When the elders came to prepare them for the death ceremony she could not let them go.

Eventually, her mother arrived and speaking softly to her, picked them up. Ocillo, staring vacantly through the dark forest, continued rocking as if nothing had changed.

The twins' bodies were washed then wrapped in tight-fitting cloth. Chil's cloak was dyed in striped shades of indigo and violet while Chel's had the colours of the rainbow. In the middle of each, where their hearts once pumped, was a large, white spot with a deep blue centre. This, the shaman explained, was symbolic of their bodies, their skin and the colour of their eyes. The blues and purples represented Chil's connection to the universe and Chel's to the rainbow and seven vortexes of energy. Each body wore a magnificent, feathered head dress that radiated outwards as a giant hibiscus flower with their little stamen heads centred as white dots. The feathers, picked from the ground under squabbling macaws high in the wild almond trees, blazed a bright message in brilliant yellows, blues and reds. They lay side by side in bamboo baskets nestling against the centre bonfire.

The dancing began. More drums picked up the beat of the lone drummer. The flerds dressed in their finest, feathered head dresses sang and wailed in rhythmic prances around the fire, led by a flamboyant effigy of a flightless condor. Bounding and swaggering like the possessed, which indeed he was, the old shaman danced and wailed. Covered in condor feathers and a mask with a large condor's beak over his nose, he impersonated the sacred bird. Two small, pinhole, yellow eyes above his black beak looked on. With feathers strapped to his ankles, knees, wrists and elbows, flapping, swaying, prancing, pouncing, he bounced like a ruptured bird in a headless trance. The captured condor looked on with indifference. It kept an attentive eye of intent on the two hapless howlers. In contrast to the majestic bird, the monkeys, quiet and subdued, looked forlorn and miserable. Bound hand and foot to two wooden stakes, they hung upside down like premature lumps of dead meat.

The shaman led the yoppa-induced dancers to such a frenetic pitch that the spirits were swimming with their souls. At some nebulous point known only to the shaman, he swept his wing in a huge sweep of the floor, then, leaving the Mother Earth he pivoted full circle in flight before landing softly on the fire-warmed earth. Standing fully erect, he stretched his wings over the two lifeless children. The drums stopped, the dancers stopped, Tree stopped. Silence suddenly sounded loud. All eyes turned towards the large, stationary bird. All except the real one, who maintained a perspicacious eye on the dishevelled monkeys with more than a casual interest.

Tree, who had been watching this all day, thought that the out-grown surrogate, bedraggled chicken had taken root and was now doing a poor impersonation of himself. He really wanted to pull up his roots, bend his increasing girth to imitate two twisting, contorting snakes and dance with the rest of them. Not since Three Toes fell out of his tree holding a branch had he witnessed such entertainment.

Inti had dropped low behind the furtively stalking Tempest Cloud that had crept across the forest canopy. Nobody had noticed. Suddenly, the shaman twisted round and cut down a monkey. With one wing holding the wretched, writhing creature high in the air, he threw back his head and wailed at the swirling spirits above. Tempest Cloud answered with a thundering clap of lightning. For an instant the forest blazed with intense light cloaked with ragged shadows as the erratic bolt hit a twitching earth. Within that briefest moment the shaman unleashed his knife and slashed the monkey's throat with one swift movement. The monkey swung limp. Held high by the shaman's wing, warm, bright, burgundy-blue blood poured from the open wound and dripped onto Chil's forehead.

The dyes and herbs on Chil's face, mixed with fresh flowers and fragranced with the warm blood, solidified, producing an instant death mask. In cooling, the colours of the mask turned to mixed hues of blue and violet cracking across her tiny face as it shrunk to a tight fit. With the monkey's job completed it was tossed onto the hot boulders surrounding the warm embers of the fire. The condor cocked his head and trained a glinting eye as the monkey's life blood freely flowed and sizzled onto the hot rocks. Tree thought, "The flerds will eat well tonight in their sorrow." The condor had no such thoughts.

The other howler's fortune was no better nor different and Chel received her mask in the same way. All the colours of the rainbow spread across her face as the different dyes reacted with the cooling blood. They were ready for the great journey to their ancestors. They would guide the flerds.

The condor, still perched behind the giant, spoof, shaman bird, watched the howlers die in an instant. His cool, regal, frame remained frozen to his shackled stave. Two piercing, black eyes overlooked a huge, crooked beak like small, dark islands in an orange sea. Other than the occasional blink there was no other sign of life inside. He kept a blinking eye on the two cooking monkeys and a wary eye on the scruffy, spoof bird.

With the twins prepared, the shaman untethered the condor and swung him onto his winged shoulders. Now free of all earthly ties the giant master soarer spread his enormous three-metre wings and dug his talons into the depleted, inferior, imitation below. Slowly he flapped his wings increasing the power until the shaman was clinging to Pachamama by the tips of his toes. Screaming in pain, he did nothing to disturb the bird, for it was the embodiment of the spirits.

The other flerds dropped to the earth in fear as the two condors rose to the skies as one. Tempest Cloud dropped to touch the trees, then released his annual load of rain. Lightning ripped across the world, lighting every tree and fern. The condor tightened his grip on the dangling shaman until he felt the bones within crumble and crack. Illuminated by the untamed electricity he luminesced with power; light bouncing from the tips of his feathers, he appeared to the quivering flerds below as angry, reincarnated ancestors. The two birds disappeared into the electric storm. In fear and disbelief the flerds remained prostrate. Pulsating, rubber-balled rain bounced from the earth; angry and tempestuous, it battered the cowering creatures.

Ocillo was unseen when she picked herself out of the mud. She walked slowly over to Chil's and Chel's bodies. Picking them up in their baskets she carried on to Wee Tree. She looked at their frail, gentle bodies in the flashing lights. There were no tears left. The gods were angry. They had their sacrifice, there was nothing more to do. She placed them under the protection of Tree's largest, lower branch and tucked them up against one of his rising buttress roots.

Flickering in the lightning she noticed something bright and shiny on the ground. Looking closely she realised it was the shaman's knife. "He must have dropped it in his fanciful flight," she thought to herself, "before he could kill the condor. Now the condor has him. We will all suffer."

She picked up the knife. Anger and grief quickly bubbled up through her. She thought of thrusting it into her own heart. It would be so easy, then all the suffering would be over. But she could not. She had failed to protect her children; now she could not even end it. She would suffer for eternity. That was her lesson, her destiny. In her frustration, fear and anger she lunged at the tree, thrusting the knife deep into the branch above her babies. Time and again she struck the tree until the strength drained from her and she collapsed onto the earth next to the twins. Sobbing uncontrollably and sick with despair, she curled into a small ball and prayed to be killed.

Tempest Cloud continued lashing the forest with its watery whips. The lightning crashed and thundered, shaking the ground by wringing its earthly neck. A loud, deafening boom split the air apart right above the camp. Ocillo leapt into the air. Freezing cold and soaked, she ran to the hut. The others were also awake. Huddled around a small fire they pulled Ocillo in towards the warmth and covered her with skins, bodies and arms.

The Rio Fly quickly began to rise. Its placid, calm surface began to boil and hiss. Its alluring, translucent waters transformed into a ginger-brown, rumbustious cauldron. Boisterous, foaming whirlpools and eddies emerged and grew into rabid, uncontrolled boils that gnawed and gobbled at the banks. Trees, small and large, young and old were dragged by their roots into the river. Its insatiable appetite ineluctably consumed the petite to the monstrous. There was no discrimination, no relief. Tempest Cloud had only just begun and continued to feed the river. He was in no mood to ease the constraints on his bloated belly.

It was a different world when the Laughing Sun appeared. The cloud had covered the whole of the land. Even the tops of the highest trees were engulfed by his water-logged stomach. No laughing beams of light glittered under his smothering, swollen belly. Only a dull, dead dawning edged out the darkness and remained for the rest of the day.

Exhausted by the long, cold night, Ocillo woke with a suddenness that made her sit bolt upright. All around her were slumped, damp, doped bodies. Like wet leaves

141

that had no stalks they had folded into themselves where they had dropped the night before. Peeling off bodies, a growing sense of panic and alarm began to spread through her slowly awakening senses. The feelings trembled through her light frame. A diffused, sallow light oozed through the hut's entrance casting nebulous shadows within the cramped, dusky dwelling. A revelation abruptly seized her shaking body, freezing it into the cold, still, granite rock of Fly Mountain. Alarmed by a sudden terrified thought, she screamed at the top of her voice. The sound shot through the forest, quenching Tempest Cloud's thunder. Animals flinched as they instinctively crouched in caution. Flerds suddenly kicked alive, believing the demons had returned to cut out their souls from their aching bodies as revenge for the lost shaman. Shock and confusion rooted them to the earth as they tried to remember where they were and what was going on. Ocillo leapt to her feet, treading over puzzled bodies. Out she raced, puma-fast, across the drenched forest earth. Her feet fleeting above the ground, touching so gently that she made no splash. Her breath so light that she hardly breathed. Her hair flying behind in wisps of fine, dark, gossamer vines. She stopped abruptly at Wee Tree's buttress roots. There her two dead babies were crying; crying uncontrollably, relentlessly, distressingly. She scooped them both up and cradled them in each arm pushing their heads close into her pounding bosom, then dropped to her knees. Her heart beating like a thousand war drums, tears pouring from her eyes, she looked up at the tree of life. Lightning was sweeping through his spreading branches, sending dancing shadows across the forest floor. An aura from the fathomless universe seemed to emanate in mellifluous, yellow hues, radiating away from the core of his trunk. Amongst the violence of the demonic Elements crashing around her, a peace filled her heart. The tree engulfed her. It comforted her. It had brought back her children. It made her strong again.

Wee Tree had grown quickly with the sun blasting his leaves. Now, with his top disappearing into the bellowing clouds and his outstretched branches spreading high, he, too, was a pillar of the sky. His thin, straight trunk touched the edges of the sky. He poured down his love onto the two babies and their mother. From the wounds that Ocillo had cut into his branches, poured a milky white, sticky sap. With the fresh, clean rain water it dripped onto their faces, turning them whiter than Monocled Moon in full face. His mask of life had trickled into their stomachs and destroyed the virus that had swept through their small frames rendering them unconscious. All night he had provided his life-giving sap to their delicate, frozen, fragile faces. With the fundamental element of water, charged and ionised by a turbulent Tempest Cloud, they had fought off the death sleep and been reborn into a life-giving world. They both screamed into their mother's breasts. Her tears poured down her face onto her naked body. With the tears of her babies, they mixed with the Tree's sap to form an eternal bond between them and the Elements.

Wee Tree remembered the words of Whale's continual reminders: be true to yourself and others will respond. An intuitive, eternal connection existed between the Elements, the flora and the animals. He had forgotten the threatening, deleterious ways of the flerds and had instinctively reached out to the two abandoned children. Nor was it any coincidence that Tempest Cloud arrived that night to light, to soak, to energise. Tempest had never thought twice about stepping out to light up their souls, to nourish, to rejuvenate. It took all of them to work together, seamlessly, simultaneously and unconditionally. Now, it was so obvious, Whale was right: everything exists together and depends on everything else to live and flourish.

Upon hearing Ocillo's cries the Indians fell out of their nests. It was a chaotic avalanche of jumbled, jumping beings. The first flew out so fast that he did not see the large rock in front of the entrance. He tripped over it with such vigour that he dived head first into the slush, the mud and the gravel. He pulled himself from the earth spitting out grit and waterlogged, dead beetle shells and looked back with dismay as his comrades now toppled down upon him. When all the flying bodies and tangled limbs had settled ignominiously into the sodden, bedraggled wreckage he looked back at the rock;

it was no longer there. He sat thoughtfully, momentarily puzzled.

Ocillo was on her knees looking up into the clouds where tree had disappeared. A soft glow surrounded the tree, which shimmered with changing colours. Her two children, now attached to her bosom ,were quiet and content. The rushing onlookers stopped abruptly, amazed at what they saw. They, too, dropped to their knees in total disbelief. The events they had witnessed over the last two days had challenged their sensibilities. They were tired and confused. Ocillo began to sing softly. One by one the others joined in. Tempest Cloud sang too, with his background, thundering bass.

Tree watched as life continued around him. The day gently sang on until the Laughing Sun dropped into the west. The clouds' heavy half-lights quickly succumbed to the black of night.

Gradually, the Indians returned to their normal routines. The children flourished in the nutritious forest. Each day Ocillo would bring them to Tree and sing. She offered small gifts of berries, fruit or picked flowers and laid them down next to his roots. Wee Tree always glowed with warmth in her company. She felt his energy, his love; a calming enchantment prevailed upon her. Chil and Chel, too, picked up on this latent energy. They rocked on their backs, their clear, blue eyes looking straight up towards the top of the towering kapok – never taking their eyes away from him. He was the tree of life.

The Rio Fly continued to rise and expand. It burst over the banks with flowing disregard for all around. Mountainous dams of torn, trapped trees constructed reluctant islands of twisted timber at every rock, slack or undertow that could catch a tree. With the expanding water threatening to engulf the small camp, the flerds packed up their belongings and moved deeper into the jungle.

Savage sat blinking under some soaking foliage. "That was close," he mumbled to himself, "There's one, enjoying the seasonal delights of the mud and the slush when hundreds of demonic banshees come hurtling out of the bush, from nowhere. Luckily for me I am sprightly, lithe and agile and," he paused for the right words befitting such a nimble athlete, "performed with poise, adroitness and finesse. Nothing ruffles Savage Foam Frog," and with that, hopped off.

Chapter XI

The Oarsmen had continued at their relentless pace with unwavering resolve. Although their body weights had dropped twenty percent they had not faltered or lost focus. Night and day they flattened the rolling waves with indifference. Vivacious Wind continued to blow south without any sign of relaxing while Rumbustious Sea pushed the four leviathans and their precious cargo with idle ease. The Elements were immense.

Whale drifted between liquid states of lucid consciousness and abstracted sublimation. The universal seas of divine consummation released her mind from her tortured body to swim in the pure energy that is life itself.

In her more earthly moments she rocked with the natural frequencies of her two enormous cradle handlers. Those huge giants cushioned her physically. Their unbreakable resolve and boundless strength stabilised her emotionally and psychologically. She could forget about the physical world, it was all handled for her. She had the freedom to let her mind explore any psychic channels that opened up. It was something she had never been able to do before. There was nowhere safer. She allowed her mind to roll back to when she was a calf when she was young and reliant on her mother for

total survival. She felt small and calf-like, frightened yet
protected. Now, as then, her physicality, her life, her
well-being was in the control of others. This time there
were four of them and they were Oarsmen.

With each day of travel her rational moments became
shorter and less rational. When not swimming the
ethereal dream, she would try to hold her attention on
one thought. She did not know whether she would
survive this ordeal, so she wanted to sing to the world
one last, meaningful message. With each fleetingly lucid
moment she focused on its meaning. Each phrase or
word was archived as they were composed, hoping it
would all be there at some later date. By concentrating
on her precise words she kept herself from sliding into
spiritual darkness. Her message would be truthful and
poignant but above all compassionate. She wanted to
give hope and significance to all who live in the world.
To understand the purpose of their lives and to believe
in the fundamental relevance of what their actions and
reactions mean to others. That those actions have
positive intent to the well-being of all and are critical for
the survival of each of us. Her emotions tangled with
her conscientiousness, her self-appointed task
continually battered by the desperation she felt to be
with her calf again. She did not want to die without
bumping noses with him. She wanted them to sing
together. There was so much to tell him. Above all
though, she wanted him to feel all her love because he
was everything. Her heart ached with a burning

passion. She knew that this event changed everything. She also knew that she might not have long to live. There had been a lot of luck, courage and goodwill delivered by many to still be here at all. Now she wanted to be with Calf. To help him understand and be prepared for the long journey on without her.

The route down had not been uneventful. Whale's brutal wounds left a trail of blood and the smell of raw, weeping flesh had attracted some big predators. All of the biggest killers arrived: hammerheads, tiger, bull sharks and the big great whites. Some of the whites exceeded fifteen metres in length and were the top predators of the seas. The great whites were more discerning than most and backed off after one look at those four titanic beings that transmuted the sea into vapour. Even if they could get close, Whale was so heavily protected by the two supporting flanks of the carriers that there was little room for manoeuvre. At the speed they were moving there was no way to get between them without risk of serious injury, even assuming it could be done at all. Many couldn't keep up, but some of the bulls and tigers could. They paid a heavy price and were severely battered by the no-nonsense, no-stopping Oarsmen. Some of the less experienced took their chances. They were all skilled, intelligent killers and proficient with unleashing their armoury. They seldom failed but until now, they had never crossed an Oarsman. They all experienced the same welcome and were battered senseless. Huge flukes would crash down on top of them, the impact instantly breaking their backs or rendering them unconscious. For those less astute, a monster fin would then sweep them, tumbling under the carriers before another battering from the flukes. The backup Oarsman would then take out the remaining stragglers with a single, crushing bite from his cavernous, bone-breaking jaws. Hundreds of tonnes of pressure would scythe through their battered bodies, splintering their spines. An indifferent, sharp shake of the Oarsman's head would snap the aggressor in two. The carved debris from the severed beasts was spat out in the same instant as the next was collected. No matter what the size of the predator or how many there were, it ended in the same way: cut in half and left drifting for their companions to further bond their communion.

A trail of carnage spread over dozens of kilometres. Most were eaten and the rest sank to the bottom to fertilise and fuel the hidden world below. It was another day for the Oarsmen, it did not slow them, it did not distract; it did, though, leave an impression.

When they had reached the colder waters of the polar seas, all the warm-water predators had long before run out of tooth and muscle. From here on the threat diminished. Here, the types of animals changed. Animals that had adapted to the cold polar waters. It was safer here, although some danger was about. While Whale was within the care of the Oarsmen there were no threats but it would not last forever. The only possible creatures that might orchestrate an attack would be the orcas. Only one pod came close to investigate. They quickly moved on, being too bright to take on anything like an Oarsman, let alone four.

For the first time since they started their mission, the Oarsmen rested. Nobody moved for several minutes. This was the spiritual home for the whales; it spread over thousands of kilometres. The Oarsman stopped to pay their respects. Their physical bodies embraced the spirits mixed with the essence of Pachamama and their enlightened souls touched the Laughing Sun. Whale, half aware, half indifferent, was still cocooned between her two carriers. She was in both worlds at the same time. For a while the Oarsmen did nothing but allow the currents to silently drift them along. They listened to the ocean sounds. Slowly they accustomed themselves to the normal Antarctic acoustics, listening for anything abnormal that might be of danger. The boobies and frigates enthusiastically circled some distance above. Sensing the cautious, uneasy atmosphere emanating from the whales they ceased their normal squabbling, quarrelling cacophony but still maintained a sagacious eye on the choppy sea.

The two free Oarsmen slowly began circling the carriers. With each separated by one hundred and eighty degrees, they gradually increased the distance from Whale until they were several kilometres away.

When they were satisfied that the area was safe they began dropping sound bombs. High intensity sonic soundings were transmitted at regular intervals. They listened, then dropped more. All the echoes were analysed. Gradually, they built up a picture of every marine animal and structure afloat or submerged within hundreds of kilometres. The sonic images were mapped and compared to known threats.

Whale was too weak to be left alone and in urgent need of food. The carriers lowered her into the water until she held her own buoyancy. Keeping her in an upright position they slowly glided her large body through the nutritious, krill-saturated sea. The Oarsmen refuelled too. A wide, empty channel developed behind the three animals as they continued forward. The momentarily lifeless passage behind was invariably re-stocked from the inexhaustible larder from the depths below. In front lay a thousand kilometres of tightly packed, whale-building food. They swam, feeding, consuming, all day, every day. Not a murmur or song passed between them.

By the time the first of the elders arrived Whale had put on some weight. For short periods she was able to swim unassisted. The Oarsmen stayed close by. When she tired they pulled together, sandwiching her, so she could continue.

Two matriarchs released the Oarsmen from their daily duty. The four giants grouped together and moved themselves away from the pod. Isolated from the others they were left alone to continue feeding.

A summit meeting was held. The elders acknowledged the Oarsmen's incredible feat of transporting the Curator. She would have undoubtedly died without their power and speed at such short notice. They took the opportunity of the rare meeting to re-establish the bond between them. Although Oarsmen were held in the highest reverence, some were afraid of the dead-black, silent monsters that shared no secrets.

In the ebbing, sub-Antarctic lights heralding a new night, Monocled Moon lay low on the freezing horizon. An eerily cold, translucent light stretched across the shimmering surface of Rumbustious Sea. It was impossible to determine whether Moon was beaming with joy or rage. He floated metres above Pachamama's rim transmitting an edgy, undecipherable message that few were aware of and none could decode. Four enormous dark shapes, re-fuelled and full of power, silently, surreptitiously swam north east, their oily wake filled with diving, gabbling, blind birds delighted by Monocled Moon's fortuitous, fish-finding light. The Oarsmen's mission in the polar sea was complete. They departed without notice.

It was many tortuous days before Calf and his matriarch arrived at the sanctuary. They, too, had seen the debris behind the Oarsmen's slaughter of the ocean's most fearsome predators. Enormous broken, bloated, half-devoured carcasses bobbing nonchalantly, innocently on the earnestly pushing sea. The remains of these creatures were bigger than him. Calf could only imagine the fearsome fights that had occurred. It was clear that the Oarsmen had inflicted awesome damage. With dread and foreboding Calf wondered, "Have their defences been breached? What damage has been inflicted upon my helpless mother?"

But then he reasoned, "She was not helpless, she was with Oarsmen. Not one but four. How could anything be so stupid as to try and take one on?"

Calf could see clearly that they had though, and not just the odd one. There was massive carnage. Bobbing carcasses littered the sea like endless flicks of Inti's light dancing off the turbulent tips of the mildly hypnotic waves. There was so much dead meat that not even the surviving sharks were feeding from it; they had satisfied their hunger and were long gone. Now the floating blubber mountains were left for the insatiable boobies and smaller fish. When all were satisfied Rumbustious Sea would claim her levy; the remains would sink to her silty floor where the deep-sea, dark-world, bottom-feeding dwellers would look in awe at this opportune abundance. Perhaps they, too, would pass a thought of wonder as to what on earth was happening above. Still, he could not stop himself thinking with all she had gone through, whether she could survive all these attacks. Each day, as they swam ever closer, his heart would give a slight shiver with the increasing uncertainty. Not that he did not want to see her, for he did. All the love in his heart was with her but there was that chilling fear that if she had not survived then what would he do? He could not foresee a life without her; there would be no point for she was everything. He could not cope with the unknown, it was beyond his comprehension. He swam hard and fast until the roaring pain in his muscles engulfed his emotions.

Rumbustious Sea was calm under the contrasting, luminescent lights filtering through the chilling polar air. The deep sea shimmered with delight as if massaged by the cool fins of a wise universe. Diatomaceous algae danced passionately with the phytoplankton and krill to produce a multitudinous world of radiating, pulsating stars flowing in a galaxy of waves. Whale was floating in a sea of ethereal beings, covered in their cool, green blue glow, enticing her to feed from a universe of energy and power. There were times it was so seraphic she could believe that she had really died and was suspended in a pool of pure, pulsating power.

Ruminant Whale was now swimming under her own power. The two matriarchs still stayed either side of her but rarely were they required to assist. The group swam, sang and swallowed hundreds of tonnes of krill each day. They bonded quickly; of a similar age, they sang anecdotes to each other from their ancient past. She quickly tired though, eventually leaving the singing to the others. Nobody mentioned her injuries. They each knew there was no need; it just was. Today was about feeding, relaxing, relishing their company in the sanctuary of a beautiful, buoyant, bountiful world.

Whale sensed a presence. She was not sure whether it was in this world or another but there was definitely energy about. The matriarchs remained fully focused on Ruminant's daily concerns. They concentrated on their occupation and the well-being of Ruminant to detect anything other than obvious threats. At first she said nothing. Her continual conscious wavering between floating through luminescent phytoplankton then gliding through the galactic star-ways became such a daily ritual that there were times when she did not realise the difference. It did not bother her; she was as comfortable in one world as she was in the other. Her emancipation from her enervated body had elevated her levels of enlightenment. The luminescent lights flashing in her worlds induced a wondrous sense of awe, but, above all, trust. She had faith in the elders, the Oarsmen, the matriarchs, the spirits. She trusted the whole universe, it would deliver. Somewhere in amongst those vacillating lights there was another being. An immense being that was closing in on her. Its presence became larger, more dominant, like a visitant energy that would not go away. The force of feeling became so potent that it pulled her into the real sea. Whale could not hold her thoughts any longer and sang about it to her two friends.

Such was their respect for Ruminant Whale that they took the threat seriously. They honed their faculties onto the ocean's sounds, searching for anything menacing. There was nothing alien there. Still, they did not drop their attention. They stopped feeding and closed in to Whale's flanks. They sang to the elders, bringing every whale in the sanctuary to full alert. Sonic soundings saturated the southern seas.

Ruminant Whale, oblivious to all concerns, continued floating serenely in her comfortable worlds. The presence was there too. It was strong and getting stronger. She relished its power.

Calf was really scared. He heard their songs, their sonic bombs. They were getting close to his mother; now there was another serious predator about. "Perhaps it's another flerd ship. She'll be easy prey for them now. Why did they let the Oarsmen go?"

Fighting back the tears once again, he mulled over this imponderable thought but kept returning to the same question, then to the same conclusion: "Why am I so small? When I get big, I'm going to be an Oarsman, then I'll sink every flerd ship on the seas."

He had forgotten his mother's teachings and through the fear and boiling rage he sought only protection for his stricken mother. The only way he could secure her safety was to destroy all those that attacked her.

His surrogate mother was also alarmed and increased her speed a little. Calf had not noticed but was racing like a wahoo through her broiling wake of exploding froth and bubbles. Throughout the night and the following day they travelled without pausing, then without warning his matriarch slowed. She had the awareness to raise her tail, knowing Calf was right behind her. Taken by surprise by this unexpected manoeuvre he continued on at full speed hurtling along her underbelly before exploding through the surface right in front of her. She laughed inwardly and Calf thrust out his fins and turned into a gibbous, unceremonious halt of cascading surf and blubber. His new mother was stationary, looking at him with fondness. She laughed again. Righting himself up he tried to regain some degree of composure by blowing a bluster of hot air and spray from his blow hole. Looking up, he saw a frenzy of agitated whales; he suddenly realised the immense danger they were all in. A flerd ship could slaughter hundreds in this environment. They swam slowly towards the hubbub of anxious hulks. Instantly they arrived, the mass of bodies began to split apart making a narrow channel for them to pass. They glided through until it opened into clear water. There in the middle was his mother and two friends.

For weeks he had been dreaming of this, how he would rush up to her and crash into her side singing his songs, but now he saw her, how frail and weak she looked, he cried. Fighting his emotions he forced himself to keep swimming. He swam alone, slowly, cautiously, scared yet eager. He was on her blind side so he swung into a huge arc to meet her head on.

Ruminant Whale, of course, knew he was there. In a small window of coherency she had identified his presence by his immense energy; she had simply forgotten to tell everybody else. It was so obvious to her. The group though, was still in a state of high anxiety of which she was unaware. Calf slowed to a drift when he knew that his mother had eye contact. Now, hardly daring to breathe in case he sank her for ever, he drifted up to her, touching her nose so gently that a sandwiched sardine would have survived the encounter. There they stayed, anchored in an emotional bond. Inti sank into the western seas and the loving blanket of the secure night wrapped their union with their own melodious harmonies.

They were still together when Inti surfaced. His wide, broad-beaming face smiled a million shards of flickering light across the shimmering, black-backed hulks of the extraordinary congregation. Calf, reconnected and energised, had overcome his trepidation and was swimming circles around his stationary mother. She no longer had the strength to batter him fathoms into the depths so he swam wildly and freely in the new, fresh morning light. He swam towards her injured side. Where her bright, intelligent eye had once looked deep into his soul, now there was nothing but the ugly, raw, ruddy red embroidered scars edging a deep, black, sinister splintered hole through her skull. Distressing, grim memories flashed back instantly instilling a lugubrious time bomb of nefarious fears. An intense feeling of hate and loathing dominated his racing mind. The rage swept through his muscles and veins like a rampant virus. It was such a meaningless, aggressive act against his mother.

Each time the same thoughts resonated through him, "She was harmless and sensitive; she loved the world and all that was in it; she sang every day to them: preaching compassion and love. Telling them of tales of the world, its history, where we all came from and how everybody depends on everybody else. Yet still they came to slaughter her."

He despised those animals but contradictorily he felt guilty because of it. He knew why. His mother had always told him to live in peace, so why could he not? During the night his mother sang to him. It was with a weak, vacillating voice but there was no disguising his mother's resolve behind those lyrics. He understood the songs she sang but where did the compassion come from? She was not just big in mass but her clemency dwarfed all on this earth.

Confused and disoriented by the speed of how those re-emerging, life-changing emotions shook him; they rattled his freshly found confidence. He promised himself not to swim on that side of her face again.

Calf looked at his mother in a fresh way. He saw all the marks on her skin. It promoted her story. A confused Calf ruminated: "Was it a visual reference to the being she was or what she had become? Was it by birth, encounters, scars of life, language, a determination of being, enlightenment, a mark of an individual, a statement of intent, a miscarriage of justice or a savage act of deliberate brutality?" Calf did not know.

"She has been marked by what, for what?" he still had no answers. He remembered his mother as the biggest, strongest mother in the world; now he looked at her hanging on to the merest threads of life with all her scars tattooed like life's medals of achievement, or should that be attainment? He did not know. He was not sure that he ever would.

He stayed on the side of her good eye. Throughout the night they had both cried until weak. Now reunited, Calf stayed on her flipper, eyeball to eyeball looking deep within each other's beings. It was a pure love, unconditional; the essence of their souls were one. There he stayed, never leaving her side. He knew one thing though - he would take care of her.

They had sung all their songs until there were no more to sing; they swam in silence. He tried not to hate the flerds as his mother talked of compassion, but he found it so hard. So hard that each time he cried. He did not know whether it was his own enlightened inadequacy or his frustration at unfulfilled vengeance. He knew not where she found the strength. She was immense.

Chapter XII

He didn't like the look of it. The weather had transformed into a wild, untamed animal. A short while ago all was calm and peaceful. Now Gruesome Gale roared like a demented being. He whipped and thrashed Rumbustious until the sea howled from the pain that it neither understood nor cared for. Unperturbed by this brutal beating, Rumbustious responded by generating monumental waves that smashed relentlessly into the ragged rocks, spitting foam and froth to the very edges of the racing clouds. Albatross, weather-hardened, life-hardened and as solid as the rocks he was anchored to, could feel the earth shake and vibrate to the thunderous forces shattering its foundations. Whether it was in terror or retort he did not know, but his resolve was undoubted. Too many miles had seasoned his feathers for one of the world's finest transglobal aviators to be subdued by a piffling, little squall like this one.

"Even though," he thought, becoming increasingly disturbed, his stomach falling into a sickening pit, "the weather I can handle, but the power pumping within the soul cannot be restrained. Those emotions that won't be tamed belittle all the Elements together." Tempest Cloud was turning black with vengeful menace. It brought back cold memories. He shuddered, but it was not for his safety that he feared. The odd returning, bedraggled bird was still defying those engaging Elements. In between the clouds and the kicking, stinging spray from the rising white-water crescents off the splitting waves, the returning birds held their course towards the rocks.

"It cannot happen twice, surely. I haven't the strength to go through that again. Perhaps it would be easier to simply step off and forget the whole thing." Somehow, he could not quite bring himself to do it. Something kept him on that rock against the full force of the rising gale. He knew what that something was. It was optimism, a touch of life-cultivating curiosity perhaps. While he could see birds on the ragged horizon, he had some hope.

The wind continued to gain in strength. It was reaching the point where he would be blown off the rock, if not the island. He would then have no hope of getting to the cliff edge again. Gruesome's power was approaching herculean proportions. The clouds now appeared to crash into the sea, or was it the sea leaping towards the dark clouds? He could not tell but kept his eyes on the confusing horizon.

Throughout the night he kept vigil, there was no sign of her. A grey, vaporous, strangled light painfully emerged. The Laughing Sun must have surfaced somewhere behind Tempest Cloud. He could not tell whether Inti was laughing or crying. The morning low lights crossed and flicked between the raging clouds like the dancing silver fish that whisked briefly on top of a fracturing wave before darting into the darkest depths of a roaring oblivion. The torpid day dragged itself through the storm.

Albatross remained immobile and unmoved. As far as the rest of the world was concerned he was that rock: stolid and attached. Although he stayed in the colony, he was not part of it. He was circumspect when choosing his friends. The other Southern Royals perceived him as autonomous, unconnected; an isolated world traveller. They treated him with respect but not affection; he was a damaged loner.

Despite the Elements' merciless battering with their undiminished, truculent bombardment, he never dropped his gaze. He never wavered nor flinched. The salt-washed winds whipped over his beak, eyes, feet; they grabbed and tore at his feathers, pummelling every cell that held him together, but he did not move. The days and nights became irrelevant. To the world he appeared as if the winds had carved him from the granite that held him. His cool, cold, rock-hardened exterior contrasted despairingly with the grim, boiling, pithy doubt that was slowly dissolving his insides. His emotions were building into an uncontrolled beast. Bigger than the seas, more powerful than the Elements, they were hauling him down, dripping feather by dripping feather, into a hell that was fuelled by all of his fears. He did not know how long he could hold it down.

In the vast, rolling waters of Rumbustious Sea, Albatross's lightning-sharp eye could determine a flicker of reflected sunlight from a sprat slapping its tail. Even perched high on his wind-lashed rock he could distinguish life from element. The odd bird was still returning. There were not so many now. They looked exhausted. A Southern Royal would rather die than not attempt the annual return home. He was ruminating on the tenacity of Southern Royals when a faint flash, a momentary sparkle from a weaving wing, caught his eye. He recognised a Southern Royal amidst the fury of the Elements. That slight over bend to her port wing disclosed her identity. Most would not have noticed, but to Albatross it was as pronounced as a full-faced, beaming Monocled Moon in a cloudless night.

Holding her course was the Southern Royal he had been waiting for. The ferocious sixty kilometre-per-hour tailwind hurled her rapidly over the thrashing seas.

Albatross's heart stopped. A mixed confusion of disjointed, incoherent thoughts raced through his mind. Would she remember him? Would she want him? Would she be able to land safely? Would she get swept into the rocks and drown right in front of him? Would he be able to stand there and watch? He had to stop thinking. She needed him now whether she remembered him or not. He felt self-conscious and foolish for allowing idiotic, egocentric thoughts to transgress. He felt he should know better at his age.

While he was admonishing himself, half a plan had been propagating in some deep recesses of his subconscious. It wasn't much of one and the more he thought about it the less he liked it, but it was the only one he had. It was fraught with danger but he considered that he would prefer to die helping than to sit and watch. His biggest problem was getting into the sky without being tossed backwards by the racing storm, then shredded across the razor-sharpened rocks. He knew that as soon as he opened his wings the wind would catch under every flight feather and toss him away like a worthless fleck of dust, but there was no more time to think. She would be here shortly, hurtling past faster than a burning meteorite. Keeping his wings tightly tucked into his sides, thrusting his beak as far into the wind as he could, he tipped over the edge and plunged towards the crashing, rock-blistered waves below. He could not open his wings too early nor leave it too late. Having never attempted this he wondered how he was supposed to know when to pull up. It seemed a bit rudimentary at this stage in his life; it was all a bit late for doubts. The dominating hand of Gruesome Gale pushed his powerless body towards the indifferent, hardened cliff face. Air pockets pounding with exploding energy ripped through his feathers, wrenching at their roots with trembling tenacity. His vibrating, shaking, buffeted body hurtled downwards, quickly reaching terminal velocity. Vaporised sea and salt, whipped into an insatiable appetite of loathing, pulverised his beak and blinded his eyes until sea and sky became a blurred, surging mist of variegated shades of light and dark. The shaking, unremitting forces carved away at his confidence. Doubt began to get to him; at some point his nerve would collapse. Through the fear he felt a slight change of pressure. Air forced off the waves and channelled up the cliffs began to catch his plummeting body. He detected a slight decrease in the speed of his descent. It meant one thing: he was close to the bottom. Instinct and experience suddenly kicked in; he felt a joy of adrenaline, an equilibrium in pressure then subconsciously he spread his wings out hard. Pushing out his tail feathers and lifting his beak he arced out from the dive and headlong into the gale, breaking through the splintering tops of the wretched waves.

Now airborne, Albatross readjusted his alignment to take control. "So, what was your problem there then, old sport? A bird of three could've done it."

It was a flippant thought but secretly he was relieved. "Even though," he mused, "it's not in your average albatross's flying almanac."

Battling headlong into the gale was more familiar territory as his bent wing would testify. Back in control, he was a master of the air and understood its every nuance. He used the vacuous gaps between the waves and the turbulent air as a tunnel to rip himself forwards. It was a struggle flying into the wind but the salt from his eyes had cleared enough to now see her hurtling towards him. She was slightly higher but her bright, glossy white plumage contrasted starkly against the mountainous, black clouds. He kept his beak pointing directly towards her. When she was almost over the top of him he dipped his wing a little, allowing his momentum to swing him upwards. The full force of the wind hit the underside of his outstretched wings and propelled his body towards her as if slung from a catapult. For a brief moment he felt as if his wings would get ripped from their sockets, but he adjusted quickly and was streaming alongside her before he could blink. They flew side by side in Southern Royal formation with the tips of their wings touching. Holding their course, they torpedoed over the cliff top with a magnificent display of aerial control. The polished performance left all on the land in awe and admiration.

Gruesome Gale shot them towards the back of the island in a flash. Locked tightly together they swung and dropped as one, landing deftly behind a small outcrop of rocks with such ease that it looked casual. All the best cover was taken but it offered sufficient shelter to take the edge off the wind. They landed with the finesse of a dancing couple.

Although exhausted she stood tall and lean. Neither made any move. He stood there with his bent wing looking dishevelled and feeling awkward. They looked at each other for some time, neither of them moving. Eventually, when he considered that she had recovered sufficiently he took a step forward. More bold now than the last time, he stretched his beak towards her maintaining eye contact all the time. He tapped her beak. Holding his breath, he paused, remaining as rigid as the rocks he stood behind. He thought, "Well, this is it: do I fly like an aviator or plummet like a rock?"

She had not moved her eyes away from him from the moment her feet touched the earth. Watching his big hooked beak come towards her, she looked him straight in the eye. Slowly stretching her neck towards him she softly touched his beak with hers and held it there.

Chapter XIII

Ocillo broke through the foliage at pace. It was a lightly used track by some of the larger mammals and heavily overgrown. Her sharp eyes and good memory had enabled her to find the track several kilometres back. Eager anticipation and excitement broke her constraint; she had left the main group long ago. Ignoring warnings to be careful, she broke into a run with Chil and Chel in hot pursuit and pushed through the ragged trail with one aim in mind.

Chil and Chel had grown. The fruits of the jungle had been good for them. Like their mother they were agile and athletic. Their hair had grown into long, silver, gossamer strands. Their skin was still as white as the forest lily. Running barefoot across the warm earth they left no prints. Nimble and delicate in flight, they brushed past leaves and branches with hardly a flutter. Even the molecules of air simply moved from their path then returned as if nothing had passed. Their flowing hair chased behind them. Eager to catch up, it flowed like flooding water over smooth rocks, but never overtook. They chased their fast, nimble mother but never lost her even when out of sight, which was often.

When the twins came to a small, heavily overgrown area thick with secondary bush they stopped instantly.

Their senses spinning, not with alarm, but a perceived awareness of massive energy flowing throughout the area. They knew their mother was near. They also knew they had been there before. Instinctively, simultaneously, they moved in the same direction. It took them towards a tall kapok towards the edge of the new growth. There, they found Ocillo sitting crossed-legged, her hands on her knees looking upwards towards the top of the tree. Chil and Chel knew at once that this was the tree of life. They would often make their weary mother repeat the story of their birth. It was their persistent beseeching to the tribe to take them to the place of their birth that caused the elders to finally give in and make the move back to their old camp.

Some were reluctant. The ghost of the old shaman would come and beseech them or worse, capture their souls and drag them screaming up into the heavens to join him. They were all scared of the twins. Already the children's powers were advanced. Some thought they were the devil reincarnated, some that the shaman had possessed their souls and had come back for them. None though, were keen to cross them. They were not from this age.

The twins walked up to their mother and sat either side of her. Nobody moved. Nothing was said. They sat meditating, looking straight up Wee Tree's trunk to the tops of his highest leaves.

Wee Tree recognised them instantly. He felt the energy around him increase. For a long time the flerds did not move, but the aura surrounding them did. It pulsated between orange and blue with all the different tones in between. Slowly the blues became dominant then turned golden yellow. The twins stood up, quickly pulling their surprised mother with them. Holding hands they walked around Tree until they had completely circumnavigated him. The twins then linked hands completing the circle with Tree in the middle. They pulled themselves and their mother tightly to the tree so that their hearts were pumping against his warm bark. Tree felt like he could grow another two metres. The energy gushed through his cellulose veins. He felt so powerful.

The three flerds also felt this power. When they completed the circle they focused it into him forcing it upwards with Tree's natural flow of sap. It roared towards the roof of the world emanating out to touch every living thing. In return the universe delivered an equal amount back. The twins charged to the touch of their ancestors. They stepped into the other world.

The shaman appeared as a giant condor and greeted them with a huge, emboldened embrace from his massive wings. Wrapping them towards his body he pulled them onto his back. Effortlessly he glided, guiding, ghosting them through the myriad of the universe's tangled highways towards the source of wisdom and enlightenment.

They swept around countless galaxies, sweeping through the dark, through the light, the hot, the cold, past the good, past the bad. Eventually he plunged them into a suffocating darkness and released them, tumbling helplessly onto a sick, black, barren planet. The big condor flew off. Alone and scared they tightly held onto each other.

They stayed wrapped together, terrified to let go in case they never found each other again. Neither dared talk. It was sightless black, death-black, dead black.

Cold and shivering they remained locked together, hardly breathing, their heart beats pounding like war drums in their ears. The lifeless, numbing cold ate into their bones. Nothing changed. Nothing existed. "Why has the shaman brought us here? Are we dead?" trembled Chel to her tightly held sister.

"We are not dead, Chel. We died once and were brought back. There is a reason for all these things. Stay open Chel. Stay alive." Chil tightened her grip on her younger sister. Though they were born almost together, being the first to arrive Chil felt her responsibilities. Even so, she was as scared as Chel.

A long time passed. Nothing changed. The twins were still wrapped around each other in this cold, unknown world of invisibility. Chel eventually spoke again, "Chil, we're going to die here. Why did the condor bring us here? I want to go home."

Chil did not know what to say to her sister. There was no point saying anything as they could both feel the other's pain. Deep within her soul though, she knew the condor would not let them die there. He had brought them there for a reason, to teach them something. Chel knew this too. Chil clasped her hands around Chel's frozen face bringing her nose into contact with her own. She felt Chel's hands against her own cold cheeks and the two girls looked into each other's invisible eyes. Their souls mingled amongst each other's minds, becoming one. They simultaneously thought of Wee Tree. They hooked into his indomitable, universal energy. Slowly, they raised their own until it filled their whole bodies. More and more arrived until it began emanating into the unknown world beyond.

Far away, a shimmering horizon appeared as a faint orange arc. A desolate planet began to reveal itself. Chel whispered in Chil's ear, "Look Chil! Look. Look what is happening."

Chil twisted around with her back to Chel and watched the brightening, empyrean light slowly walk across the dead planet. Chel wrapped her arms around her sister, completely encompassing her to protect her and to sustain their energy.

The light spread quickly around them. There was nothing to see. A lifeless, barren, parched planet stretched out towards the distant horizon. It gradually changed from deathly black to a purple desert.

A smouldering, amber sun edged itself above the perfect, unbroken sphere of the planet's rim. Rising steadfastly, imperturbably, unstoppably, it grew rounder, fuller, until it flared full-faced into a roaring yellow fire ball. Its incandescent rays began to scorch the bare, burnt, ragged rocks.

The twins stood up. Their fearful, cold, dark world had transformed into a brilliant, scorching, fire-baked oven. Within a few moments they began to roast and swelter. A new fear swept through them. With no shelter to be seen ahead, nor any water, they realised that they would burn to death with their bones crumbling into the same dust that they stood on. They both turned to look for some shade and froze as still as the dead at what was in front of them.

The dry, desolate plains stretched stitch-tight to the planet's rim. Behind them, far in the distance was a high, denuded, rocky outcrop. It was the only imperfection on a perfect, unblemished horizon. Dazzled by the brightening light they gazed with puzzled eyes at the harsh, unforgiving, lifeless landscape. Breathing in slow, deep, lungfuls of thin, burning air, they gasped at what lay by their feet.

Extending away for fifty or more metres lay the half-buried remains of a large, fossilised tree. It lay prostrate across the rock-hardened ground just metres from where they had silently shivered moments before. One dead buttress root pointed out away from the ground. Others were still attached to its trunk. Some, broken into a myriad of dull, fragmented rocks, etched with its long-forgotten figure that was its fingerprint bark. Further along the trunk a large, straight branch, broken and segmented, lay perpendicular to it as a futile, fractured crutch that had failed to support it. The twins felt its pain as they walked a slow, subdued walk along its length. The thin, torrid atmosphere amplified the sun's rays into blistering, sharp needles. In that brutal light they stopped at the broken branch. Close to the trunk lay two large, thick segments of the long branch. A ragged crack in each mirrored the other, derived from a millennium of forces that had torn it apart. They both froze in horror. Suddenly, a chilling feeling of realisation flooded through their frail, immobile frames. Tears gushed down their faces leaving crusty salt trails as the hot sun burned them off. Before them lay the tree of life: it was Wee Tree. Carved within the fossilised segments were the stab wounds their mother had inflicted millions of years before. They were standing on the Mother Earth at the same point that the Condor

Shaman had swept them away. It was not the vibrant, colourful world they left. This was a dead planet.

In their pain and sorrow they were unaware of an encroaching shadow swelling over them from high above. Within an instant the giant condor plummeted on top of them, sweeping them up with no more effort than a silent flutter from his massive wing.

Chil cried out, more in anger than in pain: "Why Shaman, what has happened?"

In a hoarse, rasping voice the condor croaked back, "Chil and Chel this is your destiny. It is yours to choose." With that said, the big bird swept a huge, sweeping arc back through the winding galaxies and rapidly left the burning, purple planet to cook as another lifeless lump of rock in an endless universe.

Ocillo, ignorant of where they had travelled, released the girls from her hold around the tree and beckoned them to follow as she walked away. Chil and Chel were too much in shock to think for themselves and lamely followed.

The Elements had turned unseasonably cold. Gruesome Gale had blown in from the south, sweeping his Antarctic tinted winds over the high-altitude peaks of the Fly Mountains. It gave that extra edge of sharpness. He swept down their eastern flanks cutting through the warm, moist air with the precision of a wild, scything blade. He swallowed the whole forest, freezing feathers and fur without fear or feeling. Gruesome only coughed up when Vivacious was feeling low. He did not come to these parts often, preferring the reclusive, frozen wastelands of the polar regions. But when he came he did so with enthusiasm and gusto. He loved a jolly romp across fresh grounds. Sweeping down those high slopes invigorated him, allowing him to pick up speed, flex his muscles and power into anything at will. He was a simple soul at heart; to run fast and strong was all he ever wanted to do. Watching those tall trees bend, buckle and break invoked a satisfying chill to his cool demeanour. Blowing things off cliffs was truly a delight. He would watch them tumble and twist uncontrollably in his powerful grip before smashing them to pieces into the earth. It was a simple thrill but he loved it. There was no better job in the world. "Who wouldn't want to be a gale?" he thought to himself. Fly Forest received a pounding.

Shap was sitting close to his fire, clad in all the skins and furs he could muster. His ornamental beads and gourds clattered around his neck, chafing his skin. Leaves, twigs, broken branches and the rest of the forest's discarded debris flew around him in twirling eddies, touching and testing as if possessed by foul and malignant spirits. They flew into him then bounced off before collecting Gale's power again to fly into oblivion.

"They know," he thought to himself, "they know and they're trying to expose me."

A desolate, disconsolate look furrowed his young features. Looking deep into two bowls placed in front of his crossed legs he poured his scorn and dismay into his despairing misery. He cursed the old shaman. "Why did he leave me like that? I wasn't ready, he knew that. He did it on purpose, to show me up, to belittle me. He was an old fool." The bitterness gushed. "All he had to do was cut a monkey's throat but no, the old idiot had to take a condor, the ethereal spirit of the gods. The highest power on this material earth and he had to parade it around as if he controlled that power. What was he thinking? It's no wonder they took him away before he did something stupid. He walked beyond his boundaries. I was his protégé. He chose me. He trained me but he didn't finish the job. Now he's left me alone here with this lot and those two alien girls. They're possessed. They will bring bad luck to us all. It is the spirits' revenge for messing about with things we know nothing about." He peered deep into the bowls as if they were the source of all knowledge. Nothing came back.

He ground up some fresh herbs and added a little to each bowl then placed them on the edge of the fire to heat up. Slowly he poured the sap from a kapok into one and in the other sap from a sudigal tree. He mixed them into a thick paste then let them stand to infuse and dry in the fire.

The flerds did not stay too close to Fly Mountain. None felt safe there. Its immense, vertical sides of solid rock dominated the land and everything around it. It dwarfed the tallest kapoks, piercing through the forest canopy far into the clear blue sky. It kept the bad from the good.

A small waterfall cascaded over the fallen boulders off the nearby cliffs. The small rapids formed the beginning of a clean, fresh stream that turned and twisted around the rocks and big trees. A narrow strip of green grassland bordered a bend on the river surrounded by ancient, primary rainforest. The flerds had pitched their camp a short distance away from the rocky banks bordering the trees. Many comou palms grew in the forest, providing a multitudinous supply of rich, nutritious fruits. It was easy living for the Indian flerds with plenty of animals seeking fresh water and shoals of strong, fighting dorado in the river.

The elders had appointed Shap as the new shaman after the condor spectacularly took away the old one. It was an ambitious decision because he had no previous experience, but after much yoppa-snorting all eventually agreed – mostly because there was nobody else.

Shap was desperate to prove their decision was a worthy one. He had had some minor successes in the past. Like the day he predicted that it would rain and they should move camp before the floods arrived. The following day the river had swollen over its banks and they just about escaped with all their belongings. Whilst this impressed the younger members of the group, some of the elders were more sceptical. They had seen the river the previous day while hunting further upstream. It had turned a mucky chocolate colour from the mud washed down by rains above Fly Mountain. Tempest Cloud was accumulating into ominous columns as quickly as Shap was prognosticating.

On another occasion, a young female was collecting berries in the forest. She heard a rustle in the bush next to her and instinctively jumped back landing into another bush on the other side of the track. Frightened and startled by this sudden intrusion, a snake that had been resting there leapt into the air and on landing sunk his fangs into her foot. Much vexed and ruffled he slithered off into the undergrowth causing several of the other berry pickers to hastily scramble out of the way. Accounts differed. Some said it was the bright, red and black striped coral snake that had been hiding amongst the multi-coloured berries. Others, that it was an emerald green tree boa and one said it was a fifteen-metre boa constrictor. The girl was carried swiftly back to camp. The shaman looked at the wound declaring it to be from the deadly, venomous coral snake. Wrapping her wounds in different herbs and binding them tightly with the bark from a cow tree he beckoned the spirits in a yoppa-induced, psychotropic dance that lasted throughout the night. All were impressed by this feat of endurance. They were even more impressed when the girl survived and fully recovered. Some of the elders had seen bite marks from coral snakes. Nobody survives. They suspected it was from a harmless milk snake that looked identical to the deadly coral. They said nothing.

It was the end of one wet winter that established his credibility as a gifted shaman amongst the indians. Mosquitoes erupted along the banks of the receding river. Cumulus clouds of black, buzzing mosquitoes plagued every warm-blooded creature within miles of the river banks. Endless drones bombarded anything that breathed. Vicious and indiscriminate, they sucked the luscious, nutritious blood; glutinous and insatiable they filled themselves daily.

Before the flerds could escape they started to fall. Sickness, fever, then ultimately unconsciousness swept through the camp. Still the mosquitoes attacked. Still they wanted more blood. Only Shap, Chil and Chel remained immune.

Shap created potion after potion. Some he rubbed over the bodies to infuse through the countless bites and septic sores that developed over their festering, blistering skin. He poured herbal soups down their throats but they spewed the foul-tasting concoctions up as fast as it reached their shrivelling stomachs.

Chil and Chel watched him hunched over his fire brewing innumerable, unpalatable poisons. He would shout back ordering them to help him prepare the medicines. They ignored him. They did not get on. Shap was wary of their powers. Since they visited the tree of life with their mother they had not spoken to him. The visit to the purple planet had engaged their powers. They saw the world with enlightened vision and they saw through Shap.

The girls had collected each of the sick as they became ill and placed them in their huts, covering them with skins and clothes. Small fires burned at the entrances which they kept going day and night. As the flames burned down they placed aromatic leaves and flowers on the smouldering embers to repulse the endless mosquitoes. While Shap smoked himself into a frenzy they sat gazing into each other's eyes, opening their souls for the spirits to enter.

Each night the Condor Shaman swept down from the dark skies and, picking them up, took them to different parts of the forest. He showed them which plants and trees to use. The twins would be awake before Shap became conscious and disappear to collect the various ingredients at the spots the shaman had taken them. By the time Shap was up they had already administered their potions and had resumed their meditative state exactly as he had seen the night before.

Gradually, the Indian flerds began to recover. Ocillo was the first to emerge. Weak and unsteady, they helped her walk into the forest and sat her in the shade of a mighty kapok. They lit a small fire and covered it with wild garlic plants to dispel any mosquitoes. During the night they had collected some cacao beans and prepared them by roasting and winnowing. Chil took a large bush knife and with a single blow notched a channel in the tree's bark to allow its sap to trickle into a gourd. She mixed in the ground beans with some warm water and honey collected from a colony of wild bees and gave it to her mother. Ocillo slowly became more conscious from her involuntarily induced sleep and looked deeply into the eyes of her two beautiful daughters. They began to tell her of the events of the last few days. They wanted her to know about Shap and his poisonous potions, the Condor Shaman, the magic herbs and the special places in the forest, but Ocillo put a finger to her lips. The girls stopped talking and looked questioningly at her. They saw her energy returning. A bright, amber aura surrounded her strengthening body.

"I know," she said quietly then sat there taking small sips from her gourd. The girls waited for her to start talking again but Ocillo said nothing more. During the induced sleep from the mosquitoes she had connected subconsciously with the girls. The Condor Shaman had also visited her, picking her languid body up with his dexterous talons. He had transported her through the forest to where the girls were busy at work. She was

185

shown Shap haphazardly mixing different herbs and she saw the whole tribe collapsed in a comatose state.

When they returned to the village everybody had recovered sufficiently to get up and walk slowly about. Chil and Chel had taken their bows and arrows and had shot two coatis. On their return they found Shap sitting on his haunches mixing more potions. The girls softly, nonchalantly, drifted towards him then dropped the two blooded carcasses on his lap. Chil looked directly into his burning, baleful eyes with a face as pure as an angel, then softly spoke, "Skin them, medicine man. Let's see if your useless magic can cook a coati."

Insulted by this show of condemnation Shap flew onto his feet in an incandescent rage. His freshly mixed bowls of herbs scattered into the earth while the two dead coatis appeared to spring into life as they leapt into the fire to escape. He bellowed in a furious rage of resentment, "You have done nothing! You left your family to die. You sat there doing nothing. Nothing! Do you hear me, nothing. I have worked night and day to save us and look, they live. They live because I have saved them and you have not done anything but look after yourselves. You are demons, useless, ungrateful, selfish demons. Get away from here. You are not from our family. You are not one of us. You are demons."

Exhausted by this final outburst, his energy finally depleted. He collapsed to the ground heaving and panting like an old, worn-out dog. Chil turned to look at her sister. Their deep, azure blue eyes met briefly before they both turned, without comment, to return to their mother.

The whole village had watched. Confusion and disbelief spread amongst them. Ocillo, too, had been watching. She took hold of their hands and walked them back into the forest to the big kapok.

She sat them down and looked into their consciousness. They knew what she was about to say: "Shap is dangerous, girls. It is not safe for you here any more. He will invent any schemes to dishonour you and he has the support of the village. But Chil and Chel, not all. Some of the elders are sceptical but afraid to publicly confront him. You must leave."

"But what of you, mother? Will you come with us?"

"No. I must stay. When the time arrives I will have to support your cause. Go into the forest and stay with Wee Tree. He will protect you. You are skilled hunters. You are connected. Talk to Ruminant, she will guide and advise you. The forest will look after you. You will grow strong there. Stay connected my children then I can be with you. Now go and do not look back."

Chil and Chel picked up their bows and arrows and within a flutter of a butterfly's wing had disappeared into the secret, dark tree world without leaving a trace of their being.

Ocillo muttered gently under her breath, "Be safe my precious babies, I will miss you both."

Shap made much to inculpate their disappearance to validate his opinion of their guilt. He snarled and cursed and danced for the spirits to destroy the conniving, evil demons that had manifested themselves as two bleached freaks in flerd form. He had saved the whole village from death, now they would follow him anywhere, even to Fly Mountain.

Tree had not noticed his companions arriving and was about to talk to Pachamama when the two pale flerds walked out of the bush. They sat down on one of his roots and made themselves comfortable.

It had been a long walk for the twins since Shap had expelled them. Many times Inti had risen in the east. Travelling light and fast during the day, stopping only briefly to pick berries and fungi. At night they slept in the trees to avoid the big, night stalking predators. They knew the jungle well and had headed straight for the tree of life.

Shortly after they had eaten they stood up and wrapped their arms around Tree's trunk. He felt their warmth, then he felt their energy. At first it was gentle as it flowed up his trunk, then he felt the power. Masses of raw energy stormed up every cell in his cellulose frame until it emanated from every leaf, rising towards Inti in a monumental column of raw energy. He could feel himself growing. His roots sucked up the nutrients from Pachamama and hurtled them through every fibre of his expanding frame as he transformed into a massive kapok.

The girls could no longer touch each other around Tree's expanding trunk. He kept growing in height and girth until he towered above the canopy. The Condor Shaman arrived and flew around the twins, his giant wings fanning the energy as if it was a fire roaring up the tree. Their ancestors followed the shaman, twisting and snaking their way in and around the flerds. They took on the forms of floating bears, snakes, whales, buffaloes, birds and multi-coloured fish. Tree became a living, floating menagerie of the dead and past.

The ancestors, as metamorphosing animals, kept arriving, flooding every tree and plant with dancing creatures. They turned and climbed, swam and flew, re-enacting the history of the world until the forest was so thick the trees could not be seen.

Tree watched in naked wonderment. Everything Ruminant Whale had sung about arrived in ethereal lights illuminating his trunk in effervescent waves of whirling figures. Throughout the night they continued.

The twins, clinging to Tree's girth, watched the ancestors teach them everything that had ever happened in the world. When a shimmer of light spread from the east the ancestors suddenly stopped and vanished as quickly as a bat's blink. Only the shaman was left and spoke softly to the exhilarated girls, "Remember all that you have been shown. Your day will come. Use the wisdom, it has been given to you without condition." With a raise of his wings he pushed them down hard against the fading, cool night air and rising silently into the night sky, disappeared.

Chil and Chel made their camp at the base of Wee Tree. They used two of his enormous, flat-sided buttress roots as walls for their hut with his trunk at the apex. They quickly roofed it with straight lengths of small, chopped branches covered with broad leaves. It was a small hut, but supported by the biggest living thing in the world.

At last Wee Tree understood. He spoke to Pachamama, "I have seen your world, Pachamama. I have seen what you are. I understand why you do what you do. I know my destiny. I know yours."

Pachamama said slowly, "You know mine, Tree, not because you are my child but because you are connected. You are nothing unless you are connected. What you didn't know before was not because the answer wasn't there. It was because you didn't want to see it. Now you are fully connected you can see. You have become a pillar to the skies. You are the tree of life, Tree."

Chil and Chel flourished with the power from the forest. They grew tall and strong. They lived in harmony with the animals. They no longer hunted them for food. Instead they caught fish, picked fruits and herbs, used the forest's abundant larder and secret store of medicines. The animals no longer feared them nor hid when they approached. Now they had learned that the pale flerds were not a threat and treated them with respect, they reciprocated by allowing them into their world. It was an expansive, enriching, educational world. The twins thrived, they grew in stature, wisdom and enlightenment. Power flooded through them, evaporating throughout the world and across the universe. The animals, trees and plants sensed it; each was connected.

Chapter XIV

When Shap first suggested he was moving them nearer to Fly Mountain, many objected. Although the mountains were sacred to them, there were also devils living there. It was accepted as part of the duality of life: the good, the bad. They believed it to be possessed by evil spirits. The Indians had always avoided Fly Mountain. Demons would lace the land with sweet fruits to entice the weak and gullible. In the dead of night when all were asleep they would be dragged from their beds and carried off into the depths of Fly Mountain. Their tortured bodies could be heard screaming and the souls of the dead would cry, begging for help, pleading for release from their torment, their endless suffering. Victims could be heard crying every morning; their soft sobbing echoed around Fly Forest. Everybody heard them. The evil spirits laughed and danced in their agony. The Indians did not like Fly Mountain.

So when Shap outlined his plans to the village they were not well received. He explained that he had inherited the powers of the Condor Shaman, that their ancestors told him to bring everybody to Fly Mountain. The ancestors had shown that the mountain would provide everything they needed; their lives would be replenished with fresh fruits, animals and clean water. Their souls would be touched by the gods and they would be blessed and rejuvenated.

So deep were the flerds' fears that they still objected. Shap did not take criticism to his authority kindly. With a monstrous strike he thrust his stave into the ground. A small, crystal skull acting as a handle flashed ominous spars of light. "The spirits have spoken. All who defy them will be damned. Like the old shaman, you will be picked up and eaten alive by demons. We are going to Fly Mountain."

It was as Shap predicted. Birds and mammals were prolific amongst the virgin trees. Many fine fish inhabited the clean river, including the much loved golden dorado. Fruits and nuts were abundant in the forest. The villagers had an easy life as Shap had professed. Additionally, nobody disappeared. No demons had materialised. The spirits had delivered what he said they would. His inspired wisdom had impressed them – to such an extent that some believed he had become a spirit reincarnated. He was connected to both worlds, his channels were open. He was a mortal god. He was their chosen one, to guide them along life's difficult paths. Some even believed the Condor Shaman had repossessed him to return to his people as their empyrean, guiding light.

Shap fed off their veneration. Both in body and in spirit he was seen as one. He left none in any doubt as to the leader he was. He dressed to the position he purported to hold. Black condor feathers were woven into his hair; they contrasted sharply with the large, white, ibis flight feathers. The message was symbolic to remind everybody of the duality of life and death and that he was in control of both. Leather bracelets made from the belly of a mature cayman and ringed with its teeth were strapped around his arms, thighs and neck, displaying a powerful message of his portal to the ancient wisdom. He walked with the air of a god; he sublimated the smell of fear.

To remind any doubters of his descent from the Sun God, he had carved two larger skulls out of clear crystal. One hung from his neck with two sapphires for eyes. It caught the sunlight and flashed blood-coloured arrows towards the unenlightened. The other had studded diamonds for eyes which beamed golden rays on Shap's command. It replaced his smaller skull on his stave to show his increased dominance.

Not everybody was impressed with Shap's performance. Two of the elders were sceptical about his miracles and godly posturing, but were afraid of him. Not only did they fear his vile temper but also the backlash they might receive from the rest of the village. They remained quiet, preferring to wait for Shap to slip up.

Ocillo, though, had no such fear. She knew Shap was a fraud. He had exiled her daughters. She was not afraid of his sham powers and challenged him publicly: "Flerds die here in the shadow of Fly Mountain. It is possessed. You are leading us to our deaths."

Shap flew into a rage at the audacity of this challenge to his authority, "You are the whore bearing those two cadaverous demons possessing your daughters. I should have exiled you too. Perhaps I shall sacrifice you to appease the spirits if you don't hold your contaminated tongue." His eyes bloated with anger as he hissed his venom. The skull with the diamond eyes flashed provocatively towards Ocillo.

She backed off and walked down to the edge of the river. The two elders approached her after Shap had returned to his shelter. One put his hand on her shoulder and said, "Hold your tongue, Ocillo. You have always been too outspoken. He is powerful now but he will fall and get a bloody nose, then our time will come. There are few of us so we need to be strong and stay together. Let Shap be."

"I am scared to live here," replied Ocillo. "He doesn't know what he is doing and he didn't do those miracles. It was Chil and Chel that saved the group. It is they that have the powers of the Condor Shaman. They would not have brought us here." She explained what had happened during the fever.

"We've suspected Shap for a while but for now we must stay quiet and be patient. He has the confidence of the village. Fraudsters always expose themselves."

Shap enjoyed the prestige that his position allowed. He had always thought the old shaman to be a fool. "He killed those twins through his own incompetency. It was the forest that brought them back. A pity," he paused in mindful reflection, "that he didn't do the job properly. Still, they are gone now and will either have starved to death or been devoured by a jaguar or preferably both. I will have to arrange something similar for that insufferable mother of theirs." He continued strolling in a half-ruminant state further into the forest to collect his daily supply of seeds and plants.

With a bountiful supply of food, the flerds relaxed in the new camp. Their initial fears had subdued. Nobody had died or been dragged away in the night and killed. The young flerds played safely amongst the trees and in the river.

A shallow, swirling, twisting whirlpool broke the single-minded flow of the river. Two groups of large, smooth, round boulders channelled the water down a rapid drop. Smaller stones created rough, white-tipped water as it hurtled down towards a sharp bend. There it deepened and widened, allowing the fast-moving water to channel into the slower depths creating a large whirlpool. It was too fast for caymans and pirañas that preferred the slower, placid stretches further downstream. The young flerds, though, loved it. They floated gently towards the two big rocks. Their speed rapidly picked up until they were swept uncontrollably down the bumpy rapids before dropping unceremoniously into the whirlpool. The affable waters swept them around until they bobbed like corks in the centre with nowhere to go. If they were strong enough to keep to the edge then the whirlpool would catapult them away into the banks of the river. Submerged and bedraggled, the waterlogged flerds would haul themselves across the stony shallows and up the grassy river bank. Once there they would run back up to the top and repeat until utter exhaustion turned them into soggy, flaccid flerd forms. They remained slumped across the sun-dried, warm grass, soaking up Inti's radiant energy until they had the strength to walk back to the camp. Their parents would have freshly cooked food waiting for them by the fires where the youngsters ate until they felt they would burst, then collapsed again until their small legs had the strength to lift them back up.

Ocillo would go down to the river at the end of each day to wash. She would wait until everybody else had returned to their huts. A narrow, worn track led from the camp to the whirlpool. When the moon was out she could follow it easily by its ghostly glow. Otherwise, she would walk barefoot and follow the path by its gravelly feel. In the darkest of nights the river emitted its own luminescence. It glowed faintly but enough to see it sliding across the lush land like a giant anaconda slipping sideways in slow motion. Once on the grassy bend she would strip off and sit in the eddies spinning out of the whirlpool. Like gyrating galaxies expanding out from the centre of the universe, the eddies oozed into her body, melting around her in a conglomeration of tiny bubbles. The universe never ran out of galaxies.

It was a moonless, clear night when she lay on her back in the shallows. She watched the Huaca River gradually edge across the night sky. To the indians, that great Milky Way centred the universe. It was the channel Viracocha himself travelled after the creation of Pachamama. She wondered if Viracocha was watching her now. The smooth pebbles gently massaged her back as the soft currents tugged and pushed her body with each visiting eddy. Her hair floated off in different directions only to be pulled reluctantly back by the flowing waters tugging in another direction. She subconsciously counted the shooting stars, more out of fascination at their tiny, finite lives than anything meaningful. She wondered about her ancestors, whether they were watching her, whether they would come and float with her and tell her stories like they used to do. She thought of her husband, the twins' father. She missed him greatly. It was more painful in the nights, especially here in the placid water. Tears welled in her eyes, she swallowed hard to suppress them. It was a beautiful night, she was not going to cry. She continued counting shooting stars, it took her mind away from the past. Tonight, though, her mind would not let her soul rest. She missed her children. It was a prison sentence living here. She wanted to hug them and feel their warm breath against her cheek, to look into their big, blue eyes, to hear them laugh, to watch them grow. Her tears suddenly burst down her cheeks, it was futile to even try to hold them back. The pain was just too much. She felt so alone.

A twig broke. The sound echoed around the pool like a thunderclap. Something was out there. Instantly Ocillo became fully conscious. Her sorrow vanished, to be replaced with a high-tensile nervousness; she was fully alert. Remaining perfectly still, she slowly pushed herself into deeper water away from the vulnerable edge, with only her face above the surface. Her eyes strained into the darkness around the tree line seeking anything that might endanger her. Images of malice raced through her mind, "What if it's a jaguar," she thought, "or worse, an evil spirit? Is it the demon from Fly Mountain that takes flerds away in the quiet of the night then screams about its victories in the morning? I am alone here. Oh no! How stupid have I been?"

All she could hope for was that the water would conceal her and perhaps the beast would see or smell nothing and look further afield. A brief thought raced through her mind that perhaps it would go into the village and take away Shap. "But that would be too convenient," she thought, "life doesn't work like that. You have to build your own path." With that single thought echoing around her mind, she waited to see what would unfurl.

The Huaca River appeared to stop dead and the shooting stars stopped shooting. Another snap. Nearer this time, but still she could see nothing. Was it stalking her? Was it waiting for her to get tired, to climb out of the river then pounce from behind and drag her into the forest before she could even scream? She had to remain calm, vigilant; after all, the chances were on her side. It was unlikely that she had been spotted, lying mostly submerged. She gained strength from that thought and was annoyed with herself for not realising it earlier. She was in the consciousness, not the beast. The tables were turning.

A branch moved. Not too far away from the edge of the grassy patch. Ocillo saw it from the corner of her eye but she did not want to move her head to get a better look in case the ripples on the water gave her position away. A bush quivered and two dark shapes crawled stealthily out. From under the camouflaged hidings of the illusory darkness they appeared large and confident. They moved with unperturbed firmness. A cool, confident determination exuded from these menacing beasts. There was a calmness surrounding them.

Ocillo shivered as she thought, "Oh no! There's two of them. Perhaps they've just come down for a drink and will move on." Fear pushed hard across her chest preventing her lungs from breathing that cool, rich air. The shapes continued slowly down to the water's edge, right to the point where she had been bathing. Ocillo felt the tension in her back; she thought it would break her in two; then she heard, "Mother, are you going to come out and talk to us or do we have to go in there and get wet? What are you doing there anyway?"

Ocillo sat bolt upright. Waves of conflicting emotions flooded through her like the ripples of the river before she finally uttered, "You idiots, you scared the living daylights out of me. What are you doing creeping up, uninvited, on people like that? I thought you were some kind of evil spirits."

"We are, mother," Chil dryly replied. "We've been breaking sticks to get your attention for ages."

Ocillo sprang from the water like a hungry cayman chasing fish, swept her two daughters into her arms and covered them with dripping, wet kisses and tears. She held them tightly. After some time Chil murmured gently into her ear, "Mother, if you don't let us go shortly you'll squeeze us to death."

Ocillo released her hold and looked at them in the acquiescent light from the stars. She could see their bright blue eyes, almost luminescent, peering at her with big smiles showing their white, strong teeth.

Eventually Ocillo spoke, "Look at you. You are so strong, tall. You have grown powerful yet still tall and lean. I can sense your confidence. I can feel your power. You are so connected. Yet, I've been so worried. I thought the jungle would kill you but I knew it hadn't. It has nurtured you. How I have missed you." The words tumbled out then she began to cry.

"Mother, do not cry. We are here. We will look after you. Concentrate now, we need to talk to you."

Ocillo pulled herself together. She knew she had to be strong for her daughters. They had risked much going there. "How long have you been here? You can't stay, Shap will kill you. He is so powerful now; still a fool but a dangerous one."

"We know, mother. We've been watching for a few days now. We wanted to see you, to let you know that we are well. The forest is looking after us and we are looking after it. Wee Tree mother, Wee Tree is so big. He is the tree of life. The Condor Shaman visits us. He has shown us the past, the future; he is guiding us, we are looked after well, mother. The universe is protecting us, but what of you? How are you keeping?"

"I am well. I avoid Shap and two of the elders can also see through his façade, they help me. We look after each other."

Chel looked at her sister and said, "It is time to go. We will return on the full moon, on each full moon. Be careful at night, mother. There is evil about. It is hungry. Do not come down here without Monocled Moon. It is not safe."

They embraced tightly, then the twins glided back into the forest without touching the floor. There was no sign they had ever been.

Ocillo was relieved to see them so fit and healthy. She also felt proud, but what had they meant? She sat for a while pondering on everything they had said, "How could they have been here days when our hunters and trackers are so good? They could find a snake in a burrow. Nothing gets past them yet they've reported nothing untoward. Perhaps the condor brings them. How is my husband, I wonder?"

"He is good, Ocillo." A gravelly voice spoke close behind her. Shocked and frightened she spun round. A huge condor, with his wings spread wide, blotted out the sky. Standing ten metres high, he looked down towards her with warmth and affection. His face had the look of an angel. Love and serenity radiated from his feathered frame. Ocillo felt his energy and dropped to her knees as she felt hers draining away. Her whole family was with her and had been with her all the time. It was all too sudden, too unexpected. The colour drained from her as she collapsed onto the soft grass.

When she awoke she was in her hut. It was light outside with Inti in full beam across the tree canopy. She felt alive and fresh. Energy was seeping from her pores, then she remembered last night. "Was it a dream? How did I get to my bed? I remember nothing after the condor spoke. It must have been a dream. My daughters, too, that was all in my head. I am alone, so alone." Sadness filled her body and the energy drained away as quickly as she had noticed it. She went outside to see what Laughing Sun was laughing about because she could see nothing. The village looked as it always did. The hunters were gone. The women and children had also gone, presumably picking fruits in the forest. Shap was nowhere to be seen as usual. "Still in his pit, hung over no doubt from too much snorting. A waste of good plants. One day it will rot him from the inside out, hopefully." She felt guilty about wishing bad thoughts onto others even if it was Shap. "Sorry," she said softly to any spirits listening, "please ignore that last message. I am feeling confused."

It was a beautiful day so she turned to air out her hut when she suddenly stopped. Her body froze as she stared at the dried palm leaves thatching her roof. Above the door, tucked under a frond was the biggest condor feather she had ever seen. She quickly untangled it from the leaves and hid it inside her bedding. Shap would not take kindly to his collection being dwarfed by this specimen and would grill her incessantly as to how she came by it. "And what could I tell him?" she thought.

Her energy returned. She was the happiest flerd on the planet.

Chil and Chel kept their promise and visited Ocillo every month on the full moon. The brilliant night light lit up their faces and Ocillo marvelled at their beautiful, lean, toned bodies. Their clear, bright eyes mirrored their intelligence. Beaming smiles and with white, light hair down to their shoulder blades which flowed like rivers in full spate when they ran. They looked at their mother and smiled. They always smiled. She never detected any concern on their fresh faces. They were as confident as the Elements were competent. The three were as one when together. Talk was idle, deeper matters were already understood.

The flerds' easy living was beginning to mark a change in their attitudes. They were becoming lazy, paunchier and irritable. Squabbles erupted over minor occurrences. Shap fuelled the male flerds with increasing amounts of strong yoppa. Each evening they would disappear with fantasy dancing in the company of spirits and each morning was wasted as they lay in bed longer to recover. The slow, languid and sluggish men grew fat in their inactivity. They could no longer track the howlers and stumbled around with the finesse of doped tapirs.

The females found themselves doing all the work. They would be up at daybreak collecting forest food, feeding their families and looking after the young. They picked up the discarded bows and arrows and brought home the freshly killed meat.

They complained to Shap. He retorted sharply, shouting them down, "You are ungrateful, whining devils! Have the demons infested your souls? I bring you to paradise with everything at your hands. Clean, running, fresh water, fish, abundant animals, fruits galore and you thank me with this continual, nauseating bombardment of complaints about mundane triviality. You are selfish beasts; have you no gratitude for what I have freely given you?"

The females backed off but Ocillo held her ground and fired back, "The males are as useless as are you. They are fat, lazy and inebriated. We have been here far too long. It's time to move."

Furious and incensed, Shap lifted his long, crystal-capped stave and struck her across the jaw. The jewelled eyes flashed venomously. "I am the embodiment of huaca. You will not address me unless I invite you to. You fall to the ground when I walk past. Do you understand? Now fall to the ground."

With blood dripping from her split cheek, Ocillo did no such thing. With a defiant look, she stared him straight in the eye. Shap raised his stave again when two elders walked from behind and stood in front of her. "Save it for another day," one said.

Shap paused briefly before turning and walking away at pace, he promised himself, "I will offer her as a sacrifice at the earliest occasion."

It was impossible to be rational with him these days. He was too unpredictable. His heavy-handedness and bad temper were becoming more prevalent. He bought the males' support with yoppa and promises of enlightenment and safety from demons. Only the two elders remained aloof. They joined Shap with the hunters but feigned inhaling the immobilising yoppa and when it became clear the group was floating into another world they crept away to help the females with the daily work.

Every day now, the males grouped around Shap's fire to snort yoppa. By the time night arrived most had passed out and those left swaying had long since left their bodies and flown off to eat sacred berries from the ethereal trees in the galaxy. The females gradually picked up all the work. A precarious impasse developed with both sides becoming increasingly isolated from the other.

One night, Tempest Cloud had blown over from the west. His chambers were fully loaded and his marauding columns marched down Fly Mountain.

Electric tension rattled the air. He was ready for a long campaign. The female flerds had prepared their huts, strengthened the timbers and increased the roof palms. The camp was prepared for the onslaught.

Thunder and lightning began the war song. It hung drum-low over the canopy. The explosions detonated in the trees, producing high-pressure waves reverberating amongst the cowering forest dwellers. The world shook to its low-frequency rhythms. Ocillo's bones were shaking apart. She slept alone these days but kept her feather close to her bosom for strength and support. She could not sleep with those fulminating roars crashing above her. The lightning lit up the forest and for a brief moment it was as bright as day, then it would collapse into infinite darkness. She sat there mesmerised by the show. It scared her a little. The power and voracity was humbling to feel and witness but she felt safe in her hut. She sat there looking through the door towards the river and trees on the other side. A snapshot of the forest arrived moments before the thunderous applause. It was as spectacular as it was frightening.

In one flash, she saw something. A large shape emerged from the bushes. It was big but she could not identify it. She stared intently in the following blackness but was blinded by the dazzling lightning and could see nothing. The subsequent dark moments lasted for an eternity. Fear tingled at her alert nerves. Her instinct told her to lie low and quiet, but curiosity wanted to know what it was. She lay on her belly and poked her head around the entrance, listening and looking. Another flash arrived but nothing was there. Several more came and she scanned the whole area piece by flashing piece. There was nothing to be seen. The thunderous show eventually lulled her into an uneasy sleep.

Screams awoke her in the morning. Flerds were running around in erratic circles. Tempest Cloud finally offloaded its payload. Rain teemed from the sky in waterfalls. Muddy puddles the size of small lakes covered the once fertile land in a brown, bubbling liquid carpet pockmarked by the pelting rain. Yoppa-saturated, dozy flerds crashed, trashed and fell uncontrollably in the sloppy, muddy wallows that was once hard ground as they staggered looking for the source of the screams.

Ocillo leapt from her bed and raced across the camp to one of the huts. A young mother sat screaming uncontrollably while trying to be soothed by her sister. Her son was missing. He had been lying next to her when they went to bed last night, now he was gone. Ocillo organised anybody capable of standing to search the village. When he was not found she sent them into the forest. They searched all the trails and far down the river but nothing was found.

From out of the clouds, amongst all the flashes and thunder came other screams. Hideous, tortuous screams mingled with Tempest Cloud's rumbling explosions. It greeted the new, frightful day to fracture the already tattered nerves in the village.

Ocillo flashed back. Had she seen something after all? She ran down to the river to where she had spotted the moving shape the previous night. The rain had obliterated any possible trail and the river had risen too high to cross safely. "Perhaps there was something here after all, but how can something come into a hut and take a child with nobody noticing? It's not possible. The child is either lost in the forest or has become caught in the rising waters and swept away."

Ocillo was lost in her thoughts. A niggling instinct gnawed away in her stomach: she was sure she had seen something last night. There was something out there; her instincts were never wrong. She spent most of the day looking for trails that the creature may have used. There was also another purpose – to keep out of the way of Shap. This was all his doing. Everybody knew there were evil spirits there.

Chapter XV

Chil and Chel suddenly popped into her mind. Were they trying to communicate with her? She sat down on a soggy log, dropping into a meditative state. She saw their big, blue eyes looking benevolently at her. She smiled. Their words came through with echoes of the past: "Don't go out in the dark nights, mother. There is evil about."

"So, it is true," she thought to herself, "evil spirits are here."

Shap was calling the good spirits. He asked for help to find the boy. A bear walked from out of the cover of the trees and took him to the base of Fly Mountain. It faded into the solid rock to be replaced by a mythical cat leaping out with huge, ivory-white fangs. Shap leapt backwards in surprise, startled by the ferocity of the animal towards him. It was a demon luring him into a trap. He fought it with his spear but the cat leapt at him again and bit his spear in half, shredding it to splinters. Shap ran away from the mountain and hid in a tree. A large, bedraggled bird flew in and perched next to him. It had a massive, long multi-coloured beak and looked ancient and moth-eaten. The old bird sat there looking Shap up and down, then with a quick swipe of his beak knocked him from the tree.

He hurtled past planets, the sun and into a cold, black void. He awoke, face down in the mud next to his extinguished, water-logged fire. Had the spirits shown him the way or were they warning him off? The mountain was legendary for evil. Nobody went there.

He rebuilt his fire and dried himself by it. Some of the elders came by and sat with him. "Shap, you would do best to be out in the woods showing the way. The tribe feel let down. They are doing all the work and you are seen sat here keeping warm. They have searched everywhere and need guidance."

Shap said nothing for a while, then looked the elders straight in the eyes, "I have travelled with the bear spirit. He is calling for action with strength through adversity. A big cat came, suggesting action without analysis and the pelican I met talked of a recovery from loss. I have been shown where the boy is. We will go in the fresh light tomorrow."

The elders left to tell the others the good news but Shap sat there, ashen-faced. "The dark side, though," he thought to himself, "the pelican could have been telling me not to misuse abundance and to be careful about our ego. Did the bear try to tell me of death and destruction on the mountain and the cat – what about the cat? Was that demon spirit trying to crush my leadership?"

Shap was disturbed and remained alone all night. Tempest Cloud still pounded Pachamama with his heavy, watery load and Fly River was transformed from a gentle stream into a torrid, angry, mud swollen, pulsating torrent. The flerds wrapped themselves up and wondered if they would still be there in the morning. Shap had a serious problem: his male hunters had been doped up for too long to be of any use. He had to call upon the females in the tribe to substitute them. It went against his natural instincts as he knew this would give Ocillo further grounds to discredit him. The women were not the formidable warriors as in the past. Today they were hunter/gatherers but they embodied the Amazon huaca of their ancestors and the elimination of the evil spirit was of more immediate importance. He had to swallow his pride.

To be safe, Shap armed two of the females to guard the village. He put one at each end and told them to stay in touch and raise the alarm as soon as they saw anything. Normally he would have fires burning all night but the torrential rains prevented that. The guards positioned themselves between the huts and the forest. Nothing could get past them and into the camp unnoticed.

Low light frizzled electrically through the heavy night clouds. It mixed with the pouring rain to produce a hazy, mystical, ghost light where shapes disappeared then reappeared in different forms. Distorted, corrupted noises buckled and mixed with the booming thunder and pounding rain. Momentarily, Ocillo heard two piercing screams distorted by the beating clouds. She listened intently but heard nothing more except rain, lightning and thunder. The sunken, depressed, low cloud challenged her senses.

The long, drawn night dragged on until a semblance of sodden daylight filtered through. The guards were missing. Nobody had heard nor seen anything. Ocillo kept her thoughts to herself. The devil incarnate was stalking them. Broken, shredded weapons were found scattered amongst the puddles and mud. Fear pervaded throughout the camp like water dripping from the trees. Two of their sharpest, female hunters taken out without a trace. "There must be more than one," thought Shap. He, too, was afraid. Never had he encountered this. The remaining hunters looked for signs in the rain saturated bush. The demons could walk amongst them without anybody noticing. "Perhaps it is Ocillo." The thought flashed through his mind but he did not hold on to it. Something needed to be done.

Ocillo could hold her peace no more, "You, Shap; you brought us here; this is your doing. We have invaded the spirits' space, uninvited. I told you there was evil here and it's here big. We must leave."

Shap held his anger at her challenge, "No! The spirit has shown me where the boy is. It is likely that our hunters are there too. We will go to Fly Mountain and we will return with all three."

Ocillo retorted, "You are a fool, Shap. You always were. They are no longer alive. The demons have them. They are consumed. We will all be slaughtered and consumed here." She walked off to her hut before she said all the further thoughts that were raging through her mind.

Leaving the elders to look after the camp, Shap set off to lead his young band of female hunters to the base of Fly Mountain. A massive array of multi-coloured feathers decorated his ceremonial headdress. Sacred stones placed around his body protected him from the evil spirits. Jaguar teeth and giant anteater claws hung from his neck. Bracelets strapped around his thighs, arms and ankles were garnished with the teeth from cougars for speed and endurance. He exuded power and confidence. His young hunters lost their initial fear and felt brave and indomitable by his side.

They wasted no time looking for the paths to the mountains. The heavy rains had converted all the tracks into small, liquid, chocolate streams. They found a little-used trail that was heavily overgrown and dripping wet, but it took them directly to the mountain. It was a long trek. It was towards the end of the next day when they arrived; the light was beginning to fade. They erected two hunting shelters against some large trees. Shap had his own as his position dictated. The hunters were relieved to share theirs – they felt safer in numbers. They lit small fires in the entrances to scare off the predators.

Teragorm loved those dark, wet, thunderous nights. She revelled in the glorious mud. She slipped down the mountain via an ancient secret passage. She could do it blindfold. Mud and puddles covered the ground. At the bottom of the rain-drenched, slimy rocks she rolled over to wallow in the collected pools of gravel and mud. She rolled around on her back until her grumbling, empty belly reminded her why she was there. Splashing away into an upright position she sloshed her way to the tree line. Her four, wide feet spread out to maintain her balance in the sloppy conditions. She made no attempt at stealth and splashed water wherever she could. It sprayed outwards and upwards, over the bushes, rocks and up towards the clouds as fast as Tempest was sending it back down. She guided her sturdy, thick legs skilfully around the big rocks, shifting her overly large, heavy, body with the finesse of a dancing butterfly, or so she liked to think. The thick armour-plated scales on her powerful tail, thrashing all and sundry behind her, added to the muddy fountain blowing into the air. How she loved those dreary, drenched, dripping nights.

When she thumped to a stop by a very large tree root she slopped onto her belly and stuck her head over the root. She could smell flerds. "What joy," she thought to herself. "What absolute joy. They are so near. I don't have to tramp about the woods all night and without that infernal sunshine I won't get burnt up in the morning. How I love these dark days."

Teragorm picked up the scent and trotted off with a spring to her step. For a big beast she could be surprisingly agile, deft and nimble. She quickly scooted off around the mountain along the trails she knew so well. It was not long before she saw the flickering lights from smouldering fires. She could feel the warmth, "A bit of heat too," she thought, warmly.

The smell of flerds was strong; many were there. It was an intoxicating feeling; her head began to swirl with expectant ecstasy. She was an efficient killer and quickly assessed the numbers and their positions. No time was wasted pontificating over the tactics. She was on home ground, it was all hers, "And rightly so," she thought to herself with a small grin. The nearest hut had the most in, so she dived out of the black night as a silent, over-sized falcon swooping on the unsuspecting.

With powerful limbs and razor-sharp claws she landed on top of the slumbering flerds. An astute guard near the entrance saw nothing. She was instantly severed in two as the three-tonne monster flew straight into her. Her scalpel-sharp front claws shredded her as they would a wet leaf. The hut was demolished; bits of flerd flew everywhere. Her flaying feet, hooked bill and thrashing tail maimed, slaughtered and ripped apart the nearest hunters within a hiss of her saliva-dripping tongue.

The screams from the savagery echoed around Fly Mountain. Shap leapt up with his spear to hand and launched himself through the air towards the dark, mauling monster's middle. He aimed for her heart but Teragorm was aware of his threat from the other hut. With Shap in mid flight, she swung her heavy armoured tail cutting the air with the speed of a cracking whip and caught the hapless Shap across the ribs.

Shap bellowed in pain as his rib cage collapsed from the crushing force and he was thrown thirty metres into the forest. The collision with a large tree collapsed the other side of his rib cage. The impact broke his arm and he fell to the ground breathlessly trying to suck in air. Teragorm looked up to see her attacker disappearing into the darkness but decided not to chase him. There was enough here.

Within the brief distraction of Shap's interference two hunters rolled away. Teragorm noticed but let them go. None of them were any threat and she could take them any time she wished.

She sat on the disassembled remains of the hunter warriors and ripped them apart with her hooked bill. The fresh flesh slithered down her raw throat producing a cooling ecstasy; her eyeballs rolled back into their sockets. It dropped into her rumbling belly with a gentle plop, slowly filling the vacuous cavity until it began to stretch out the sides. Nothing was left – flesh, skin, hair, bones, clothing and some green leaves as an aside completed a very fine, wet night. Collecting two broken bodies, she climbed back up the secret passage. "I'll have them for breakfast," she thought placidly to herself, "I should be feeling in need of a bit of a pick me up by then."

At the top she collapsed into a gratified, peaceful slumber. It was not long before the rich flesh began to putrefy in her fierce, gastric juices. Clouds of methane bubbled up inside. Teragorm rolled over and began groaning as the pain stretched across her abdomen. A vacillating light crept above the mountain ridge and Teragorm roared in pain as the rotting flesh began to work through her bowels. Condor circled high above while the mountain goats maintained their guard on the edges of a nearby scar. How she hated the new day, the morning day.

The escaped hunters had been badly mauled. Ripped skin and loose flesh hung from their battered bodies, but no bones were broken. They found mosses, leaves and herbs with antiseptic properties and bound them over each other's wounds with strips of bark. Every muscle and fibre in their torn bodies burnt.

Shap had found his breath and called to the hunters. After a short search they found him slumped against a large fig tree. He was too badly injured to do much with, so they made a light stretcher and carried him away from the mountain. They were keen to leave. Nobody had the stomach for another night there. The tormented cries of Teragorm echoed around the forest as a deadly reminder that they would not survive another night. It took them five days to get back to camp.

At the village the others were stunned into a frightened silence as the tale was unfurled. Too scared to talk, too horrified to move, they sat in disbelief with their hands covering their faces as their vulnerability became apparent. Nobody had seen such a creature. Many myths existed but nobody had lived through an encounter with the demon.

Ocillo was not short on being forthright. She thundered her fire towards the crippled shaman, "You didn't listen, you fool! Now you will. We are leaving here at first light providing we survive the night. If you object I personally will stake you to the ground as a sacrifice to the devil. Perhaps he will take you and leave us in peace."

Everybody looked at Ocillo but nobody spoke. They either agreed or were too shocked and scared to say anything. Shap, too, said nothing. He hurt all over and had neither the strength nor stomach to fight her. It was all he could do to draw in breath; each lungful shot spasms of pain across his chest. He made another mental note to deal with Ocillo once and for all when he recovered. First, though, he had to get through the night.

The dark night arrived quickly with Tempest Cloud hanging so low over the treetops. Torrents of arrow sharp rain continued to pelt the sodden ground. Each hut lit their own fire. They knew it was no deterrent. A psychic fear from deep within triggered an inbuilt dread of being taken in the dark. It came from the very centre of the flerd being: to be pulled down by an unseen predator from behind in the pitch dark, it sent tremors through their already traumatised bodies. The light from the small fires gave them comfort. At least they could see their attacker and take some solace from a sharpened spear pointing towards it.

Nobody slept. Many of the young, strong hunters were dead or injured. It was pointless having guards. They were an offering, not a deterrent.

The night was long and slow. Nothing happened. The rain continued. Some slept where they sat with a gentle heaviness to their breathing, but most sat with wide eyes peering into the unpredictable dark. Spears and shields lay by their sides, more for an emotional prop than anything promoting defence.

There were no strange sounds, no unusual occurrences; night life continued with its familiar hum. Suddenly, the night clouds disappeared outside one of the huts. Two gleaming, yellow, inimical eyes appeared, hurtling silently, iniquitously towards them out of the dark. The hut was demolished in an instant. The occupants involuntarily screamed as one being. The lightning green, yellow eyes flying through the door were the first they saw of anything and then they were gone. She landed in the middle of the huddled, shrieking group and picked up one of the elders in her crooked beak. The flerd's broken body flopped down either side of her beak, his blood-curdling screams briefly bellowed for help before spluttering into a gargling groan as the air was crushed from his lungs. Teragorm stood up high onto her back legs, sweeping her tail through the wrecked hut as a scythe through dry grass, cutting through anything it hit. Some of the braver flerds arrived, throwing rocks at the armoured beast to try and get it to release their comrade. They bounced off with no effect.

Sweeping around she turned to take her meal back to the peace and sanctity of Fly Mountain. The stone-throwing flerds ran off to hide in the dark as the monster turned to face them. Teragorm stopped in her tracks. Beyond the fleeing flerds were two fiery lights floating slowly towards her. She spat out her food and roared at the steadily moving lights. The timbers of the forest shook from the voracity of the noise. Life stopped breathing. She blasted out her bill, billowing venomous, contaminated spit towards the incessant, oncoming flames. Children and adults alike cried aloud. They felt that the essence of life itself was being shaken from them. That the gods were testing their mortality by sending this evil presence to them. Teragorm continued spitting fetid bile with all the power and angst stored within her mighty, rancour-fuelled belly. The lights, which were impervious to her venomous fire, continued at the same, slow, relentless pace. Her serrated, dagger-sharp claws excavated the watery earth into cascades of flying mud as she prepared to charge them down, smothering them with her explosive attack before ripping them to shreds.

The lights were unperturbed and continued unabated. Teragorm wanted to pounce but strangely found herself faltering. The lights continued – slowly, composed and unruffled. Normally everything fled in terror. She had not encountered anything like this and was not sure what they were. Maybe it was her intuition, curious that she wanted to see what the lights were. She snorted and puffed more bile, shaking her head violently from side to side, but the old, vindictive vigour was not there.

The lights came very close to her; still she did not strike. She was not afraid. She was afraid of nothing. She had survived for millennia. Two little flames did not bother her. What bothered her was why two little flames were not bothered. Now they were so close that the background fires from the huts cast a shimmering, hazy view beyond them. Two slight flerd forms became apparent, each holding one flame. A knowing, satisfied snarl tore from her beak from the realisation that more food had offered itself.

Hidden in her hut behind Teragorm Ocillo screamed, "Chil and Chel, what are you doing?" She wanted to shout more but the thoughts would not connect as the image contradicted all her natural feelings. Her fear numbed her functions as she watched her two daughters face the devil. Immobilised, her mouth opened and closed but nothing further came out.

The twins moved up close to Teragorm and put the burning torches aside. Two pairs of burning, blue eyes replaced the fiery lights. She continued to roar and bellow but now it was more from posturing than from malice. Chil and Chel stood, lean and strong, tall and confident. With their long, white hair tied back in tight plaits and as white as the spirits themselves, they stood erect and motionless looking directly into the creature's soul.

Teragorm's spit and thunder dried into sticky phlegm in the back of her throat. Unable to move, she stopped roaring and sat back onto her haunches and looked at the two silent, spiritual effigies staring straight back. The other flerds hidden around the camp hardly dared to breathe. They wanted to scream but the sight of two slender children just metres away from this enormous, uncharacteristically inert evil spirit was incomprehensible to their senses.

Teragorm stopped feeling aggressive. Gradually, a warmth of affable contentment pervaded throughout her. She was not sure why, but felt quite happy. She was usually happy, unless it was morning, but now she felt sublimely happy. The two beings in front of her seemed friendly; life felt good. She could not remember ever feeling like this. She was sure it was to do with the two skinny, white flerds and felt a longing to protect them. They were so frail, almost transparent. They looked so fragile. She leaned forward and put her giant head on the ground and looked up at them. Both girls walked towards her, one on either side and laid their hands on her head. Teragorm closed her eyes. She had never felt such peace. The girls whispered gently in her ears then moved back a couple of steps. Teragorm gracefully pulled herself to her feet and trotted off into the dark forest, but not forgetting to drag the battered body with her.

Chapter XVI

The indians watched from behind spears, barricades and trees. Frozen through fear, they watched as still as stone, staring in a terrified state of amazed admiration. They expected a token fight, a few arrows fired or a thrown spear or two before the twins were ripped apart and consumed. Ocillo ran out and hugged her girls then dragged them back into one of the bigger huts to get out of the rain.

When Shap was fit enough to move, the girls approached him, as he was mixing potions by his fire. "We have news for you Shap. It is your turn to live in the forest. Your follies and sham practice are exposed. We are the shamans now. Go!" Chel was indifferent with her delivery to Shap, with no hint of any expression on her face. Shap briefly thought about killing them on the spot with his bush knife but had an uneasy feeling. He promised himself that one day he would. Saying nothing, he packed his belongings and left.

The twins instructed everybody to pack up and get ready to move on. It was a decision they could not act on quickly enough. They moved far away from Fly Mountain. Chil and Chel had no fear of Teragorm but they knew that she must eat. Flerds were her staple diet, that was not going to change. They took the group far downstream to where it joined another river. It merged into a wide, slow-flowing river. Many different species of fish and fauna lived in this part of the forest. It was a long way from its mountainous birthplace and its odd inhabitants.

Teragorm could not stop screaming each morning. Her belly simply reacted that way with flerd meat. Although the crippling pains doubled her up in agony, she could not forget those two wispy flerds. They connected with her in the same way that Ruminant Whale did. They made her feel important, needed and loved. All other flerds were a screaming, hostile, bellicose lot, but these two were different. They could see her finer-tuned sensibilities. They touched her soul. She liked it and wanted more.

"I will find the pale pair," she mused to herself while racked over her comfort stone, although she had no idea how, or even what to do if she did. She just knew that she had to see them again. Some ancient, primitive instinct was telling her to find them.

Whale often sang to Teragorm – usually on some of her more bellyaching mornings. Teragorm would lament on why such fine cuisine would cause her so much digestive infliction. "Could they not change their diet to make their meat a little more palatable?" she would whine while gripping her rock of consolation.

"But, Teragorm, you love your food. You've sung about it so often. You have a wonderful, synergetic relationship with the flerds and you're so connected with them. Look at your history, they have been feeding you for millions of years."

Whale and her calf had travelled around the southern polar waters of Rumbustious Sea. The food had been plentiful in their sanctuary and Whale had recovered much of her previous power, although the encounter with the flerd ship had traumatised her beyond her consciousness.

Calf clung to her like a limpet. He, too, was growing in power. Tonnes of daily krill, together with an almost psychotic attention to his mother, had built him strong beyond his age. He swam around her incessantly. Always singing to her. Always attentive to her desires. Always protecting her from all and anything. He had become fearless and confident when confronting danger.

When orcas arrived he would stay on her dark side and would take them on with indomitable aggression. He did not know that they were really stalking him, he feared only for his mother. They expected him to hide, dormant next to his mother and would try and run him to exhaustion. Ruminant and Calf, though, never played to this tactic. Initially Whale was terrified they would get to Calf and would try to outrun them, but Calf did not stick to the plan. When they least expected it he would unpredictably swerve out at a rapid rate of knots and ram one of them under their ribs, then tuck back in under his mother. If he hit the right spot and judged his timing correctly he could feel their ribs breaking around the front of his jaw. His power and timing improved with each encounter. The tails and flier games he used to play had developed his muscles to maximise his acceleration. His mother's mock attempts at sinking him had built up his lung power and stamina. The toned muscles hidden beneath his body fat provided surreptitious, raw, athletic tension in his flukes and fins; his power defied his size.

The battered orca's cries suddenly echoed through the water as it would roll over to one side from the pain of its cracked ribs. It ended any attack before it started. The other orcas backed away from the combative calf, collected the crippled orca and escorted her away from the rancorous cetacean.

Calf would rejoin his mother who had carried on swimming to distract the main pod. Neither sang anything. She knew from the orcas' distress calls that Calf had found his spot. She was immensely proud of her brave, ambitious baby.

After several of these attacks all the local pods learnt to avoid the dangerous one, so they left Whale and her vicious, ten-tonne baby to it.

Having defied death and regained her strength, Whale resumed her duties and continued to sing to the world. She sang about how she had felt in those dark moments after the harpoon had hit her. She recounted each moment and thought, not so much to warn the world about the dangerous flerds – because most knew anyway – but more to give other whales an idea of the tactics she used. If more could be saved by following her example then the world would be a better place.

Tree was perplexed on hearing Whale's songs. He was relieved to hear her again but also distraught at the pain and trauma she had gone through. After months without the wisdom of the Curator it had been a quiet, dark world. Now she was back to her former self. Tree was so jubilant he sang back to her, "Your flerds murder, kill, and maim for just the fun of it, but I have met two here that live with every living thing. They connect at all levels. We combine our energies and are the stronger for it. They hear your songs and sing to you. How can they be the same? How do you know the good from the bad?"

"Your flerds are special, Tree, as is the place where you live. You are the pillar for the skies, the tree of life and the forest is full of trees where you all support life. Without any of you, the world would change and most animals would die due to that change. Your flerds realise this. That is why they live in harmony with their surrounds, why the spirits guide them and why they give you energy. You gave them life when others discarded them. There is no nobler action, Tree. Run with your instincts, they will never let you down."

Wee Tree was going to reply with a whole host of questions but was too confused to know which to ask first. The more he thought about her words, the less he understood. His mind kept returning to the same questions, "What does she mean, 'without any of you'? How can there not be any of us, we are everywhere, we are the source of life, so where would we go? It's not as if we can get up and run around or go eating, killing or maiming everything else. It's a pointless exercise and yes, I gave them life because that's what you do. Why wouldn't I or anybody else? It's not noble, it's what you do. It's instinct. 'Run with my instincts!' I'm rooted to the ground. I would like to run. That would be great. So how do I know a good flerd from a not so good flerd?" His thoughts trailed off into an unknown, nebulous world where nothing made any sense, but he did feel joyful that he had saved the two pale flerds. He took in what Whale had said and made a mental cellulose note to run with his instincts.

Chil and Chel had positioned the camp on the junction of the two rivers. It was here that other Indian flerds navigated the waterways in wooden dugouts. Much trading was completed in their camp with many different groups moving through. With Shap's influence halted, the males returned to work around the camps;

their former fitness levels returned. A work ethic was instilled throughout the community with everybody engaged to re-build their lives. The two elders who had entrusted Ocillo presided over the building work providing guidance and support.

News of their encounters with the evil spirit spread throughout the jungle. Their miracles and cures became flerdlore, but mostly it was the encounter with the Teragorm. Flerds came from far away to seek their advice or look for healing. Some came in awe of them and just wanted to touch them, believing it would connect them with their ancestors who would show them the way. Others simply wanted to hear the stories about the Teragorm, the Condor Shaman and their rebirth by the tree of life.

Shap remained alone. Villages either had a shaman already or had heard of his reputation and the conflict with the pale, spiritual twins. It had taken him a long time to recover from his injuries. His arm was now permanently bent where it had broken and he no longer had the strength in it that he used to. He never stayed in one place too long, preferring to keep moving. This, he believed, would minimise his footprint on the land and reduce the chance of anybody finding him. In particular, he was in no rush to meet up with the Teragorm but he was very keen to meet the freaky twins. They had destroyed his easy life, exiling him to a solitary existence. They had made him look an incompetent fool.

He cursed them and spent his days and nights plotting their removal and his resurrection.

A small, rocky escarpment poked up above the canopy on a sharp bend of the Rio Fly. Surrounded on three sides by swirling, white-tipped water flowing rapidly through the narrow ravine, it stood naked, high and proud above the green, fertile background. The forty-metre drop towards the river was denuded of trees. Its bare, rocky scars showed its hostility towards the Elements with constant mud slides. A long, narrow strip of heavily congested trees, rocks and thick scrub provided the only means of access. Shap had cut a small, meandering track up the arduous, steep slope to the summit. He had built a sturdy timber hut hidden between two large rocks; he felt secure there. A new moon peeped above the tree line, cracking a slender, white arc in the blue-black sky. "The beginning of a new dawning," he thought purposefully to himself. He stirred his yoppa powder in a slow, meditative way next to a smouldering fire.

A thin-cut moon travelled across the tree-strewn horizon as his hallucinations travelled across the ancestor-strewn universe. Animals danced with his soul, pulling and tugging him every which way until, confused and exhausted, he burst a waterfall of frustrated tears. The Condor Shaman mirrored his imagination. He swooped down and carefully placed him onto his back. They swept past countless galaxies until they reached the centre of the universe. There to greet him was the ultimate god of creation: Viracocha. Shap could not see his face but only a silhouette of a dark profile surrounded by blinding, multi-coloured lights. His form constantly changed from flerd, to earthly animals, to mythical beasts, then finally an outline of a small tree emerged. Slowly, it began to grow, getting taller and thicker, its branches sweeping across the universe. Cucura-shaped galaxies hung from it like succulent fruits. Radiant rays of exploding light spasmodically torpedoed out of its branches towards the distant reaches of the universe. Its roots spread out, twisting and turning like demented snakes with their tails on fire. They wrapped themselves around Shap, coiling and writhing, they crushed his lungs. The roots constricted tighter, strangling, asphyxiating him until they sucked out the air and his life from his crumpled body. He raised his spear to beat them back but then weakened as fear and terror crippled his muscles and bones. Tears poured down his contorted, confused, crucified face as he finally exhaled his last dying cry, "Why?"

Inti was burning into Shap's prostrate, naked body when he regained consciousness. The sun was high and its scorching power had blistered his skin into red, suppurating sores. His head throbbed with pain and the intense light blinded him into a sightless darkness. He scrambled around, scratching at the Mother Earth for something recognisable before crawling into the hot remains of last night's fire. He screamed out loud, his reflexes shot him away; rolling onto his back he hugged his hand and knees. Whimpering in pain he lay there sobbing.

The trip disturbed him. "What did it mean? Nobody gets to see Viracocha. No mortal dare even say His name. Yet," he paused to shuffle his burnt frame into a more comfortable position, "yet, the Condor Shaman took me to meet Him. Only the sons of Viracocha meet Him. Am I His son? Am I His chosen flerd? A demigod on Pachamama to lead the flerds to their enlightened path?"

He paused again as he moved position to relieve some burnt spots and allow other burnt spots to take the strain. "Then there's the tree. What's that about? Why is He a tree? Are all trees the essence of Viracocha? Then He tried to kill me. What have I done to deserve that? I am His simple disciple. I am His only true follower of the ancient traditions. The traditions passed down through generations of our forefathers. I have offered sacrifices and followed His ways to the word. Why kill me?"

He sat in the shade of his shelter, shuffling occasionally, musing over Viracocha's message. "That is it," he shouted aloud, leaping to his feet, "I am His appointed emperor, descended from His son Inti, to lead these flerds. He made me feel His pain so that I understood the message. I must lead His flerds to Him." With that revelation Shap walked into the cooler forest to find herbs and sap to embrocate his burnt body.

Although young, Ocillo had been brought into the circle of the elders. It was a controversial move as elders were always male, but her two comrades upheld their beliefs and argued on her behalf against all objections. The biggest objection was that she was female and tradition never had females as elders.

During a heated and confrontational meeting the two elders finally said, "She is the mother of Chil and Chel. You have accepted them as shamans – not just the first females to be shamans but also the first time to have two shamans. You have accepted them for their achievements and foregone tradition. The precedent is already set. Ocillo, their mother, has raised them, giving birth to them twice. She is wiser than us all put together and she is connected to Chil and Chel. Was it not her alone that confronted the idiot Shap? Was she not correct? She will benefit us all with her wisdom." There was no argument returned against these points and Ocillo was unanimously, if not a little uneasily, appointed an elder.

On the junction of the two rivers the Fly Indians prospered under Ocillo's prudent and practical guidance. Trade increased dramatically between the land-based Indians and the water traders. Beads, berries, fruit, hides, teeth, claws, herbs, medicines and baskets were exchanged for fish, vegetables, alpaca wool, tools, yarns and clothing from tribes spread far away along the river. Everybody benefited from this budding, bartering economy.

Chil and Chel provided spiritual support and medicines for villages across the whole river basin. Flerds from far away would spend days travelling with sick friends and relatives for their healing and guidance.

Such was their reputation and providence that many shamans were outcast. Disgruntled elders and headstrong young males were not benevolent towards females instructing them, especially two very young flerds that looked alien to their kind. Fear of their power and the influence that the pale ones were able to manifest across the forest sat uneasily with some. Alone or in small groups they trickled away from the villages. They walked the old hunting trails, never staying long in one place. They inadvertently migrated towards the more isolated parts of the forest and mountains. Many died from illnesses, poisonous bites and attacks by larger animals. Some, though, joined together to form small outcast groups and set up new communities.

Chil and Chel challenged traditions. Slowly they began to show how living with their fellow animals was better than killing them. They taught the practices they had learnt while in exile, that by living off easily sustainable foods like vegetables, fruit, crayfish, shrimps, eels, catfish and insects, you did not have to kill the animals that shared your forest. The flerds in their village took time to understand this, but as they were low on hunters it was a practical solution to their short term needs. Gradually, the previously hunted creatures lost their fear of flerds and began to walk through the village, taking no notice of the inhabitants' activities. Flerds were considered no different to any other peaceable creature. Chil and Chel taught about the importance of conservation and showed how it helped everybody involved.

This, too, benefited the flerds. They felt more connected with Pachamama and took enjoyment from being close to the animals. It gave them a feeling of peace by living in a much bigger community than a single species can.

Word gradually spread throughout the forest of this new way of living. Visitors enjoyed sitting next to slumbering tapirs or watching parrots land on their shoulders to take wild almonds from them. The village became a model of enlightened living. The songs from Ruminant Whale suddenly made sense and all would stop and listen to her whenever she sang. A feeling of serenity pervaded the village and all who visited. Slowly, other villages along the river adopted this model and animal life flourished and migrated throughout the forest.

Not everybody was happy. Many arguments developed between traditionalists and the embryonic native conservationists as they adopted this new way of thinking. It made many feel better, but some of the young hunters wanted to hunt. It was what male flerds did and besides, what else could they do? Fishing and picking flowers was for children and females. Males hunted; it was their destiny. The elders were resolute in following Chil's and Chel's methods, so the uncompromising, young hunters began to leave in favour of wandering the hunting trails in small, nomadic groups.

Shap was a magnet for these lost, meandering hunters. In ones and twos they joined him in his lofty camp until it gradually became too big for the escarpment. Shap did not really want to leave. He still felt safe up there, but now he had many strong hunters around him he knew he had to move on. A plateau was found further downstream. Some large trees were removed to make room to shelter everybody and Shap was careful with which ones they took down. He remembered, all too vividly, his meeting with Viracocha and was certainly keen not to offend him. Only some of the very old or weak trees were removed. This, Shap hoped, would appease the Mighty Creator.

Some young females found their way into camp, attracted by the large number of virile, strong males. They admired the finely tuned skill of the hunters and liked the taste of roasted monkeys, jungle chicken, coatis and anteaters.

The females were very popular and Shap could see that this could become troublesome amongst the group. He encouraged the females to grow corn and brew chicha, a strong alcoholic drink. Each night he would bond with the hunters around fires by drinking chicha and snuffing yoppa. The hunters soon became intoxicated from the deadly mixture and danced around the warm fires with the spirits of their souls before crashing into Pachamama where they lay until daybreak. Shap kept them in these induced states of exhausted highs to stop them thinking too much.

The nearby forest was quickly depleted of its fauna. The hunters travelled further afield to keep the burgeoning camp in food, sometimes spending many days travelling. Often they returned with nothing. A meeting was held and they decided to move. Shap followed the river down to where a small island had been created by an anabranch from the main river. They removed many trees again but this time Shap paid no attention to discretion as all the land was needed.

The administration of the group was becoming a tiresome, endless burden. Quarrels were common and maintaining a food supply became a daily chore. He found himself spending all his time as arbitrator, doctor, counsellor and leader.

After everybody had gone to bed, or passed out, he sat on a log watching the low flames dance above the orange embers of the dying fire. "It was not meant to be like this. I am their emperor not their public servant. I wish I was back on my rock. Life was simple there, it was peaceful, but Viracocha wanted me to lead them towards His light. Now I'm fixing their every problem. Things must change." He pontificated into the night, working through his options until he came up with a plan. He went to bed promising himself, "We start first thing in the morning."

It was not long before light came. Shap was already up and walking meaningfully around the camp. He woke some of the older hunters that had a little more intelligence than the others and took them for a short walk along the river. Sitting on some washed-up, bleached tree trunks embedded into the sandy banks, he outlined his plan. Well, he outlined a part of the plan.

"The great God Viracocha has chosen you to become the tribe's wisdom by becoming the elders. You will make the decisions when dealing with the others. I will provide your spiritual connection to Viracocha so that we walk along His path. I hear that there is an abundant supply of food to the east of here way down the river. We will build canoes and set up our new village further downstream."

"But, shaman," protested one, "that will take us into Ocillo's part of the forest. She does not allow any hunting."

Shap's temper began to flare but he shut it inside him and aggressively said, "I am emperor of all the flerds! I was appointed directly by Viracocha Himself. I determine who hunts and who doesn't. Do not tell me what I can and cannot do. Do you understand? Or I will make an example of you."

Nobody said any more and they returned to the camp to prepare the canoes for the journey east.

Ocillo came up to the twins as she did every day. "You look worried, mother, what is on your mind?" Chil was always straight to the point, ignoring any formalities. She did not find the need to say much but when she did, she did not waste her words.

"I have not said anything yet, Chil. What makes you think there is something on my mind?"

"I saw your aura one hundred metres away. It is weak and dim. You are clearly concerned over something."

Ocillo did not waste any more time arguing with her daughters, she always lost. "It is Shap, Chil. Some of the traders have told me that he is coming to build a camp near us. The hunters will kill all the animals, destroy the trust we have built with them and we will be back to where we started. I do not trust Shap. He is evil and ambitious. He will kill us if he has to."

"We know, mother," replied Chel. "We have been visiting Wee Tree. The Condor Shaman lives there. He has shown us."

Ocillo paused for thought. She was confused by how lightly they were taking it after everybody's effort and was perturbed that they had not thought to tell her of something this catastrophically important. "Sometimes," she thought, "I do not think they are mine. They are in another world." Resigned to continual exacerbation she sighed, "Were you going to tell me at all or just wait until he walked into the village and destroyed all that we have accomplished?"

The twins stood tree-still with enormous, broad smiles spread across their radiant faces, looking at their exacerbated mother with love pouring from their hearts. Ocillo dropped her pained expression and smiled with a resigned look and when she was sure they were not going to reply she said, "Let me guess, the spirits will guide us." Without waiting for an answer she turned around and walked briskly back to get on with her daily business.

Ocillo was long gone before Chel turned to her split second older sister and said, "What are we going to do, Chil? He will kill mother."

"He will kill us too, Chel." Chil bluntly replied without looking at her.

Chapter XVII

Shap's canoes were built from the tallest, straightest kapok trees. They were strong and light and could carry up to eight flerds with room for luggage. The scouts had found a suitable camp site on the periphery of Ocillo's area. The land was stripped of trees and bush on Shap's instructions. The hunters spent many days building shelters for all of his followers.

Shap left his elders to organise the removal of the village. He set off on a pilgrimage to his old escarpment. All the huts were still standing when he arrived and he went straight to his original between the two rocks. After lighting a fire he settled down to wait for nightfall. The stars emerged, shyly at first, but as they became more confident they spread across the whole night sky as an iridescent, flickering blanket. Shap rocked on his haunches as the yoppa infiltrated through the veins to settle conflictingly between his consciousness and subconscious.

The starlit sky slowly began to vibrate. Animals and insects crawled amongst the pinhole lights, pushing and shoving them out of the way. Spirit toads began infiltrating from the edges, devouring all the insects and animals until the whole sky was covered in jumping toads. They dropped towards the forest, swimming around his head and leaping on his feet. Shap swam with them, in between them and around them. Still more came. The skies and Mother Earth became so thick with crashing toads that it was impossible not to collide with them and just when he thought he would be crushed, they all disappeared.

A large tarantula walked over the Huaca River as if it was its guiding path. It used the countless stars as stepping stones to march across the spangled sky. It stepped off the bright stones and dropped to the earth. On landing it stopped and looked up at Shap. Another came and did the same. They stood motionless, looking at him. Soon thousands were dropping off the star-crusted highway to stand frigid and still, looking Shap right in his eyes. Frozen through fear, Shap could not move. The earth had wrapped a tangle of roots around his feet. On an unheard signal the tarantulas all moved simultaneously, seductively towards him, never taking their eyes from him. No sound came from his mouth as he screamed in morbid terror to be saved. They loomed above, their mandibles clicking with delight, then their forms dissolved into falling rain. The rain thickened, battering the earth in torrents as it stung his eyes and cheeks with the ferocity of angry, swarming bees. He felt water lapping against his ankles so he pulled on his feet but the Mother Earth kept hold of her tenacious grip anchoring his sapling legs in the rooted ground. The water rose past his knees up to his chest and splashed against his neck. He stretched tall, looking straight up towards the twinkling stars. It continued rising. When it touched the lobes of his ears Shap found his voice and screamed for the Condor Shaman to save him. The rains stopped. Shap stood, tall, still, so still for fear that if he moved the water would run over his mouth, through his nose and drown him vertically.

With nowhere to look but the stars he saw pirañas floating down. They dropped in their millions. Cascading from the sky in wave after wave, flashing brightly coloured under bellies of vivid reds, yellows and greens. Millions upon millions dropped into the water. Their splashes echoed around Shap's flooded ears as they dived towards him in frenzied, savage shoals. The waters boiled from their delirious excitement. The skies emptied and the stars returned; for a brief moment the waters went calm and the splashing noises subdued. The silence was absolute. Shap thought that perhaps they had gone and waited for the next spirit animals to arrive, hopefully in the shape of a condor. Suddenly the water around began to boil and bubble. The pirañas tore into his body, ripping out chunks of raw, bloody flesh, their teeth grating against his stripped bones. The pain paralysed his disintegrating body as the frothing mass of frantic fish pulled him down into their dark, wet, deathly world.

Shap awoke in a cold sweat but hot, very hot. Inti was high and he had begun to cook on top of the baking escarpment. Drenched in his own fluids he crawled into his shelter. His head thumped and his body ached as the toxins from the previous night began to flow through his veins with the sole intention of poisoning his muscles and joints. He collapsed, panting on his bed while Inti cooked the rest of his life from him.

It took several hours to stagger down the track to the river far below. He stumbled over rocks, wobbling into thick brush, taking wrong turns, becoming disorientated amongst the strange trees and collapsing through dehydration. Reaching the limits of his endurance he reached the river bank and slipped into its cool, reviving waters in a sheltered eddy behind a large, smooth rock. Holding his head in fear that it would fall, he lowered it under the water. The salubrious, cool waters washed away his fears, the pain and the intolerable, throbbing war drums pounding his brain. He pulled himself up and drank until his belly, filled and bloated, could hold no more. Perched on a rock under the shade of a small bush, he paddled his feet in the placid water and his mind flapped flaccid thoughts into last night's events.

"The spirits are playing with me," he thought. "What did they mean? Toads – mean long life and changing luck or is it hidden poison? Poison for whom, me or others? And the tarantulas, what of them? Their ability to shed their skins and transform their creations, or to spin a web to entrap my enemies? Then there were those fearful pirañas. I nearly died! They are symbols of

248

savagery to tear apart my enemies but also a service to all life in the river. What are they telling me and where was the Condor Shaman? I needed him."

Shap splashed the water with his feet as he used to do as a child. The sensation brought back happy, carefree memories of when his parents were still alive. In the sparkling splashes that sprayed coolly up his calves and disrupted the placid, flowing surface, he saw their smiling faces. When he stopped kicking, the splashes washed down the river and their faces dissolved – to be replaced by his reflection. He looked old and tired. He kicked the water with angry ferocity. His face disappeared. It pleased him. Slowly, unwelcomely, another face shimmered through the glittering drops. It gradually built up amongst the cascading water until it beamed back at him in its full, unambiguous entirety. It was the Condor Shaman. "Remember the principle of duality," he said, simply. "Do not forget."

Before Shap could reply, the face broke into thousands of tiny water droplets, each with a disintegrating face of the Condor Shaman, then vanished into the welcoming river. Again he kicked the water with frustrated rage and when he stopped his weary, washed-out features looked blankly back.

"Duality?" He murmured to himself. "Black, white. Good, bad. Day, night. What is he babbling on about? It is the animal spirits I need to know about. What do they mean? Not the principles of life." He paused, looking deeper into his own image. The spirit animals flashed through his rattled mind.

Suddenly it all came together. "Hidden poison, entrapment and savagery! That's what he's on about: the duality of life. We have been living in peace and cohabitation. That's not the way forward. Now I understand." Rejuvenated, fresh energy flowed through him with this revelation. He marched back to the river village.

The forest around the new camp was inundated with animals. The hunters were returning every day loaded with animal carcasses. Nobody could ever remember it being so prolific. Nothing went to waste. The meat was cooked or dried and the pelts prepared for blankets or coats. Shap had two jaguar skins made into ornamental robes fitting his position as the future emperor.

Laws were passed making it illegal for anybody to wear a jaguar skin without his authority. Only emperors could wear a jaguar skin, but he did not tell anybody this. Other tax laws followed. Everybody living in Fly Forest was obliged to pay Shap directly a proportion of their trade in gold. In return he would protect them from invaders.

Hunters were sent out in their large canoes to all the villages along the river. Many of the elders were bribed with fine pelts, bracelets and necklaces of teeth, claws, gold and crystal figures. Banquets were held in their honour and pipes were shared around the yoppa bowls. The elders became part of the Fly brotherhood. Fly images were tattooed down their necks and across their chests to show the world that they had been selected and respected. All were sworn to recognise Shap as their emperor and Shap made sure they profited by it.

His name and reputation spread along the river and far beyond. His power increased, backed up by his loyal, hunter henchmen. Only Ocillo held out. Shap left her alone and isolated. Gradually he killed all the game around her territory and threatened anybody who contacted her, strangling her trade. He had plans for Ocillo and left her until the end.

With more wealth coming into his possession than he could ever have imagined, he built a temple to Viracocha. He constructed a large tower from a combination of rocks and timbers that soared higher than anything in the forest. Only Fly Mountain, far to the west, was taller. On its pinnacle he placed a large crystal skull fixed on top of an ornately carved pole from a kapok tree. His foundations were ready to appease the gods, to show to Viracocha that he lived by the principle of duality and followed His teachings as given to him by the spirit animals. A sacrifice was all that was required and he had three in mind.

His hunters stormed Ocillo's village at the darkest period of the night. They found Ocillo sleeping. Binding her hands and feet together over a stout stake they carried her back like a captured animal. She remained bound to a stake in a remote hut away from the village. Two hunters guarded her day and night.

Shap was furious when they returned without the twins. He roared at the hunters, "Why do you insult me like this? I ordered you to bring me all three. I get one. Why did you disobey me?"

Nobody was keen to speak for they could see he was about to explode as would a violent volcano. One, unable to look directly at him, reverently spoke, "They were not there, Emperor. We searched every hut. There was no sign of them."

Shap glared, spitting back at them, "Search again and do not return until you find them."

Shap interrogated Ocillo for many days but knew that she would die rather than tell him. He waited weeks for the hunters to return and when they did they had no news of the twins. Raising his crystal-topped stave, he swung it down, striking the hunter that told him. He stormed off to Ocillo.

He remembered the tarantulas' message from his trip: spin a web to entrap your enemies. "Your daughters evade my best hunters. I will sacrifice you, then they will come to your rescue. I will have the pleasure of slitting all your throats for the creator Viracocha. I will then be crowned Emperor of Fly Forest. Do you like my plan, Ocillo?"

Ocillo cast her eyes briefly in his direction, "You are mad," then returned her gaze to the floor.

When Shap announced his plans to the people of his empire not everybody was happy. Ocillo and her daughters were still deeply loved by many. The thought of human sacrifices was abhorrent. Rituals of this kind had not been performed for centuries, but Shap had Ocillo too heavily guarded for anybody to consider a rescue. The land was controlled through fear and violence. Many had preferred the ways of love, compassion and acceptance as practised by the twins and Ocillo. Life was happier when living peacefully.

Chil and Chel had made camp by Wee Tree. Although hunters had looked for them they had raised their energy levels and masked themselves with Tree's elevated energy. The hunters did not see them. They followed the hunters to their camps where they listened in to their conversations. It did not take long to find out what was happening. They returned to Tree and called the Condor Shaman.

He swooped down and picked them up. Taking them through the galaxies he took them back to Pachamama. They saw Shap sat on an escarpment calling the spirits but it was not the spirits that came. They saw the toads, tarantulas and frenzied pirañas. They saw him drowning in his own tears; the animals were demons but Shap had not realised this. They had infested his soul.

The Condor Shaman took them on to the future. There they saw their mother strapped to one of three poles. Shap was dressed as a jaguar with a condor's head. His fingers had grown into long, razor sharp talons. The condor flew on, taking them high above Fly Mountain. He circled slowly in the rising thermals. Below lay Teragorm, bloated and in agony, guarded by the mountain goats. He flew off into the sun.

Chil and Chel stood facing Tree. They could no longer spread their arms around him and touch each other, so they stood with their hands spread wide against his rough bark. All three effervesced energy. They used each other's energy to magnify their own, which they fed back into the Mother Earth, each growing in power and wisdom until they could no longer hold their combined energy and it burst from tree as an exploding star. All three connected with the Elements, the animals, the trees and the ancestors.

Whale felt their power and sang to them. She told them about the misuse of power. How empires had collapsed. How greed and consumption had destroyed all who valued it. She showed them that there was a path where all could survive in mutual respect, that enlightenment was the only weapon they needed – enlightenment and compassion.

Tree did not quite understand all of that and was about to ask Ruminant but felt that perhaps this was not the best time. He had a feeling something important was going to happen and did not want to be held responsible for distracting their energies. He spoke to Pachamama, "Greed, empires and destruction, what's all that about?"

Pachamama shuddered. It would take her a fortnight to explain all of that and she had a couple of earthquakes to manufacture, "It's complex Tree. Essentially, if nobody listens to Whale's songs then history has shown that the world changes and readjusts and not necessarily for the best for all that dwell on it. Watch and see, you will learn something here. Now, I'm getting the shakes, I must go."

Tree thought that a bit glib; how can a world collapse? "Pachamama is the world. She's enormous. She is the mother." But she had gone before Tree could collect his thoughts together. "Oh well, let's see what happens then. These flerds feel so good, there's so much energy about them. I wonder what they're all on!"

255

Decorated in his finest skins and feathers, Shap strutted around his hut. It was the day of the great ceremony. The day they would offer their first flerd blood to Viracocha for centuries. It would be the day he would be enshrined to immortality as the Son of Inti, chosen by Viracocha Himself. Shap thought to himself, "Today I will become a deity."

Despite all the preparations, he was disappointed Chil and Chel could not be found. His plans to ensnare them had not been fulfilled, they had not turned up. He was preparing himself for the great day for the spirits. He wore the skins of jaguars that he personally had killed. Although the hunters had trapped the beasts, it was he who had plunged his spear up between their front legs so it did not mark the skin. He had felt the life from the angry beasts drain in an instant as his spear split open their hearts and their spirit melted on the ground before him. Power flooded through him as the big cats' life's blood ebbed into the earth. He felt good. He placed the large, black, condor-feathered head dress onto his head, fixing it securely with leather straps made from the soft underbelly of a cayman. Laced with bracelets and necklaces of feathers, teeth and claws from the largest predators of the sky and land, his body emanated the power that was symbolic of the land and universe. The final decorations of crystal skulls and sacred stones exuded the power that was his dominance. Two gloves had been made from the front feet of a giant anteater and were strapped to his hands. The claws had been meticulously shaped and sharpened into razor-edged knives capable of slicing deep gashes through warm skin and muscles with a single swipe. He allowed himself some self-adulation as he rehearsed how he would rip open Ocillo's throat and collect the blood for the offering. He secretly hoped, "Perhaps they will come to rescue their mother while she is strapped to the altar, then my guards can easily take them. Viracocha will be pleased with me to offer three of the same blood and two so pure. Will they be so brave and stupid? Perhaps so, they will not abandon their mother or their journey will have been a futile one." A thin smile spread across his face, but not so broad for it to crack his face paint.

Every Indian in the forest had arrived. Most were in fear that if they did not they would be punished. Shap's heavily armed guards were everywhere. Each village's elders and dignitaries had been given seats on elevated platforms around the square. From there they would get an unobstructed view of the ceremony. Afterwards a huge dinner would be prepared. Gifts would be exchanged and Shap would ensure he had their undisputed acceptance as Emperor of the Fly Flerds.

Towards one end of the square rose Shap's mighty tower. Three hundred and sixty five steps led to the top; one for each day of the solar year. Shap walked alone when he left his hut. The outskirts of the village were deserted. Guards lined his route to ensure his safety. The small path widened as he approached the centre of the village. Crowds were packed around the central square but the guards held them back to allow Shap unobstructed access to the tower.

The busy murmurings of the Fly Flerds stopped as Shap approached. A gasp rose in the stillness of the forest air as they witnessed for the first time their future Emperor. Dressed in his jaguar skins, feathers and sparkling crystals, he looked like the emperor he was about to become. The native Fly Indians had never witnessed such luxurious finery.

On each step of the tower two sentries, dressed in feathered head dresses and furs, stood tall and erect, each with a ceremonial drum. The crowd remained silent, even the forest was quiet as Shap approached the tower. This was his moment. His foot touched the first step and the silence exploded with all seven hundred and thirty drums beating together as one. With each step the sentries beat a single, synchronised strike that echoed with the power of malevolent thunder. Power that symbolised and reinforced Shap's strength. Slowly, this continued until he reached the top. The beats echoed around the square.

Shap gave a long, tedious speech about the rules of his empire, its future and its destiny. Any defamatory vociferations or vilifications of the gods, which incidentally included himself, would be met with death. It was meticulously punctuated with self-adoration and his visions of glorification and immortality. It continued all morning. The Fly Flerds stood in silent apathy. Towards the end children began to complain but were quickly castigated by their mothers.

Shortly before noon Shap stopped transmitting. He signalled to his guards to bring the sacrifice. Ocillo was dragged out of her hut and bound hand and foot to a stave again. Four guards marched her up the tower to the synchronised beats of the drummers. She was tied to the central, sacrificial pole. The crystal skulls caught the Laughing Sun and danced multi-coloured rays through the heavy midday air. Ocillo's heart was beating fast but she was not afraid. She would not let Shap see any emotion in her face, only contempt.

Shap did not look at her but stood facing the crowd. He was hot in his robes and tired. His long monologue had exhausted him. Disappointed that the twins had not arrived, he now wanted to finish the job and relax in the pools near his escarpment before the banquet later. He turned to face Ocillo but did not look her in the eyes. He could feel her loathing emanating towards him. It rallied him further. "This will be so satisfying," he thought to himself. He raised his massive claws to the sky, the bent arm lagging a bit below the other. The drums beat fast and furious. The crowd screamed in astonishment, then as suddenly as they started they stopped. The drums, too, stopped beating. There was complete silence. Shap was incensed that the drummers had stopped before he had killed her and turned wildly around to threaten each with lashings when he, too, stopped short as the crowd began to part.

Through the middle walked Chil and Chel. Dressed in pure white cloth, with their white hair flowing freely behind, they moved with tranquil assurance, with calm confidence, in no hurry. The crowd stared transfixed in astonishment at their beauty – simple and pure: ethereal spirits in flerd form. The twins looked at no one. Their faces were as emotionless and as pure as the radiant sun. They took each step of the tower with such nonchalant ease that it appeared they were floating above them. They glided to the top and faced an over-heating but exuberant Shap.

Shap was first to speak, "You are unarmed, so you have come to die with your mother. That is very noble. I knew you would come because I am too strong for you. I have seen Viracocha, He has guided me and you to me. I will send you to Him. He will be pleased with me for such an offering. I thought you would have made more of a fight than this. I was looking forward to showing the flerds how weak you are. How they have chosen the strongest ruler. A ruler embraced by the creator of all life: Viracocha. I am too powerful for you. Guards, strap them to the posts, tightly!"

Chil spoke to nobody in particular, "If you touch us, you will die a hideous and painful death." A gasp rose from the crowd and hung in the tense atmosphere.

Shap spoke back, equally composed, "If you do not touch them you will also die a hideous death."

Perplexed, the guards looked at each other. The conflicting instructions upset them. Whichever way they moved would result in a hideous death. They had seen Shap's vicious hand. But Chil and Chel they knew. They knew they were truly honest and caring. They would not crush an ant, it was not in them, so why would they say that?

For a moment nobody moved. Chil spoke, "Your Condor Shaman came to see us. What you saw on your escarpment was nothing but your alter ego. You had manifested yourself as your own divinity. You did not see the reflection of your soul, you saw an illusion. You saw power and ego. You saw yourself, nothing more. You saw the toads, spiders and pirañas for what you wanted to see. You saw them servicing your own needs. But we sent them, Shap, not the spirits, not the condor, we did. They were demons and you did not see that. The toad was poison. Not to us, Shap, but to you. The spiders were telling you of entrapment. You took that to mean us, but the message was to defend our land and that the environment would conceal and protect us. Why do you think your hunters couldn't find us? We were here all

261

the time. And those pirañas that nearly killed you Shap, were not about savagery. They were warning that they are protecting the river as are we. We are working together. Your ego was what you saw, now the demons have your soul."

Shap could not understand how they knew these things. Chel picked up from her sister, "We have not come bearing arms, Shap, because we are stronger without weapons. We can achieve more with trust and honesty. You are free to go."

A black, choking anger flooded through Shap. Incensed and boiling in rage he raised his claws to strike them both down dead and finish this nonsense before any further doubt was sown. The crowd below screamed again. It was fearful, terrified screaming. Shap, thrilled that he had made such an impact, animated his gestures to further entertain the expectant crowd. Panic spread through the crowd as they flooded the streets in all directions, like a torrential river that had burst its banks. Colliding, tripping and falling, they clamoured to get away from the tower.

The screaming was replaced by a stomach-churning roar. The tower began to shake. The roaring became louder and nearer. Mighty, timber beams could be heard splitting and splintering and the tower trembled to a beat from a monstrous pounding. All the guards sprinted down the shaking steps, dropping their drums and weapons as they fled. Shap looked frantically around but could see nothing. Chil and Chel stood there motionless, unconcerned, burning their azure eyes into Shap.

The vehement screams appeared to come from right under their feet. The timbers of the floor splintered into pieces. A large, scaly, clawed foot swung from underneath followed by a hissing, steaming, snorting Teragorm. She raised her head to the skies and bellowed an ear-piecing scream. Shap screamed, waving his claws above his head to protect himself. His knees buckled through fear. Teragorm lurched towards him and with one voracious snap of her jaw took off Shap's feathered head. Spitting out feathers, she roared again, lifting her head high to swallow the lot. When the vile, poisoned meat hit the pit of her belly she roared towards the Elements. The village was empty.

Chil and Chel remained unmoved and simply looked at the enormous beast. Ocillo, still tied to the stake, felt the calmness in her daughters and looked on in awe at the beast's incredible power and size. Teragorm continued roaring and shaking her head violently from side to side. When she realised that all had gone and there was nobody left to impress she stopped to look at the two thin, pale flerds. Slouching down onto her belly she lowered her head to rest it on the floor. Her two big, bulging eyes looked over her bloodied beak to see the flerds at their level.

Undisturbed, the twins walked across to the hot, snorting beast and laid their hands on her head. Teragorm closed her eyes and once again felt complete peace flood through her. She knew she would see the pale ones again and she knew she always would.

Chel, sitting on her thick, scaly, outstretched leg, whispered in her ear while Chil untied Ocillo, "You shouldn't have done that, Teragorm. What are we going to do with you? You must be the biggest, most brainless glob on the planet." Teragorm, oozed and soothed by her gentle words, melted under the midday sun in utter contentment.

Ocillo picked up the warmth between them and walked up to the brainless glob and kissed it on the nose. Reaching behind her back, from inside her sacrificial robe she retrieved a large condor feather. She tied it around Teragorm's neck with the twine that had shackled her.

Ocillo had returned to her village with the others. Shap's followers had dispersed back to their original groups. A rebuilding programme began based on Ocillo's original model. This time everybody backed it. Apprentice demigods had scared them. They saw the wisdom of living together with compassion and understanding.

Chil and Chel followed Teragorm back to her mountain. She showed them her secret, mountainous passage.

They climbed through steep crevices, across waterfalls, through underground caverns, before finally climbing a steep, rugged, rocky path to the summit. The twins scrambled out of the cool gloom into bright sunshine. There, another world opened up in front of them: a large, water-filled crater surrounded by tropical trees and plants. It was an unknown paradise.

Teragorm showed them her rock of amelioration. The girls sat on it holding each other's hand and each touched Teragorm's tough, ragged beak with the other. Teragorm relaxed into a soporific state. The Condor Shaman dropped from the circling thermals and swept them back into the cosmos. He travelled through the universe back to the purple planet they had visited many lives ago. Chil and Chel did not recognise it. They were standing on a precipice of a large mountain looking out over a huge, green, fertile forest. Trees and rivers covered the landscape. Macaws, howlers and cicadas could be heard far below. One monstrous tree far away was noticeable by its immense size. It poked out high above the canopy. Birds circled it, resembling a hazy swarm of spiralling bees. Behind them lay a large lake surrounded by trees. Herds of teragorms proliferated, half submerged in the cool waters to escape the burning sun.

Black jaguars floated above the trees and around the mountains. They walked up to them and roared into their faces then turned and ran towards the lake. The twins could feel the heat from their breath, the scent of their being, their power and their force, but they were not afraid.

The Condor Shaman turned to the twins. "It is for you to choose. Jaguar is the earth father. He moves without fear of darkness. He is the protector of the unknown. The primeval forces that feed the mountains, which emancipated their tectonic powers, is the same force that came from the black sun. The sun that shines upon the underworld. Jaguar is the warrior of destruction. His roar shows his mastery over the future – his alarm or defence. He has the gift of sight; forewarned is forearmed. Use your psychic sights, shift shapes and control chaos. You alone can cast light. It is for you to choose."

The big condor flew high above Fly Mountain until he became a small, black dot, then disappeared. Chil and Chel found themselves back with Teragorm, holding hands on the rock of amelioration. Chel looked down on the grit-ridden ground and scuffed the gravel and stones until she found what she was looking for. Dusting them clean she sat up, looking directly at her smiling sister. "This one is for you, Chil and I will have this." She handed her one of the gleaming white jaguar teeth. "You must wear it around your neck. It will guide you. It is the gift of sight."

Chil looked straight into Chel's eyes and said, with a hint of mischievousness, "You worry me, Chel. Are you the reincarnated Shap? Have you become a demigod too?"

The twins laughed.

Vivacious Wind leapt high during the night. Monocled Moon was nowhere to be seen so Wind crept up surreptitiously without anybody noticing. He blew in from the unpredictable south west carrying traces of Tempest Cloud's intent. When Inti flicked on his hazy, milky lights from under the horizon Vivacious was in full force. He dragged with him an earnest Tempest who had turned a shady black and had thickened, high and glum. He sang a whistling song towards the turning seasons.

Chapter XVIII

Shap was a terrible treat to eat. A lifetime of yoppa had flavoured his stringy flesh with an acrid toughness that bit into Teragorm's taste buds with the sharpness of chewing thorns. It came as no surprise to her that, when the streaky high lights emerged with the new dawn, she was doubly racked with pain across her favourite rock. How she howled.

Tree was used to each day starting with Teragorm wailing from her disagreeable, nutritional jaunts in the night. On this particular day her wails seemed more acutely penetrating and carried on far beyond the point where she would normally cease. When the cicadas hit full volume she had faded a little but her agony could still be felt. By mid morning she collapsed, exhausted, vowing never to eat a shaman again, even a sham shaman. She crept into the dark recesses of the mountain to sleep it off. The cicadas were left to compete between themselves.

Just as the forest was settling down again and Tree was drifting in and out of different levels of awareness, another noise wafted itself between the cicadas. It started slowly with the odd grumble then gradually picked up in intensity until it became a constant snarl all day. When the light began to fade, it stopped as quickly as the jungle did. Wee Tree thought that with its beefier, throatier, guttural growl, it was a larger, brawnier and bulkier version of Teragorm with possibly, worse dyspepsia. Tree had seen Teragorm through the eyes of Chil and Chel but struggled to imagine anything fiercer or larger. It growled all day. It was perpetual. He spoke to Pachamama. "You know Teragorm screams all morning until she collapses with exhaustion and the cicadas vibrate and whirl all day until Inti drops too low? Well, now I can hear something else growling and grumbling all day. Like Teragorm, it sounds very far away, so must be huge and angry. Does that have bellyache too? Can you hear it?"

Pachamama could. She knew what was making the noise. It was a long way off though, so she decided to keep her reply simple, "Yes Tree, I can and it is a long, long way away. That's why it sounds grumbly. Kilometres of forest have muffled and diffused the noise to sound like rough growls. It is only some flerds in one of their camps living along the edges of the forest."

"Oh no! It's not another feathery one with some wacky notion that he is an indestructible god?" Tree exclaimed, quickly adding, "Two pale, thin ones come to see me occasionally. They show me all these things. We have massive energy sessions together. I grow every time I meet them."

Tree was on a roll and Pachamama was impatient to get off before the conversation became awkward again. Tree continued before Pachamama could get in, "It's odd, I get a warm feeling from them. We have tremendous power sessions together. I feel nothing but positive energy when they are here. When Ruminant sings her stories of life past and her recent events, the flerds she meets make my trunk tremble. It's like different animals; confusing really!"

"Yes, it is a bit confusing. Nothing makes much sense when there is a flerd involved." In some ways Pachamama was relieved it was flerds making the din. With their reputation and ambiguous, unpredictable actions nobody expected anything of benefit from them. Most avoided them to be on the safe side. Pachamama was a bit concerned that Tree had befriended two of them and thought it best to offer a gentle warning given their erratic behaviour. "Now Tree, I know you have two flerd friends that appear a little odd and give you lots of energy, but do be careful. They're an erratic, fickle lot."

"Yes, I know Pachamama but I get such a warm feeling from these two. The others that Whale sings about, scare me. These two are more on a par with Tat and Three Toes, with the exception that they embrace me and make me grow. That's why it's confusing!"

Pachamama mumbled again to be careful and went off, concerned that Wee Tree, although prematurely colossal, was still very young at heart.

Teragorm was bloated from her dietary excesses of flerds. Fodder was abundant currently. She had no idea why, even the thought had not crossed her mind. She just carried on eating. It is what any Teragorm would do. Consequently, she was so full that she could not move and stayed slumped over her rock. After a few days it was a relief for her digestive system and her larynx when her gastric fluids stopped boiling. It was also a relief for every other living thing within earshot.

In her shrouded, mystical world, hidden in Tempest Cloud's high loft, she, too, could hear the monotonous, gravelly growling. The high, unobstructed mountain air was a good propagator of sound and the low-frequency noises echoed crisply against the naked rocks. Now the stabbing pains had gone she thought, "Perhaps tonight, another flerd, maybe two. What if there are more? The more, the happier the Teragorm." She trilled the thought around her mind in a continuous, happy ditty, forgetting the crippling cramps that Shap had inflicted upon her.

Tat and Three Toes were both active in stationary ways. Tree was watching both and decided that with Three Toes anything involving an eyelid or more was activity. With Tat it was more to do with what she was up to than what she was doing and what she was up to looked devious.

She had found a low-hanging branch and was herself low hanging from it on its underside. She was disguised as a moody shadow on Tree's underworld. It wasn't so much a hang as a spread-eagled grip secretly blending in with the dark shadows against the dusty brown and black markings of the tree's smooth bark. If Tree looked really carefully then eight, dark globes could be seen the wrong way up. Occasionally, a pair would twitch. The question was, what was Tat doing upside down? Normally, she'd be the other way around or hiding under something with all the eyes looking up.

Tat's brain could process proceedings in any orientation. Any of her eyes could spot a slither of a movement, the flick of an eyelash or the stretch of a claw. Once detected, her head would turn locking her main eyes on to the target giving a full, binocular image to her fast-processing brain. Hopefully, anything producing a blink or a scratch would come in the form of a plump jungle chick. It was Tat's view that by hiding from above she could spring an aerial attack whence they would least expect it.

It had been discouragingly quiet on the path below. She thought perhaps when dusk appeared, the shadows lengthened and the humid, warm air lifted, then her little path would become a motorway of entrapment.

The very thought made her pulsating heart jump at the exciting prospect of it all. She clung on for the rest of the day, giving each leg in turn a regular shake before the serious business started later.

From where Tree was rooted Tat looked like she was barking up the wrong one. The ground below had not much foliage for anything to scratch around in and it appeared a little open to a non-chicken-hunting tree. "However," Tree mused, "Tat is a masterful tactician and she is so cool." Full of intrigue, she had Tree's full attention although he kept a wistful eye on the slippery sloth.

A sweet scent of ripening cucuras had caught the soft air currents drifting idly high up the trees. A whiff had also nonchalantly wafted down to some split branches and right up Three Toes' highly attuned nostrils. Instantly opening both eyes, he rocketed into action. Releasing each of the three claws from his right front leg, he unhooked from the branch above. He had to move fast. It was his concern that the rest of the forest had also acquired this valuable piece of information. The cucuras were his, not that other lot of thieving reprobates'. From where his bed lay to the larder of cucuras was a full branch away. After some considerable deliberation he estimated that if he hot-trotted it now he could be there before nightfall. Given, too, that all those devious night creatures would also get a whiff of his larder then the best place to spend the night would be in the middle.

Without further thought, he set off at a blistering sloth speed. High in the trees Three Toes was moving.

Three Toes had made surprisingly fast progress and he was in the middle of his ripening larder of treasure before you could blink. Well, at least a sloth blink. With each stride the succulent, air-hung aroma, wafting gently into each nostril became stronger, beckoning him on. In a stupefied, intoxicating dream the rich, sweet fruits lured him into their sanctuary. Whichever direction he turned his head there were cucuras, big, fat juicy cucuras.

"It is a dilemma. The biggest, ripest one is towards the furthest extremity of this branch. To get to that I may knock off the nearest ones that are not quite ready, but if I wait until tomorrow so that I can eat my way towards it, then it might fall to the ground, or worse," a tremor of uneasiness vibrated across his consciousness, "it might get eaten in the night."

"This is serious business," thought Three Toes. "All these cucuras are likely to be ripe tomorrow and, as their caring, diligent guardian over the last few weeks then rightly they are mine." This, argued Three Toes to himself, was the crux of the matter. He did briefly consider the option of eating the lot now but that had serious bellyaching risks of acute discomfort. Also, it was getting dark. Although he had a stomach of iron from eating tonnes of ficus leaves all his life, he was reasonably certain that a couple of dozen, unripe cucuras would take the wind right out of him.

"However, the ripe ones will never make it to the morning as there are a load of unworthy, despicable, underhand, wretched, ignominious, scurrilous, shameful, robbing, winged and four-footed throwbacks in this forest. I need to get to reach that big, juicy one before nightfall without breaking off the others. It is a quandary."

Unfortunately for Three Toes he never had time to resolve his quandary. Green Iguana had, unbeknown to him, scurried up the trunk. Luckily for Three Toes, the iguana, in his eagerness to reach the forbidden fruit along a branch above him, knocked away a dead branch. There was an enormous crack, then a clattering clamour, as the branch smashed its way down through other branches and leaves before thundering into the soil with an earth-shuddering thump. Green Iguana sat on his branch completely unconcerned about the destruction of the tree. After all, branches fell off all the time underneath him. Iguana was also oblivious to a mortified and by now seething three toed sloth who was eyeing him with malicious intent.

Tree nearly jumped out of his roots. He was placidly watching Tat, wondering whether she had lost the plot and had completely forgotten about checking on Three Toes. On looking up, he saw that he was no longer there, but somehow throughout the day had absconded along the branch and was now hanging close to the middle. Not only that, but Green Iguana could be seen demolishing a cucura on the branch immediately above him.

Wee Tree briefly pondered on another of the forest's paradoxes, about green iguanas being brown, when the only thing green about him was to turn a placid, peaceful living sloth into a livid, green one. "You really do not want to do that," thought Tree to himself.

Three Toes dropped his grip from his front legs, then as his body dropped he used his momentum to swing up, pushing from his back legs to catch the branch above with one claw. The iguana, taken completely by surprise because he had thought that lump of mould below him was a pile of decaying moss, could not turn around quickly enough. The enormously, squashy cucura, which was half pinned to the branch with a big, scaly claw, was somewhat restricting him. The other half was disappearing into his cavernous, chomping mouth. It was not a good time to be besieged. Before he could swallow, a huge, hairy, freely flowing, front left leg of a sloth with three heavy, sharply pointed toes slapped squarely into his abdomen launching him into free space, still holding onto the cucura.

Astounded, Tree looked at Three Toes in a new light. Never, in all these years of watching, had he seen such rapid movement. Normally, to exert that much effort it would have taken him over a whole week to expend the energy into those powerful, ponderous tree-climbing limbs.

Now hanging with one arm attached to the branch above him, the other idly swinging languorously below and his two back legs stretched to the limit on the bottom branch, he had half a smile on his face. With casual ease he swung his back legs up, then hung upside down contemplating the righteousness of life's rich rewards. It was while in this hanging position of blinding inspiration that the most productive idea about how to save the rest of his stock arrived. When he thought about it, most of his blinding ideas swept into his slothful brain while hanging upside down and hanging upside down must be an exceptionally brainy way to live as all the blood flows from the legs straight into the head. He thought, "By definition then, I must be one of the most intelligent animals in the forest, if not the whole world. Subsequently then, those that stroll around on the ground must be quite dumb." He gave himself a self-congratulatory, imaginary pat on the back and was very thankful he was a sloth.

Without any further pontificating he set about his fine plan. Moving steadily along the branch he continued until he reached the first leaves. It was here that the branch started to bend downwards. Three Toes had anticipated this as he was one of those lucky, brainy, swinging, intellectual types as opposed to the towering, land-based, dim sort. Slowing down to a more sloth-like speed, so as not to damage any vacillating cucuras, he inched himself along. Each step bent the branch a little lower. At the point where he considered the branch to have reached a critical point with gravity, he released his right front and back legs and grabbed the branch below. Now with his weight distributed across two branches he carefully continued towards the ends of each branch ensuring that he did not trap any fruit along the way. "What a masterful sloth you are," he beamed inwardly at his cleverness and, looking up, there, too, was the sweetest cucura in the whole forest, just inches away. He leaned over to snap it up but as he did so his weight was distributed further out, lowering the branches even more and the whole world sagged a little further towards the ground; the cucura was no nearer. It didn't seem to matter where he moved, the whole world around moved with it, including the cucura. He moved ten centimetres, the cucura moved ten centimetres. "Interesting," he thought, "just an anteater's tongue away and happiness reigns. However, this is not the case." He went into a gently oscillating, meditative state. It did occur to him that he could be stuck in this softly fluctuating world for quite some time. Not that it was a hostile environment, it was just that he could not reach the cucura.

Something bit him on the left flank. Reacting impulsively he brought up his right arm and gave it a good whack followed by a soothing scratch. With each scratch his right leg twitched. The twitch rippled through his body to the branch below which then bobbed in harmony. This travelling energy reached the big, juicy, ripe fruit and it also started swinging. Three Toes kept this going. Eventually the fruit swung completely up and over the branch like a crazy spider monkey, then with one mighty swoop with his free arm Three Toes was the proud owner of the sweetest fruit on the tree.

Wee Tree branched out and applauded, "Three Toes always gets his cucura. Nothing gets past the slowest animal on earth. Imagine what he could achieve if he was the fastest." It was with this thought that Tree decided he had gone beyond the realms of tree imagination and with much admiration flowing through his sap, he returned to look for Tat again.

With night time in mind Three Toes returned to his original plan and aimed towards the middle of the branch. Continually slapping his lips with his tongue he tried to remove all the juices that had run down his jaws, across his neck and down his arm. He didn't care, all that remained was to get back into position for the night raiders then he could spend the whole day tomorrow deliciously cleaning up and not just himself.

Although it seemed a good idea, things didn't work out like that. All those succulent, fruity vapours must have travelled through half of Fly Forest, for in the next instant a screeching cacophony was heard over the canopy as eight garish, multi-coloured, raucous macaw parrots swept in uninvited. Tree sadly saw sloth sigh although it was impossible to confirm with the feathered rumpus and mighty din. This was not good news. It was an obstreperous landing with reds, blues and yellows flashing in all quarters. Three Toes didn't know where to look first; they were coming from all directions. It was an outrageous explosion of ostentatious colours, claws, beaks, flapping wings and squawking birds.

He was not going to take this hanging around. It was his larder and he was going to save it. Quite how, he had not worked out, but he knew macaws and he had about ten seconds before the lot would be gone. His body was in motion but it was going to take a lot longer than ten minutes to get anywhere. A kind of odious, sickening feeling developed somewhere between his head and his tail. He wasn't too sure where, but it appeared to be in his stomach. He was about to give the nearest macaw a bit of slothsome advice when suddenly they all shot into the air and landed on the other side of the clearing.

Sloth preened his fur. "Formidable or what?" he thought. "Nobody fools around with the mighty sloth. The slightest movement and the fearful flee. My indomitable reputation spreads far afield." It was at this point of Three Toes' ruminations that the first of the howler monkeys swung into sight. Normally, you could hear them several kilometres away. Within the fracas he had missed them sneaking across the treetops. Before he could mop the scowl off his face the rest of the family dropped in. "This is going from bad to worse. A whole group of howlers! Now what am I going to do?"

In the absence of any inspiration he decided that the best thing to do was nothing. Well, not quite nothing. This was now a case of damage limitation. After a hasty climb towards the middle of the branch, he hung by his back two legs to protect some of his valuable cucuras. Being an upside down kind of creature had huge advantages over lesser-brained, upright versions. One being that he had, for his size, exceptionally long arms and legs. Additionally, on the ends of these were three formidably strong and sharp claws. Not only could he give a sharp tap to a cranium on anything within tapping distance but by physically blocking access to the cucuras he could be sure to offer any miscreant with bad intent a sharp rebuke.

For a while there was deadlock. The howlers had not come across an aggressive sloth before. Sloths are known for their pleasant, placid affability and their peculiar and unchallenged appetite for indigestible ficus leaves. They all seemed to smell a bit, which was another good reason for leaving them alone. Here though, was a sloth behaving very aggressively to protect a bunch of cucuras that they normally would turn up their noses at. This display of abnormal behaviour had put the howlers on the defensive and for a while both sides just looked and stared, which was good for Three Toes because the longer they stretched out the daylight, the sooner they would have to go away to make their beds for the night. "Preferably, far away," he thought.

As was normal when living in a rainforest, nothing remains the same for long. Instantaneously, all the howlers jumped to their legs and started howling like demented banshees. Three Toes nearly lost his grip, then his senses; his ears rang. It was only his back leg that stopped him falling down. Even Tat's eyes nearly rolled out of their sockets. At first he thought it was an attack and hostilities had begun, but the monkeys remained where they were and kept leaping up and down still howling like, well, like monkeys.

Perplexed, Three Toes kept his eyes on the suspicious howlers. The howlers kept their eyes on the four ocelots that had just arrived at the base of the tree. The ocelots looked up at the howlers to see what was making that unearthly din. They instantaneously all thought the same: dinner! Tat screwed her eyes back into their sockets to look only for jungle chicks. Tree watched everything with engaged interest.

Ocelots do not normally attack sloths. Partly because of their size and weaponry but more so because they do not smell that good. Ocelots prefer their food fresh, not mostly decomposed. Now, a howler monkey, that was another matter. Three Toes was not too worried about the cats. They did not eat fruit and he was not averse to giving one a firm clout if it became too inquisitive. He kept the howlers under strict scrutiny.

The howlers had now lost all interest in stealing Three Toes' cucuras. All attention was on the ocelots and when one started to climb the tree pandemonium broke out. Uproar ensued. All the monkeys leapt into action by swinging around from branch to branch, howling and screeching at full volume; teeth were flashing and arms and fists waving frantically. The ocelot seemed impervious to all this and continued steadily up the trunk as if it was a casual walk along the ground. His three mates had all sat down at various positions around the tree, looking upwards with optimistic delight.

Undeterred by the showmanship of the antics above, the ocelot continued steadily upwards. When he reached the branch that Three Toes was occupying he turned an inquisitive look towards him. Being a hospitable creature, Three Toes smiled back. The ocelot ignored him and continued up. The howlers hit fever pitch. The whole tree seemed to vibrate with their jumping, skipping, prancing dances. Before anybody could stick their claws into their ears, they disappeared across the forest's swinging canopy. The wails and screams diminished slowly into the distance. After a freshen-up and a bit of a scratch on an adjacent branch, Ocelot returned to the others. They all strolled off into the dark depths of the forest as if nothing had happened.

Tree could not believe what he had just witnessed – three attacks in one afternoon and Three Toes the undisputed victor. He had beaten all those fast-footed, moving, flying, swinging animals by hardly moving. Three Toes was clearly a tactical genius and indomitable warrior. Wee Tree thought, "Perhaps it is all that hanging upside down!"

"At last," thought Tat, "that cacophony above has finished and night has arrived. Maybe we can get along with something a little more interesting than hanging about this place listening to a bunch of over-excited, swinging tree dwellers." She was also pleased that Monocled Moon was not out tonight. That would make her clandestine activities much easier.

She didn't have long to wait. Her eyes quickly adjusted to the dark and scanned the highway below with an ease as if it were broad daylight. Only, now, she had the advantage of complete invisibility. The thought made her heart bounce up and down a few beats faster as images of gullible chicks came running into her mind. She was contemplating such a delicious, edible outcome when a pair of eyes picked up a small movement toward the edge of the path. Tat's heart stopped completely.

Fortunately it started again. She focused her main eyes firmly on a small clump of grass. Every so often, a blade would twitch or tremble as if a shiver had run up its spine, then another, then it would stop. After a short pause another piece would tremble. It might continue or it might stop. One could not tell. This continued for a considerable length of time.

Tat was beginning to lose patience. It was also a little too far for an aerial attack. Whatever it was would have to reveal itself and take a short walk to admire her tree before she could pounce. "Still, there is nothing more happening so I might as well just sit here and will it to happen." She willed very hard indeed. It must have worked, too, because from the other direction strutted the Banded Anteater. Tat's heart dropped, "This will blow it," she thought. She was right. Whatever it was lurking under the clump disappeared when it felt the earthy vibrations of a nonchalantly, happy go lucky anteater sauntering past.

Three Toes had comfortably settled himself between the two branches. They swayed up and down a little but he felt the effects were generally in a soothing motion as opposed to a catastrophic one. He was not particularly in a mood to reflect on the day even though he had come out of it rather well. His mind was focused on tomorrow's exuberant bonanza in juicy city. It was almost mouth-wateringly too long to wait. Wait, though, he must, for he knew the fruits were not quite at their peak of lusciousness. He relaxed towards what he hoped would be a quiet night. And it was quiet for a while. The diurnal animals settled into their newly made beds and the nocturnal ones were tasting the air for food or danger.

A band of white-nosed coatis were on the rampage. They had been scavenging around the undergrowth for some time. With the dying light they began climbing the trees. This was partly to stay out of the way of Jaguar and partly to find more tasty food. It was then that they detected a delicious aroma emanating from a fortuitously near cucura. Climbing along the roof top branches with nothing more than a delicate rustle from a brushed leaf or two they homed in towards the succulent fruit. Unbeknown to them was an expectant, camouflaged, warmongering sloth. They, too, became confused by the mixture of sweet and rotting odours strongly emanating from the tree. Their confusion was compounded by surprise and fear when a hairy collection of sticks leapt up from under some rotting vegetation. Flashing, flaying claws and fierce, fire-bright, yellow eyes materialised from the inner depths of a strange, secret, subterranean world. This aggressive, decaying alien was surely from the dead demons of the afterlife. The coatis scattered unashamedly. Branches and leaves cracked and broke as they exploded away in every direction. Their fear-ridden, high-pitched screams trembled throughout the

swung around and focused on the favourite dish of the night. It was chicken play for a wily Tat – as much as she was inspired at the brilliance of her snake plan, it was impossible to ignore a jungle chicken. Slowly meandering, the randomly wandering entourage edged its way gently towards her. Pulling her legs close in she hugged the branch as if it were part of her body. She nearly dropped twice, but the aimless chickens dithered and danced in all directions. With panic about to overcome her as the chicken train was due to pass without so much as a pounce, she dropped onto the last one. Before it could squawk a warning she had dragged it down a large hole under the tree's root.

It was a prolific night: two jungle chicks, four mice and a young forest rabbit. The rabbit only just fitted down the hole. It was so tight down there that she could barely squeeze herself out. There was enough food for a month and yet, the procession of animals continued.

With the morning light slowly edging its way over the forest, the nocturnal creatures stealthily disappeared into the shady shadows of the forest's secrets. Now the only hint of their presence was the multitude of differing prints in the dry trail together with a few feathers near Tat's hole. Tat was exhausted. She could not work out whether she was tired from the furious activity or the high-adrenaline thrill and excitement.

The Laughing Sun always touched the tips of the high trees first and Three Toes was up there waiting. He stretched his long limbs in the early morning warmth. A few industrious ants had invaded some difficult-to-get-at parts of his body during the night. With some deft manoeuvring, by hanging from the branch above with one arm, he twisted himself into various positions that only a long-limbed sloth could accomplish. His three, strong claws made a good ant-bite scratcher. Happy with his daily preparation he slowly turned his head to peruse last night's war zone. Spinning gently on one hanging arm he scanned the whole tree. A slight, satisfied grin crept across his face; despite the attacks, it was in good shape. It had been a triumphant night. Without any further delay he pulled himself up on to the branch and began the journey towards its end. Breakfast would begin when he got there. Along the branch he mused about that day's options. There were not many to consider. One was whether to stop after breakfast and have a kip. The other was to eat all day without stopping until the tree was empty.

With some determined highly focused, operational manoeuvrings Three Toes reached the first cucura. He still had not come to a decision regarding the day's actions. He thought best to leave it for the time being until the first branch had been cleared. Depending upon his proclivity for further consumption he would then make a stomach-aching decision.

When he reached the end of the branch, he paused. A momentary, blithe thought of appreciation crossed his mind that he was perhaps the most fortunate sloth in the forest. Not just for protecting a tree full of desirable fruit but also for the ingenious tactician he truly was. Gliding slowly but meaningfully towards the ripest, most beckoning fruit he placed it between his smooth, slobbering lips. He squeezed it lovingly with his teeth. An explosion of delicious, aromatic flavours squelched around his mouth, covering his taste buds in cucura ecstasy. His whole body instantly melted into a gently swaying, soporific compost heap.

Breakfast was proceeding admirably. Several of the largest, juiciest cucuras had slipped down his slothful throat to the joyous delight of a gracious, grateful stomach. He found that, if he slopped his tongue around his chops with sufficient momentum he could mop up much of the draining juices that had attempted to delay their ineluctable end by congealing into his matted facial hair. While savouring these gastronomic delights, in the planes of hypnotic ecstasy, a loud, raucous squawking from the heavens above brought him shuddering back to the forest. The macaw parrots had returned for vengeance and cucuras.

With a pile of cucuras now infiltrating throughout his system Three Toes was feeling coolly unsociable towards his new visitors. Additionally, his victorious, combative exercises had evoked a slight sense of self-righteousness now that he had truly become the accomplished guardian of cucuras. In his mind he was the ultimate psychological deterrent against all intruders and had proved his position. He had many scalps to his name. He was a master strategist and defender of the righteous. "Sloth rights, that is," he idly thought. "Right sloths perhaps," he added as an afterthought, now slightly confused.

While all these worthy thoughts were weaving through his mind he had lost three cucuras to the squabbling parrots. So he pulled himself from his self-idolising ramblings and took a short-cut to the top by swinging upwards branch by branch. In an astonishingly short time, for a sloth, he was in the middle of the menacing macaws and inflicting havoc on their tail feathers by smacking them with his big claws against the tree.

Surprised by this sudden turn of events, all the macaws simultaneously screeched into the air with such a hullabaloo that it stopped the forest again. Three Toes was the embodiment of command and control. Now having completely forgotten about any previous plans, he sat down where he was and ate all the cucuras in reach.

Tree had been listening to the rumpus in the night. When Inti lit up the tops of the trees he scanned for the combative sloth.

Wee Tree was mightily impressed and full of admiration for the slowest yet mightiest tactical warrior in the jungle. He had sounded so heavily outnumbered in the night. From what he could hear, it was a long night of ferocious fighting. He was sure he could not have defeated all of those nightly bandits – there were so many of them.

Wee Tree spoke to Pachamama, "It was so busy last night. Three Toes went demented and Tat stuffed herself homeless. There were animals everywhere, high and low; we were inundated. Three Toes turned himself into a ravaging savage. His fearsome reputation spread throughout the forest at about the same speed as his fleeing victims. Many attacked his larder. They all received the same greeting and left rattled and frazzled. Most were so disturbed by the harrowing experience that they've had to lie up somewhere far away from the area, believing it to be inhabited by devils. Now they are all nervous wrecks. Yet still, hundreds of animals kept arriving, even shy ones like peccaries and Jaguar. What's odd is that they are all coming from the same direction. What's going on?"

Pachamama considered her reply cautiously. Experience had shown that she had to be diligent when dealing with Tree. She answered carefully, "Ah, yes!" then paused before saying yes again, then paused without saying anything. Eventually, she managed to say yes for a third time then added, "Yes," just to be sure, "Three Toes is an enigmatic creature who seems to have built a formidable reputation amongst some of his more mobile cucura lovers. When some amicable, placid soul suddenly turns into a maniacal, warmongering, thrashing beast it upsets the delicate equilibrium of what most would consider rational. Teragorm may be a little odd but she's consistently odd, so nobody minds. When something goes mad with feet like that then everybody keeps out of the way."

"No, I didn't mean Three Toes, Pachamama," replied Wee Tree. "I meant all the other animals. The only reason Tat stopped stuffing her larder was because there was no more room to put it all in, otherwise she would still be stuffing. The animals just kept coming. What's happening?"

"Ah, those. Yes," she said again, "there is a disturbance on the far edges of the forest. Some of the animals have moved away to find quieter areas where they will be less bothered."

"Why?" tree replied, forever curious and much to Pachamama's dismay.

"Because some trees have come down like they did here, only on a bigger scale. Some of the animals in that area are moving this way. You know those new noises that you have mentioned before, well that's where they're coming from."

"So the noises are sending the animals away. There's a lot of them. Will there be any more?"

"You know that each tree is home to thousands of animals. They will take some time to find new homes. Keep your eye on them. It will reduce eventually."

Tree was thinking to himself, "There must be a lot of trees down to displace that many. The animals from our fallen trees imperceptibly diffused into the forest with little effect. The cicadas took a while to sort themselves out but they eventually managed it." He dropped into a meditative state of meaningful contemplation. His gaze dropped idly down to a big leaf below him that appeared to be doing some odd things.

Savage was having a field day. He was simply sitting there in the shade under a big leaf picking off the stridulatory crickets with nonchalant ease. Thousands were manically leaping past in all directions. While unseen by all except a tree and an ever attentive spider, Savage's long, sticky tongue uncurled from under a dark leaf at whiplash speed. An unsuspecting cricket was swiped in mid flight and instantly whipped back under the leaf before an eye could blink. Tat, who had been sitting on top of some fallen leaves digesting parts of her larder, didn't blink. She saw it all. Nothing got past Tat.

"Still," she thought to herself, "I'm staying out of tongue shot of that monster," although she had to admire the indifferent efficiency of the technique. The inanimate animal continued lashing crickets towards the back of his throat at will.

"If he continues at that rate he will never move again," hypothesised Tat, now fully entertained from an idle spectator's point of view and then thought, "perhaps he doesn't need to. His body is just an anchor for a very long tongue and a depository for cricket disposal." With that, Tat decided to have a slumber, keeping all eight eyes fully focused, of course.

Chapter XX

The ocean air, purified with ozone, trembled with clouds of invisible ions. Excited by thunderous hurricane gales, it swept over the broiling transmutations of a bubbling, electrolytic sea. A moody irascibility pervaded the electric air serrated by erratic lightning bolts. Conductors of evil struck destruction towards their helpless target. Tempest Cloud and Vivacious Wind were still mercilessly hammering the death ship. There had been no let-up since it all began. Rumbustious Sea was still producing gargantuan waves. Even Laughing Sun was yet to laugh as he continued to charge the sky with blankets of nuclear particles. Tempest found it easy to strike with such infinite power flowing through his towering, black columns.

Beneath the bellicose Elements four very dark, black shapes slowly manoeuvred close to the ship. Nobody knew they were there. It was a clandestine rendezvous. Rightly or wrongly, the Oarsmen had decided that a job started was a job to be finished. The flerds had tasted the Elements' wrath; now they could sample the Oarsmen's. They were in no mood to watch the Elements. They had seen the damage the flerds had inflicted on Whale. It was a cowardly, unprovoked attack. Nobody attacks a Curator. Without a word, they decided it was time to show the flerds another power.

The Oarsmen grouped some distance off the leeward side of the stricken ship. Synchronising themselves, they quietly worked together as one big machine. Side by side they lay exactly two fins apart. Battle formation, long rehearsed and practised, requiring only one thought to produce four actions. Their tail flukes edged together so lightly that the finest fish's fin would not pass between them, neither did they touch. Spanning over forty metres, they slowly began to pump the roaring Sea. Such was their power that the sea succumbed into submissive foam. Together, as one giant paddle, they propelled their six hundred tonnes into a welcoming sea that made no demands and offered little resistance. As their speed increased the frequency of their flukes increased. Trails of eddying bubbles lay in their wake. The bruised sea was flattened by raw Oarsman energy. A tense mood hung in sinister expectation with the latent smell of menace. The dark blue sea parted over their enormous hulls producing a flooding coruscation that oiled the Oarsmen's tenacity. Within two hundred metres of the crippled ship they had reached forty knots.

The ship's sonar, working on an emergency battery, picked up a moving mass. A small siren sounded. A lone flerd lookout saw an unknown, mountainous shape spraying water high into the bellicose storm. It hurtled towards him at incredible speed. In the depths of the ship the radio operator, alerted by the siren, picked up his satellite radio handset to issue another Mayday call.

He never managed to add the last "Mayday" to his alarm call. It would have made no difference as the huge electrical storm had blasted all radio reception.

Rumbustious Sea, on picking up the Oarsmen's intentions, squeezed a freakish, rogue wave from nowhere. The living, all-consuming well at the wave's snarling foundations sucked air, sea and life to feed its voracious, deep and darkening desire. Its leading face as flat and as vertical as a canyon's dark side, it showed no emotions towards its sentencing intentions. Solid as the granite earth it sped towards the ship, sandwiching it between the wave and the four oncoming Oarsmen. The timing was Element-exact. The Oarsmen hit the ship's port side as one, staving it into the wall of the racing wave. The tremendous impact blew the remaining decks towards the heavens. Debris hit the roaring wind and scattered, before showering unceremoniously back into the welcoming waves. With its superstructure compressed into a thin strip of corrugated carnage it slipped under the waves, flip-flopping back and forth like a peaceful pendulum with all the time in the world.

The rogue consumed. Dead, dying or disintegrated, the indomitable Rumbustious Sea welcomed all without a shiver of prejudice.

After impact, the Oarsmen split as a fanfare and plummeted nose first, each following the ship from the four compass points. For several minutes they tracked the vessel sinking hundreds of fathoms towards the darkest corner of the earth from where nothing except an Oarsman returns.

When the pressure from the great depth had crushed their girths in half, the Oarsmen levelled off and, with no sign of effort, turned to face each other. The flattened ship sank on in meaningless silence, lost in the depths of an unpitying ocean. Aligning themselves to the power axis of the earth they slowly advanced towards each other. At the precise point the ship had dropped they met. The four most colossal, mightiest animals on earth stopped within metres of each other. When each of their eyes aligned they connected their souls. They inched forward until their heads touched as delicately as a fish's fin. With the ring of brotherhood connected, they stayed reasserting the strength of their alliance as befitting the world's guardians. The power of Pachamama rippling through their massive frames increased their energy, energising their vibrancy to the highest levels of enlightenment.

Re-energised, they bent their backs, pointed their heads upwards then simultaneously swiped their flukes down to begin the long ascent. Gradually they drifted further apart, increasing the distance between them. Eventually, as the fathoms began to decrease and the world above became brighter, their speed started to increase. Their vision was impeccable and although they had no forward sight they could detect the minutest details over huge surfaces of the sea. They could perceive a piece of flotsam rocking dementedly in a wild sea or a kicking flerd. This time, there were two kicking flerds. All four Oarsmen breached simultaneously at speed. They shattered through the ruptured sea like vomiting volcanoes. Their night-black bodies lifted, turning their dark bellies towards the hidden Laughing Sun showering the Elemental world. Waterfalls of crashing water concluded their final assault. They acknowledged the Elements' efforts and displayed their respect with absolute commitment. Hanging from the jaws of two of the Oarsmen were the bodies of the last two flerds. Each had manoeuvred to clear up the debris which had been spotted fathoms below. They smashed through the sea's surface with their jaws wide open before closing their hull-crushing, tooth-studded mandibles around the last two floating flerds. Their spines snapped as they were ripped into the air by the unrepentant whales, their limp bodies flapping like torn flags against the granite black, obdurate mass of an Oarsman's pococurante head.

Chapter XXI

Princess stretched her wide, blue and black wing-tips to the very limits of her breath. A small tear rolled down her face and onto an orchid's stamen. Its large white, fleshy petals with electric yellow spots looking like tiny eyes, were speckled with orange stains running down their sides. The freckled effect resembled dripping water running down the petals, complementing Princess's tear. She swayed gently in the hot, humid jungle air. Wee Tree was so close he could feel her faint breath against his outstretched leaves. Landing, feather light, on the tip of the petal she burst into floods of tears. "Look at me," thought the sad Princess, "my colours are fading, my wing-tips frayed. I'm short of breath, my legs are bent, my wings buckled. I can hardly fly any more. But look, look out there – those beautiful, young butterflies. Look how they ride the edges of the wind. How they twist and twirl, their wings caressing the currents as the sun illuminates their iridescent colours, shimmering, flashing, poised and elegant. The males chasing them from one flower to the next. And here I am, old, tattered and tired with nothing more to give. Nobody chases me, nobody looks at me. I'm washed out and unwanted."

Tree paused briefly. Curling up his leaves and cocooning the frail butterfly, he reached out to her. Feeling her grief and her soul he sighed tenderly, "Ah Princess, I see you looking at those youngsters; those young things may fly the fantasy, but it's all show and promises. Look behind you Princess. Along the lines of trees and shrubs. Look at the dazzling colours of the flowers. The multitude of shapes and sizes, the variations of the radiance and beauty they give. It is you that has produced and prolonged their lives. All the world weeps at their splendour and sees you as a part of that magnificence. You will remain in their hearts, for it is the world's legacy and you are as integral to it as are the Elements to its survival. The world loves you Princess; it always will." He wrapped his leaves around her delicate body, where she peacefully died.

Three Toes had been unaware of Princess far below. Had he known he would surely have dropped to the floor without a thought for caution or cucura. He would have offered to die for her.

After a long day climbing up, down and over the tree, plucking, eating, plucking again, he finally devoured the last fruit. It had been a consuming affair and not without the odd hiccup in between. He had seen off most of the villains in the night, leaving them with permanent psychological problems. At least that is what he hoped and that any association with cucuras and feeding in the night would bring back instant trauma attacks. "Rightly so," he thought, "one has to safeguard one's assets. If word got out that I was a pushover then every beak and claw in the vicinity would be here and the more who believe that demons protect cucura trees, the better for me."

During the day there were a few hopefuls who decided to try their claw or beak at the remaining, forbidden fruit. Not that they knew it was forbidden but they very soon found out. Two collared aracaris made some noise about it but a foul, miasma-emitting throwback to a bygone age soon shifted them upwards. A kinkajou and four squirrels also received the same treatment. To add to the fleeing creatures' despondencies, Three Toes had mastered a technique with such meticulous elegance that he was able to collect the odd fruit in the process and consume it in front of them. The recipients of this animated performance were so startled that the sight of him casually munching a tantalising cucura just added to the trauma. Pleased with his efficiency in the face of adversity, it gave him a warm, tingling feeling from tail to nose.

By the end of the day there was also a warm, tingling feeling in the depths of his belly, a point of which, he noticed, had expanded rapidly in the latter half of the afternoon. Some of the branches that he had been swinging on all night and day now appeared to be bending more than they used to. It had become obvious that the dozens of cucuras had added a few kilograms. His rotund belly was so bloated that it was impeding his movements and he could no longer swing his arms or legs quite as freely. It was with some relief when the last one was finally eaten and he could sink into his bed for the night.

The next couple of days floated past in a blissful state of comfort and self-satisfaction. The cucuras, some of which had been on the hospital side of ripe, had induced a soporific sensation of euphoria, partly due to his self-gratifying performance but mostly due to the gradual fermentation that gently matured within his acid-loving frame. It finally manifested itself in grandiose illusions of masterful gracefulness. While lying in this gentle, floating world he noticed other sloths waving at the end of the branch so he jumped up and danced along to greet them.

Three Toes wasn't the most agile of movers but he was the sturdiest. Now he felt as light as a butterfly and danced along the branches, tripping daintily on his two back feet and waving majestically to anything interested. Arriving at the end of a branch, he performed a pirouette as lightly as a hummingbird spinning around a flower. With his arms outstretched to welcome his friends he looked around but, oddly, they had gone. Confused, but with the grace of Green Iguana, he pirouetted again, which was one too many, tripped then tumbled to the ground. Floating gently down he thought of Princess and flew, for a few seconds, around the aromatic orchids before hitting the earth with an almighty thump.

Three Toes lay there, gently blowing bubbles into the air. They drifted off before exploding into thousands of multi-coloured cucuras. He burbled some more, then, rolling onto all fours, he found a tree. It was so like his old one that he began climbing it. After a short time, or it may have been a long time, he didn't know, he found a bed in between two branches. It was so like his old one that he dropped into it and passed out. On waking up he felt sore all over. He leapt up and quickly whizzed around in a tight circle four or five times looking for the creature that had hit him. Finding nobody about and not understanding how he could have been hit when seconds ago he was dancing along the branch to meet his friends, he swiped wildly at the air in case they were about to come out from their hiding place and hit him again. Losing his balance he flew down again with Princess. He disappeared under a pile of vegetation.

He wasn't sure how long he had been there, but something wet and warm snorted in his ear; it woke him up. It was not unpleasant but on the other hand, he didn't know what it was. Scraping back a load of dead leaves and branches that somehow had covered him, he eventually clambered into free space. Walking away was a big, black bottom. A stubby tail was connected to it; it waved at him affably. He waved back then fell over. Staggering back up, he looked around. The big, black bottom had gone but he was lucky enough to find a tree like his old one and worked out that it was possible to climb up. Miraculously, at a junction between two branches he found a bed just like the one he left earlier. Dropping into it he slithered into unconsciousness.

Wee Tree watched placidly as Three Toes tried several times to kill himself. After watching the same performance with each successive one becoming ever more ragged, he wondered how many thirty-metre drops Three Toes intended to do. Never before had he seen a sloth, not even Three Toes who was after all a master sloth, dance with delicate finesse along a bouncy branch without gripping with his two front claws. On the last fall he had failed to move for over an hour. Tree decided he was dead. Tree was wrong. A groggy sloth dragged himself up and climbed back up the trunk again. Finding his bed he passed out. "It must be," he thought, "that the sloth has gone mad. Maybe he now thinks he is the Green Iguana and the easiest way down is from where you are. Unfortunately, unlike Iguana, Three Toes is not built like a sack of rocks and will surely die."

On his return to consciousness Three Toes' head was spinning. For some reason he was sore and bruised all over. In fact he was so sore that he could not move. Desperately, he tried to recall what had happened. He thought to himself, "I must have been in a desperate fight with some devilish creature trying to pinch my cucuras to be in this state." The more he tried to remember this creature, the less he could remember anything. With a blinding headache he decided to stop thinking as this was hurting as much as his body. He curled into a ball and went back to sleep.

A large, charcoal baird's tapir idled past early one morning with her knee-high khaki and beige, two-tone stripe-suited son. She took a rest next to a pile of fallen leaves and branches. "Always a good place for something tasty," she idly thought. She pushed her long, wet, shiny nose in and had a good rummage about. It did not last long. It stank of rotting compost. They quickly moved on.

Further down the track she found a clump of wild garlic growing over a large rock. She stuck her inquisitive, probing nose in. Savage had never moved so fast. Something larger than himself had decided to drop in on him. It was nothing less than athletic as he bounded his cricket-weighted carcass outwards before the giant lump descended. The developing dust cloud exploded into the moist air at the point of impact where the tapir decided to drop down for a rest. Her small, suited son munched a few garlic leaves for a while then settled comfortably next to his mother to sun the rest of the day away.

Savage, disgusted by the audacity of the impertinent beast, thumped off as loudly as he could to register his discontent on the matter to anybody that cared to listen. Which, as it turned out, was only Wee Tree. He was more bemused with the fact that something had just

out-thumped Savage. Still, Savage was not one to brood
over life's thumpings. He sniffed the garlicky air for a
short while then decided where the next best place
would be to plant his honed and grossly tuned body. He
found one near a tree with a conveniently, low-hanging
branch stretching close to the trail. Crawling on all
fours, he was just able to get under it and resume
impersonating a large, grey stone.

Tat was furious. This formidable lump of a frog had not
only muscled her out from hanging under her branch
but had now bunged the entrance to her well-stocked
larder with his ever-expanding belly. She thought about
giving him a large bite behind his neck, then thought
otherwise as the beast was one hundred times her size
and had a gaping mouth large enough to fit a young
tapir. She thought best to leave the obnoxious creature
alone. In a huff she slipped from under her branch,
darted across the path to the other side of the clearing
and found a hole under Wee Tree. After some digging to
transform the place into something more comfortable,
she lined it with moss and moved herself into her new
home. Positioning herself at the front door, with a few
dried sticks pulled across, she pushed out her eyes to
search and seek the next meal. Dreaming about yummy
flycatchers and stumbling chickens she soon forgot all
about the over-fed and over-sized frog.

The resident group of howler monkeys pitched
themselves atop an almond tree. They kept away from

the bedevilled cucura tree and busied themselves snapping off leaves and branches to make their beds for the night. Twigs, sticks and nuts rained down on all below. The crashing racket could be heard from far away and kept all awake. Eventually, to everyone's relief, they all settled down.

In the morning they greeted the new day with monster howls. The wails echoed off the forest's trees as they reinforced their right to home territory. They crunched, gnawed and gnashed their way through all the ripe nuts. A constant rain of debris clattered down in lumps to the ground below.

Another displaced group of migrant howlers swung in over the treetops. They settled in a large kapok on the far side of the clearing. They were hungry and also wanted a share in the nuts. The dialogue began with both groups out-shouting the other. Some of the bigger male monkeys moved closer to each other – not so close for physical contact but close enough to see the colours of each other's eyes. Which were not pretty. A confrontation began. It seemed to Wee Tree that the tactics of the howler monkeys were to perforate the other side's ear drums before their own, then to take control of the almond tree. After an insufferable amount of time, the home group won. With a screaming banshee finale, accompanied with excited waving of arms and sticks, thumping of feet and flashing of teeth, the visitors were escorted out of earshot with much ballyhoo. Much to the relief of Wee Tree.

The noise had unsettled the dozing Baird's Tapir and her striped, two-tone son. They were peace-loving creatures and so moved on after the sun went down. Savage was also disconcerted by the racket but liked his new abode and was licking up crickets with earnest glee. He stayed where he was. Tat, too, was indifferent to a move. She had overcome her bad feelings towards Savage's eviction order; her new larder already had two sweet forest mice bundled up ready for dinner later.

Tree had been watching the changes and feeling the earth through his roots. A sensitive, interconnecting fibrous network connected every tree and plant. A living, complex, underground communications system existed that enabled all the trees to identify each type of flora, its health and the means of combating infections. It was an ancient, slow communications and health system but it served the trees well. Wee Tree could feel that many plants had disappeared. He felt their pain in their last, dying moments. Ancient trees from the primary rainforests, the highest and oldest pillars to the skies, had been removed. Large areas of woodland had become bare.

Tree was uneasy, "I have a nasty feeling. I can't put my leaf on it but something is not right. Everything around is saturated with insects, birds and migrant animals.

Tat's highway has a constant run of traffic. On top of that Teragorm's demented wailing is being drowned out by this relentless, grinding flerd noise. Now the forest communications network is indicating massive changes. Changes that have never been sensed before. It was once such a stable structure. What's going on?"

Tree put this to Pachamama. She thought quickly, then decided that Tree deserved to know the truth; in the end, he was going to find out one way or the other. She began slowly, "There are some flerds, that is, not the native syntonic sort like your two energetic, pale ones but like those in Whale's songs. They have been destroying forests for many years. They chop down the large trees then remove and burn all that is left. Nothing is left but the bare earth. The rains come down each year washing the thin topsoil away, leaving it barren and infertile. In this way they consume the forests. It happens all over the world."

"But why should they wish to destroy the trees? Surely they know we support the sky and give them life," said Tree.

"I don't know but they like to destroy a lot of things. It is not just trees or whales, it is land, rivers, mountains, fish, animals, almost everything. Even my mineral-rich veins, buried deep below, are excavated and consumed. Ruminant Whale has already explained how every living organism exists in a delicate balance so that all can coexist. Each gives something back to the world so that others can flourish. In this way a complex, interactive chain is set up. What is in place has been developed over millions of years and is fundamental to species existing. When one animal takes more than the chain can offer then the balance is broken and it forces unknown changes. The flerds are breaking that balance and changes are occurring. Even the Elements are adjusting to their behaviour. The Elements don't care. They will always be around but it will not be to everybody's advantage."

Pachamama paused to give time for Tree to dwell upon this, then continued, "It is another paradox of life that the brainless Teragorm who has isolated herself in the Fly Mountains survives to this day because flerds cannot see her although she can see them. For something so stupid as to eat food that is so indigestible to her, to have survived so long, is perplexing; but that is the paradox: there are so many flerds that she will always have food and a safe place to live. Perhaps the ignorant flerd and the stupid Teragorm have a well-matched, symbiotic relationship. They feed her and she picks off their infirm, sick and lame. Whether Teragorm will survive, nobody knows, but the Elements will remain and a new balance will arrive."

Tree was struck dumb by this unexpected explanation. Never had he imagined that such futile destruction would be caused by such selfishness. Hostility to the very pillars that kept them all alive. Dark forces from the dawn of creation were alive and had infested the soulless, contumacious and obdurate beings. While the likes of Whale swam in the seas of an enlightened world, there were those that did not understand and only wished to destroy what they could not perceive. "There is a madness about," he concluded. So deep was he in his thoughts that he became unaware of the daily, grinding noises.

Chapter XXII

The Laughing Sun laughed and laughed and laughed. In a petulant gesture he swung his burning cloak in blazing trails across the horizon. The denuded, raped, barren earth glowed in trails of crimson gold as Inti beamed across the forest treetops.

Along the forest edge Wee Tree dominated the forest canopy, diminishing all around; he watched as Inti's blinding light illuminated the flattened landscape. "Now," he thought, "I watch Inti sink below the trees. His light dances so brightly whatever it falls on. He never changes. He continues as he has for millennia. How can he do that?"

He did wonder if anybody else noticed but nobody did. Nobody seemed to notice Laughing Sun; nobody seemed to notice all the animals missing; nobody seemed to notice all the trees missing. Today he watched the setting sun wondering if it would be the last time he did. Wee Tree had no more questions.

The great trees, some older than four hundred years, were felled and removed. The thousands of plants, climbers, ferns and lichens that depended on them were hacked to bits and burnt. Nothing was spared; the land was razed. Light filtered in towards Tree. Not from above, as before, but from the sides. It was a new light, an odd light. The walls of the forest had been removed and Inti shone in from the angles. Tree felt this new energy but it was the wrong sort, it did not work on him any more. He knew that his turn was to come. There was no further point in pushing up to the skies. To become a pillar to support the world was now a lost dream. The flerds did not want him, Whale, nor any of them. He did not understand, he no longer cared, neither did the others. They could not flee like the animals, they had to stay and hold the ground until their time arrived. Only the Elements could stop the flerds, like they had with Ruminant, but there was no sign of their calling.

Tat, Three Toes, Savage and the others had long since fled. The noisy cicadas that signalled the start and end of each day had also vanished. The forest was as quiet as the dead when the morning arrived. Each cicada's incessant, long-gone racket was now replaced by a flerd's machine of destruction. An unholy, tiresome noise with spitting, black smoke and fire. Their vitriolic breath poisoned the atmosphere, flooding the pores with toxins and fumes.

Wee Tree looked across the barren, scarred, mutilated earth. The roaring machines shattered his thoughts. He was numb. No longer would he be a proud pillar of the earth. While he was musing on yet another paradox of the forest a flerd arrived and sprayed a red cross on his trunk. What did that mean? Whatever it meant he was sure that it wasn't healthy.

Others followed the red cross flerd; these were carrying ropes and chainsaws. They walked along the freshly cut tree edge, stopping at the red crossed trees. The chainsaws roared into action spitting contempt and acrid smoke at the docile, passive trees as they sliced into their bark. The savage lacerations cut through to the heart of each tree. Bleeding and slashed they felt their life's sap drain from them; the cut trees cried aloud. In their last moments of dying, pathogenic pain ran through their roots for all the forest to feel. The voracious, indifferent blade continued through the massive trunk, with its arteries severed, it could no longer hold itself tall and proud – slowly it tipped over, crashing heavily onto the ground.

Like monstrous, noisy ants the flerds swarmed over the dying tree, cutting off its branches with their screaming machines, devouring every leaf, strip of bark and branch. The denuded trunk remained dead and lifeless on the ground. Other monstrous, grunting beasts chugged towards it, snorting, puffing, heaving to drag it away. Each tree standing waited, resigned, for its own demise.

It was a dead night in Fly Forest. Tree did not think. No more thoughts were in his mind. He waited for the Laughing Sun.

When Inti arrived he beamed brightly in the clear blue skies above Fly Forest. The desolate landscape lit up to declare a single message: there were no more secrets.

Tree looked out across the empty space. There was nothing. Nothing for hundreds of kilometres. Where there had once been life, noise, animals, Tat and Three Toes, now there was nothing. He could feel it in his roots; everything was gone. He could feel his roots being pulled by an invisible force, a force sliding him from the tangled, rooted forest of his youth towards an empty space with nothing but the burnt remains of an uprooted, ancient past. The discarded remains of his peers were left cut and upended, their roots spilling from the burnt soil like giant, dead animals that had rolled over onto their backs and left to die.

Today Wee Tree was ready for the flerds. They approached with their noisy cutting machines gargling and humming, producing hot, burning air. Fires were started behind the mechanical beasts as all the scrub, brush and undergrowth was transformed by the flaring flames into heat, ash and pungent smoke. The atmosphere followed the smoke, changing into a darkening gloom of gaunt fatalism.

A loud, long whistle cut through the thick air. Tree had not heard that before. It was from no creature he had encountered. He looked around but could not see where it had come or from what had sung it. The flerds, too, were surprised and also looked around. The machines cut dead. For a moment everything stopped.

Chil and Chel walked out from behind him. Tree had no idea they were there. Normally he would have felt their energy way before they came into sight. They stroked his trunk as they walked past and stood in front of him, looking straight out at the surprised flerds.

The flerds had not seen them arrive. It was as if they had dropped from above like two white doves. Their white, untied hair dropped low behind their backs revealing beautiful, pale, unblemished faces. Two sets of blue eyes stared wide, open and unblinking. They made no demonstration nor acknowledgement of the flerds' existence. Roots spread from their feet and anchored them as securely as the trees behind.

The tree-fellers started shouting and waved their arms for the twins to move. The twins ignored the frantic arm-waving and warnings of danger. Resigned to a confrontation, a group of the fellers walked towards them. Work stopped. The noxious fumes stopped. An exasperated group of flerds congregated around the twins telling them it was dangerous and that they must move. Chil and Chel stayed as silent and as stationary as the trees behind. The willowy twins looked so frail that the felling flerds thought of lifting them up and physically planting them elsewhere. Something stopped them. Something tangled around their minds that laid heavy upon their souls. It was a deep heaviness; it mixed with the uncertainties that clouded their thoughts.

Suddenly and without warning Fly Indians arrived from behind the trees. Ocillo had contacted every village. Soon thousands lined up behind Chil and Chel. Nobody said anything. No noise was made. Arriving from every corner of the jungle they mysteriously appeared out of the canopy like hidden butterflies dropping from every leaf.

In contrast, Teragorm could not drop from anywhere without a cacophonous racket. Within the trees the sound of breaking branches shattered the awkward silence. From behind the dark, hanging shadows of the sequestered woods she emerged into the blazing sunlight bellowing and roaring from the depths of her vile stomach. The felling flerds fled. They ran so fast they could not lift their legs quickly enough. The knotted tree stumps and tangled roots from felled trees pulled at their ankles, dragging them into the barren earth. Dishevelled, hot and bloodied they raced back to the safety of their machines.

The roaring multiplied as another hundred teragorms crashed through the bush. They roared their discontent towards the heavens, breaking down the felling flerds' rapidly disintegrating rationalities.

Chel turned and walked back to Teragorm. The big beast stopped roaring and looked down at her with a pleased demeanour in her eyes. Chel placed a hand on her nose and said, "Quiet," then added, "thank you." She looked warmly at her, patted the side of her face and then noticed a cord tied around her thick neck. She pulled it up and was surprised to see the condor feather still attached. "So, you, too, Teragorm, are guided by the old shaman?" She walked back to Chil.

The other teragorms looked at Chel and also stopped roaring. The forest returned to a strained quiet with the exception of a background of heavy, hot breathing emanating from an excited bunch of teragorms.

Chil and Chel walked peacefully to the flerds hiding in their steamed-up machines. Approaching a vehicle with red flags on its roof, Chil gently tapped on the window. A hot, sweating, nervous flerd slowly wound it down.

Chil spoke, "My name is Chil, this is my sister Chel. Welcome to our home. Look before you. There are Fly Indians, teragorms and trees. Behind them, hidden deep within the forest are billions more animals and plants. This is their home. It provides food, comfort and medicine. You kill the trees, you kill us, you kill yourselves. Do you understand?"

The chief feller scanned the thousands of Indians standing, silent and still. He looked with fear and horror at the monstrous teragorms, then finally shifted his look towards Chil and Chel. "Girls, I am paid to do a job. The government says cut the trees, so we cut the trees. What can we do?"

"You can look again. You are killing us. Did your government tell you to kill us?"

The chief tree feller looked again. Above the trees the Elements had begun to congregate. Tempest Cloud had been building up and was slowly lowering. As he looked, big drops of water began splattering against his windscreen. They hit the dirty glass and exploded into tiny pearls of sparkling light then disintegrated against the grubby surface. It was not long before Tempest would unleash his load and the sky transform into a tropical waterfall.

Nobody moved. The Fly Indians, the teragorms, the flerds, all watched Chil and Chel. The twins did not bat an eyelid. They remembered the Condor Shaman, the black jaguar, the animal spirit of destruction; they saw the future. Pachamama was lit by a dark light from the black sun. They burned their eyes deep into the tree-felling flerd's soul. They reached his inner being and showed him the purple planet, past and future.

Whale sang. Her messages of compassion floated through the baffling, bent, paradoxical air.

Somewhere above the black, raging columns of Tempest Cloud Inti beamed. He shone his brilliant rays for all to see, fully aware that sometimes not all could see the light. He laughed and laughed and laughed.

******

Harry Roseblade lives near Bristol when he is not travelling. Losing his wife at an early age, then having a bit of a battle with cancer, sent him off around the world in a somewhat traumatised state.

However, he quickly discovered a love for the idiosyncrasies of this diverse earth, together with yoga and meditation. After travelling to the rain forests in Costa Rica, Ecuador, Venezuela and Papua New Guinea he discovered another love.

In his début book: The Elements, you will discover what that love is and perhaps, lean a little towards it yourself.

www.roseblade.info

Lightning Source UK Ltd.
Milton Keynes UK
UKOW06f1617211015

261112UK00001B/1/P